Healing
the Circle

Terry,
Thank you for your
Interest!
Best Regards
Richard
Gibson

RICHARD L. GIBSON

PAGE PUBLISHING, INC.
Conneaut Lake, PA

First originally published by Page Publishing 2020

ISBN 978-1-6624-0971-4 (pbk)
ISBN 978-1-6624-0973-8 (hc)
ISBN 978-1-6624-0972-1 (digital)

Printed in the United States of America

To my wife, Teri,
who taught me what love looks like
and how to do it right. I'm learning every day.

Contents

The Time Before

In the days before European people moved to North America, the continent was known to the native people as Turtle Island. It is said the first people came to be on the continent soon after the last Ice Age, when a bridge of land known as the Bering Strait was still above the seas. It was located between what are known as the Asian continent and the North American continent. Ask a native person and they would tell a different story. They would tell of their origin story and how the people have been on the continent from the beginning of the world. In this time before, the people who would come to be known as the Native Americans lived in close relationship with the animals, the forests, the mountains, and the plains. They lived within a rhythm nourished by the earth herself. The European people disturbed this harmony when they began their colonization.

On Turtle Island, the people had been living for uncounted generations within this sacred circle of life. They lived with and respected the spirits of the animals, the grasses, the trees, the wind, and the water and all the beings of this world. They had long ago learned to honor the spirits of life that brought the whole of their existence into being and sustained a balance in all the pathways of life.

From this place started the new world revolution, where every type of pollution was dumped into and onto the earth, the atmosphere, and the space surrounding the planet. Finally, the civilized world had gone too far. The world was set upon by a chain of catastrophic events that set into motion the destruction of their society.

In a few years' time, their cities lay in ruin, and their populations were devastated. These catastrophes spread on a global scale and effectively ended the societies, governments, and nations that had wrought havoc on the planet. Small pockets of people survived and set about building a society that would once again bring the people into harmony with the earth.

These people built small sustainable villages in areas where they could best take advantage of the topography and their natural surroundings. They built away from the most polluted areas of the destroyed past.

It happened that a few of the old teachers remembered the ways of the people before the Europeans. So began once more the passing of and learning of skills. Many of the villages reverted to a simpler style of life. In the Midwest portion of the continent, the people lived in seminomadic bands. Their shelters were made at first from materials they could scavenge in what remained of the devastated cities. As these supplies wasted away, the people began to rediscover the natural materials that were in use before the time of the devastation.

Enough people remembered the old ways and survived to teach, bringing back the more peaceful, simpler ways that had been a part of their past. They began to work with the earth to mend the circle of harmony in small pockets around the continent.

In the mountains, the people lived in small villages of log or stone houses to protect them from the long, harsh winters.

Along the coasts, they used these same materials to build small sea craft. With these they learned to mindfully harvest the sea life that had become more and more abundant as the earth healed herself. Trade began slowly and on a very small scale, as the peoples discovered they were not alone in their communities.

The plains people established more quickly than in the coastal areas. The philosophies and habits of the people there became an example to the rest. On the great plains in the years after the devastation, the buffalo and the elk, the bear and the eagle reclaimed their land, water, and skies. The horses that the Europeans brought back to the continent flourished once again.

These changes took many generations to become habit to the people. They had to learn and discover what was forgotten so many years before. As it was in the old times, the people came together in council to discuss what was happening in their lives. They planned as a group in order not to repeat the same mistakes their ancestors had made.

The people developed craft guilds to make the tools that simplified harvesting food and the building of their villages. They made a deliberate decision to discard many of the implements they felt had contributed to the downfall of the previous society. They made a choice to use no firearms but simpler tools for hunting game.

Metal was used for the shoeing of horses and for making farm and home implements. Wagons were built for transportation when foot travel or horseback was not practical. Gradually the people adopted a quiet, simple, slower style of life. So much time had gone by, it was not easy to remember the greed and the disregard for the land the people before them had practiced. Stories were told from family to family, however, so the world would remember the mistakes that had come so close to destroying their planet.

A bartering, or trade system was developed across the continent. Goods were traded for goods or for work done. Coin was used where it was practical. The coin was stamped with the mark of its denomination. Gold coin was marked with a twenty, silver with a ten, and copper with the mark of a five. Thus, the coins were commonly called marks. These coins were stamped by a guild of metalworkers that distributed them in trade for goods, and so the coin was put into circulation.

Vast areas were set aside by mutual agreement as preserves for wildlife. Here, the game and other animals the people grew to depend on would live and reproduce and again populate the earth. In these places, any person or group was allowed to hunt and to discover as long as the rules set down by society elders were followed. No one was allowed to set up residence there for more than the time it took to collect the animals or plants that were needed. There were no permanent structures allowed in these areas, only the lodges of the plains people, or other temporary tents and wagons were allowed to be used for shelter. In a few spots throughout this vast area, simple cabins were placed that could be used by hunters or travelers for emergency shelter.

Soon, the plains were again filled with enormous herds of buffalo. It was not hard to find bear, elk, or the other animals that once roamed the plains. Few chose to disregard the rules set by the elders. On the rare occasion this did happen, warrior societies composed from several villages would come together to deal swiftly and harshly with those who broke the laws.

The old ones who taught the people to survive also taught them how to be thankful, to show their thanks to the animals that were responsible for their food and shelter. This story takes place many generations after the devastation changed the world. This is the story of the healing of the circle.

Spring Hunt

Bren Redhorse lived with his people on what had been known as the Great Plains. He was born in the shadows of the black hills. His people had lived here for uncounted years. Even before the devastation, they had been here. His family carried the blood of the first nations in them, as well as that of the Europeans. He was of mixed ancestry, as was almost every one of the people today. He had dark hair and skin and the high cheekbones that made his native heritage obvious to those who remembered. He was told time and again through his life to remember his past. This lesson was in him down to his spirit, and that spirit would not let him forget.

Bren was at the age when he would be considered an adult. He was born to the plains, on the day of summer solstice eighteen years ago. He still lived with his mother, Thora, and his father, Ben. Their home was a buffalo hide lodge, where they lived with Bren's younger sister, Aria. Just this spring, however, Bren's parents informed him they were going to build a second lodge. This lodge would be for Bren alone. He would learn in it how to live as an adult, even though the lodge would be set up as close as he cared to have it to the camp of his parents.

He had been raised since infancy on the back of a horse. He was on a horse quite literally before he could walk, as was the custom for all the children of the plains. He caught, trained, and cared for his own small herd since almost before he could remember. To Bren's people, their horses were not only a livelihood but a way of life, and he took this responsibility very seriously.

The early spring morning was cold, and Bren's breath was visible as he made his way to the meadow above the grassy creek. There were spots of snow in the shadow here and there, but the meadow grasses were up, thick, and green.

His job this morning was picking out the horses he and his father would take on the hunt. He knew, without asking, which buffalo pony to choose for his father. Because his father would always choose the roan with the white socks. He himself would choose the dun with the wide nostrils, the mark of a runner. Bren called his dun horse Stone Foot because he could run all day and never have an issue with sore feet, even where other horses would become lame.

Stone Foot always proved to be the fastest in games between the young men of the camp. Bren had been through several successful buffalo hunts on his back. After a quick morning meal, the men of the village would start for the hunting camp. Bren was to choose two horses each for him and his father and two pack animals for each of them as well, eight in total. They would carry their equipment and carry hides, as well as some of the meat, back to the temporary hunting camp. His mother, Thora, along with most of the village, would arrive in camp several days after the hunt began. She would bring horses of her own to load and carry. Thora would also bring a wagon to carry meat and hides, as well as a lodge for the family to shelter in while the hunt continued.

From long practice, Bren knew how to prepare for a hunt. Many seasons he and his uncle Don, his father's brother, had spent their days in the woods, watching the sign the animals left in passing. They stalked deer, elk, and all the animals of the forest or the grassy plains the people used for food. They watched these animals read the ground they walked on in order to move safely through the world. In this way they learned from the animals to track and interpret the stories the earth told. They watched them taste the wind. They learned to judge the weather by how the wind blew and from what direction. His uncle taught him from early childhood that if you watched the world around you, it would teach you how to live well. The words

Don repeated to him so many times became a litany in his mind: "If you watch and listen well, the living world will teach you to live your life in a sacred manner."

Today he carried his old, worn belt knife. It wasn't much to look at, being worn thin from years of honing and use, but it was a good knife, given to him by his grandfather. He also carried the first bow he had ever used. The bow had been given to him by his uncle Don. Don made it with his own hands, while Bren watched and learned. It was strong and short, made of the Osage tree the people preferred for its flexibility, strength, and power. His quiver was full of arrows he'd made himself, during long hours of practice and apprenticeship with Don. The quivers' soft fox hair was soothing as it rustled with his steps.

He crossed the creek that surrounded the horse meadow on three sides and softly whistled to alert the horses to his presence. The dogs that guarded the horses had heard him coming long before he crossed the creek. The meadow was close to ten acres in size and backed up to a steep, thickly wooded hillside. The creek as well as the hillside kept the horses from wandering too far during the night, most of the time.

Bren stepped onto the bank of the creek, where he sat on an old gray cottonwood log to pull his moccasins back on. He saw Whisper and Badger, two herd dogs, running toward him across the meadow. The dogs were large, bred with wolves for their size and temperament. They bounced up to him and greeted him with licks on his face and paws in his lap. The black and tan male and female stretched and lay down in the short grass in front of him. Logan, the owner and trainer of the dogs and the night guard of the herd for this past night, strolled up and greeted Bren.

"How was your night, Logan?"

"Quiet enough," he said. "The dogs let me sleep for the most part. They check the horses several times a night and wake me if they hear something or think something's amiss. It's an easy chore to watch the herd, and we enjoy it when it's our turn. It's been a long time since we had a problem with a bear or wolf. You getting ready for the hunt?"

Bren answered, "Yes, I came for the horses we'll need. You're going, aren't you?"

Logan answered, "I'll be there. Right now, I need to get the rest of the horses moving toward this end of the meadow. The other hunters will be showing up sooner than later. You need help here?"

Bren told him he would manage and watched the young man slip silently through the trees with the dogs.

He was bent to tie his moccasins when he felt warm breath in his hair. He looked over his shoulder into the muzzle of Stone Foot, the short, stocky runner that was his favorite hunter. The horse pushed gently on the side of his head and delicately pawed the ground, anxious for the day to begin. His breath felt wet against Bren's face, steamy in the morning air. Stone Foot knew why Bren had come. He gathered the rest of the animals he'd come for, while Stone Foot followed closely behind. Bren strung them together loosely with a rawhide rope he had stuffed in the sack at his waist.

He mounted Stone Foot bareback and led them across the creek, stopping near a large boulder in the center. Bren looked downstream to gaze at a thin ribbon of fog that hung in the middle of the watercourse. It was a waving translucent curtain as far as he could see, following the water around a curve and out of view. Once across, the string of horses followed Stone Foot at a leisurely pace toward the village. The horses stayed close to Bren on the way back, anticipating what the day held, each of them willing workers.

The sun was not long up, and there was still a nip in the air as Bren rode into camp with his small remuda. It was early spring, and he had dressed himself in buckskin pants with a long-sleeved elk hide shirt that was tanned, smoked, and decorated by his sister. She had learned the old way of using the brain of the animal from their mother. Although she was only fifteen, her clothing was becoming famous for its resistance to hard work and artistry. It was sought after throughout the plains villages.

Bren hobbled the horses in a clearing close to the lodge and made his way there. He saw his sister, Aria, at work on a new shirt. Her long dark hair flowed over her face and partially hid her expression from view as she sat working in the early morning light.

"You're up and about early this morning," he greeted her. "It looks very nice, Aria. It appears you're almost done."

"Very close to it!" she answered without raising her head from the stitch in progress. "Maybe an hour left in it and it'll be ready to wear. It's meant for you to wear on the spring hunt!"

"Thank you, Aria," he answered her. "I can't wait to wear it."

She looked up and smiled at him as he passed.

His mother and his aunt Seela, he knew, would be close by, getting ready for the upcoming hunt. His father was with the elder council, making last-minute plans. This was going to be the first big hunt of spring. It would test the horses and hunters as well as the whole of the village. They would find out during the next few days if their skill had waned during the winter months.

The grasses were up well enough by now, and the ground was beginning to dry from the melting of snow. The larger animals were moving from their sheltering places in the hills and out to the plains. It was time for babies to be born and time to start putting on the weight that would last them through the coming winter.

Bren filled his traveling pack with a change of clothes and a few extra pair of moccasins. He wouldn't need much for the weeks ahead, when they would be away from the village.

He set the pack outside the lodge door and looked around at the mountains to the west. He loved this place. His people had been coming here for every spring hunt since before he was born. In fact, he was born here in this very camp spot, almost nineteen winters ago.

Bren belonged to this place by birth. He felt the closeness of it in his heart every time they returned. He was in the heart of his Paha Sapa, the black hills. The clean light grays of the granite and the deep green of the pines contrasting with the red soil were engraved on his very soul. The lighter green of the spring oak leaves contrasted beautifully with the deep red of the earth.

The spring hunting camp was only a few days' ride from their present home. It was on the border of the plains. He hoped their hunt would take them close to where Bear Butte stood out starkly against the backdrop of the clear blue bird sky. The butte had been revered for uncounted centuries by the people as a place of magic and power. A little farther north and west was the place the ancient ones had named the Little Big Horn Valley, or the greasy grass. The people sometimes camped here for the summer, when the wild vegetables could be gathered. This was a place where the corn, beans, and other foods could be planted within easy distance of the creeks that watered them.

Bren stirred himself and went to look for his father. Ben was a leader of the Elk clan, the elder society that would be leading this hunt. Bren sat himself with a small group of young men who would also be accompanying the hunt. They thought the same thoughts, anxious for the close of the meeting.

Bren's friend and hunting companion, Airik, greeted him with a slight nod.

"I have my horses and bedroll. I have my bow and a full quiver of arrows. What are we waiting on?" he asked Bren.

"We're waiting so you can practice your patience, Airik. The elders need to be certain everything is just so. We can't afford a mistake this close to winter's supplies being exhausted. You know how it works." Bren paused for a moment to make sure his friend was listening. "I hope you've packed your warm hunting clothes, my friend."

"I'm always ready, Bren. I brought the new bow I finished last week. I'll bet a hindquarter and the hide of your best-looking elk that I draw first blood."

"We shouldn't be betting meat that still runs on the plains, but you have a bet," said Bren, and several of the other young men acknowledged the wager. "I'll bet a pair of my sister's moccasins that my bow kills first." They sat in the early morning sun, trying to practice their patience and waiting for the elders' meeting to end.

Moving Camp

The meeting concluded after a few moments, and the village went to work with eager purpose. The hunters would ride within the hour. Everywhere about the village people were saddling horses, packing bedrolls, and making other last-minute preparations for the journey. At last all was ready, and they assembled in the meadow east of the village, riding slowly toward the north. The leaders of the hunt rode first, as was custom. They were followed by the young men who had hunted before. These were followed by the youngest of the hunt, trying their hardest not to push toward the lead and risk being scolded.

As always, the job fell to these youngest to care for the horses, making sure they followed the main party safely. These young initiates earned their right to participate in the hunt with solemn concentration and attention to every detail. The older boys were in a more jovial mood. Having nothing to do but look forward to the hunt, their conversation was more animated than their younger companions.

Bren felt the early morning sun on his back. He relaxed into the rolling movement of the horse under him as he looked around. The mountains reached down from the foothills in gentle sloping fingers to the plain. He could see gold and white flecks of the antelope in the distance. Ever aware, these fleet footed running machines ambled slowly away as the group moved closer to where they browsed. They didn't seem to be the least bit concerned with the closeness of the humans. They knew they could retreat quickly from such a large party. Bren thought of the hides of these animals. They were most prized as summer shirts and dresses. In the hands of a skilled tanner like Aria, they produced a beautiful soft material for lightweight summer dresses or shirts.

The group rested at noon on the bank of a wide creek. They gathered the horses in a large meadow nearby, leaving several young men to watch them. The younger boys fished with spears cut from the cottonwoods and the older men lay in the shade chewing on jerked elk, buffalo, or pemmican made from dried meat, wild plumbs, and cherries. Bren took a moment to look over the weapons he brought with him.

The Osage wood felt warm and familiar in his hands. The sinew backing was smooth and solid. He knew the value of keeping his tools in good shape. He had boiled horn and hoof for hours to make the glue that held the sinew to the face of the bow. The string was made by his mother, from rolling and doubling sinew again and again until a strong chord was produced. He stored several replacements in his hunting bag. He had tried other materials that were being made in the east but found nothing worked as well. He took his skinning knife from the belt at his waist and checked the edge. This was an old knife but sharp. The once broad blade was worn from use but had served him well through his childhood.

Bren was planning to buy a new knife at the fall gather. Gather was the time when people would get together from villages near the sea, from the mountains, and from the plains to meet, to talk, to trade for the things they would need to get through winter.

As he rode, he thought of his many hides tanned and ready to trade. He looked forward to seeing the folks he had met last year. This year there was a special reason for him to do his best at the trade. He had met a young girl with hair the color of golden wheat and eyes the color of glacier water under the sun. She was a farm girl from the other side of the big river. Her family grew grains and brought wagons of flour to trade. Her name was Sara, and never a day went by that he didn't think of her, laughing with the other girls or running with the huge wolves that were her constant companions.

She surprised him with her interest in his ways. He took her hunting for fresh camp meat while at gather. Sara asked him thoughtful, quiet questions as they sat by her family fire, cooking the meat while she helped him scrape the fat and excess flesh from the hide. She seemed to be interested in everything he did and learned quickly. She had stolen his heart with her quiet smile and flashing eyes.

Since she was a young girl, she had raised and trained the big wolves that her family brought with them everywhere. Thunder, the large male, and Winter, his slightly smaller sister, seemed to be her favorites and were always by her side. The big male watched Bren with what he was sure was a bloodlust. The bond Sara had with the two beasts intrigued him. He noticed the small, almost imperceptible signals Sara would give and the eyes that followed her every move with keen interest and instant reaction. Thunder would bring her small tools at the asking and seemed almost to know what she needed before she asked.

Bren's thoughts came back to the present as his companions began to get under way. Airik stared at him with a knowing look as they rode.

"Why do you always think of that tiny girl, Bren? You know, I think I heard from a traveling trader that she was married late in the winter months."

Bren knew his friend was testing him, but that didn't stop him from feeling a twist in his gut. He was, however, determined to show nothing of his discomfort to Airik.

"She'll wait for me, Airik. You and I both know she'll wait. She told me as much, and I trust her word. Besides, I was not thinking of her at all. I spend my time making my weapons ready, while you fill your face. I'll be ready to hunt, and you'll be too fat to sit your horse." He turned to his friend with a stoic smile, and Airik echoed his grin. They had known each other since almost the moment of their births and had grown up learning the ways of the plains people as brothers.

Bren noticed a small band of a dozen antelope about eight hundred yards out from their traveling group. Again, they were paying the travelers no mind, and an idea began to form in Bren's mind. He found his father and told him of his plan.

"I would like to get a few more antelope hides to sell at the gather. You see that group out to our left front? If you would ride toward them slowly in about fifteen minutes, that would allow Airik and I time enough to work our way around the other side of them. The wind is right, if it doesn't change. When you get close and they start to move, you might move them right into us."

Ben liked the idea and told them to go find a place at the bottom of a draw where they could hide.

The two young men rode to the rear of the hunting party and around, into the rolling prairie behind the antelope. Bren got off his horse once and checked on the animals to make sure they were still where he expected them to be.

"They've moved a short distance but are still just grazing," he told Airik. He remounted, and the two hunters moved a bit more away from the small group just to make sure.

Soon they found themselves at the bottom of a small draw about two hundred yards downwind from the animals. They dismounted and walked the horses around the next draw, where they tied them to an old cottonwood stump. They walked back to the steeper draw and carefully worked their way into position where they believed the antelope would most likely move to get away from the mounted rider.

When they were set in their spot, Bren sent up an arrow with a small piece of red cloth tied to the shaft. His father would be watching for this signal both as a marker of their position and to tell him they were awaiting the antelope.

They set three arrows each onto the ground and got their bows out and ready. Bren looked carefully over the crest of the draw and saw his father break away from the main party. He was walking his horse slowly in the direction of the antelope, but at just enough of an angle that he wouldn't panic the group.

Bren counted all twelve of the antelope as they started to move slowly away from his father and toward the spot where the two young men lay waiting. He looked at Airik and quietly said, "I see the whole group of them coming. They're in no hurry, so if they don't panic and start to run, they should come out about four horse lengths to our left. Let's get out one more arrow each, in case we get lucky. Move downhill from me a few yards and wait for my signal. We should both fire at once. There are two good-looking males in the lead and one more at the rear. You let loose at the closest one, I'll take the other, then make your bow ready for a second. After that, we'll try for as many more as we can, if they're not gone."

Airik moved carefully downhill from Bren and again set his three arrows on the side of the draw next to his feet. He knocked one arrow, as did Bren. Then they waited. The sun was warm as they leaned against the earth of the hill that hid them from the animals they waited on.

Bren took in the smell of the prairie dirt and the feel of the warmth radiating off the earth. He watched the clouds in the sky sail on the slow west wind over the vastness of grass and away. He checked the wind at ground level and felt it still coming with the antelope. They wouldn't smell the two hunters, hopefully, until they were upon them.

The timing in his head told him the two males leading the group should be at the head of the draw any moment. Bren slowly moved his body into position for a quick draw and release. No more than three breaths later, he saw an antelope head move into view beyond the draw.

One of the bulls had pulled ahead of the other and was walking slowly into view. The second was no more than four paces behind him. Airik and Bren carefully raised their upper bodies into position and drew their bows back just as the second bull's front legs came into view. Both arrows sang off the strings in unison and hit their marks. The two leading bulls fell without a hop or a kick. They hadn't settled to the ground before the next arrows were knocked and released on their path.

Two cows jogged up to the downed bulls and put their noses to the fallen leaders of the small herd. The bows sang once again. Airik's cow fell immediately, and Bren's cow took three strides before falling to her side.

The young hunter's arrows flew again, and two more cows fell. The remaining animals were panicking now and didn't know which way to run. They were able to get one more arrow each into the herd before they hit full stride and were gone across the hills. The remaining antelope ran full speed across the hunter's field of view, and they let them run. They moved very fast when motivated, and there was not a good chance of a killing shot, so the men sat and watched them disappear into the prairie.

Bren and Airik looked at each other and smiled. Four animals each! That hunt had turned out better than they hoped! The men checked all eight animals to make sure they were dead. They retrieved their horses and rode back the short distance to the kill site in time to see Ben ride up and get off his horse.

The men let the horses' reins drop, knowing they wouldn't stray, and got to work on the antelope. They carefully cleaned out the chest and stomach cavities and took the hides off, laying them out on the ground to wrap the meat in.

"All six well-placed shots," Ben said. "That was a very well-planned hunt!"

"Yes, it went as good as could be expected," Bren said. "We were lucky the wind blew in our favor, and you pushed them just enough. They knew you were there, but they weren't worried enough to run."

They made short work of cutting up the meat. Soon the three hunters were walking their horses across the prairie. They would take their time catching the rest of the hunting party, who continued to travel. This kind of short hunt was done often enough as the hunters moved toward their evening camp.

That first day, the group covered twenty miles over the undulating prairie. Late evening found them nearer a slopping valley, and they made camp. The cook fires were just getting started as Bren, Ben, and Airik rode into camp. They gave the meat from their hunt over to the fire tenders to add to the grill for dinner. All three men started to work on carefully scraping the fat from the hides, in preparation to be salted. From there they would be put away for Aria to tan later. Antelope hides are not as thick as elk or buffalo or even deer, so it was a tedious job. Bren didn't mind, however, as he knew a good antelope hide was worth much more, for summer clothing, when it was well done.

This first night they slept on the bare ground. They had nothing more than a buffalo hide blanket between them and the grass and stones to wrap around them as protection from the cold. Bren sometimes felt he liked this manner of living more than an established village, no matter how transient or seasonal the village might be. The peace of being close to the ground and hearing the earth settle during the night was special to him. He heard the dogs and small creatures moving through the camp. He liked the smell of the grass crushed under him and the trees and sage all around him as they released their scent into the coolness of the night.

Bren fell asleep quickly and woke to the smell of the cook fire. The sun had not yet risen over the horizon, and the air was still wet with the dew of the night before. He loved this life. He loved the smell of the smoke and hearing the familiar voices of family and friends he had known since birth. He lay in his blanket for just a moment, thanking the spirits that he was born in this time.

Bren dressed quickly against the cool morning and packed up his bedding. He hurried to make sure the night guards hadn't fallen asleep, letting the horses wander too far from camp. He was back in time to see the last of the fish spitted and placed around the fire and two flanks of antelope meat taken from metal rods, still sizzling. He sat with the others and accepted a mug of coffee from his uncle.

He wrapped his hands around the thick clay mug and felt the warmth radiate into his fingers. Several of the village ladies were well-known for making fine pots and other utensils that were fired in beehive-style ovens. These ovens were made from rocks mortared together or hardened bricks of the same clay. They worked for hours on end in the summer camps and during the long winter months. The highly prized bowls, mugs, and other implements would be traded at gather. Bren was pleased with the weight of the one in his hands.

At Sara's House

On that same morning, Sara stirred under her bed covers as the sun lit the window in her room. Thunder and Winter both stood and laid their muzzles on the covers at the side of the bed. They looked at her with plaintive stares.

"I take it you're both ready to get the day started?" She smiled as she spoke to them. Their tails moved slowly back and forth as they looked at her. "Back up then and let me get up." They did as they were told, backing up until they were out of the way.

Sara had found the two wolves on the prairie one spring morning four years ago. As she walked across the prairie, she heard the whimpering of the scared and starving pups. She saw a nose sticking out of a hole in a small hill. She coaxed him out with a bit of jerked meat from her pocket. She heard more noise deeper in the hole and, after a few moments, had coaxed another pup out. Both pups were skinny and scared and not used to human contact, but they were also desperately hungry. Thunder was tan with a black saddle and muzzle, and Winter was snow-white, with blue-green eyes. Sara wondered what had happened to the mother of these two wolf pups.

She had to see if there were any more pups in the hole, so she dug and squirmed her way in. She found the back of the small filthy den and felt her way around until she was sure the two were alone. She backed out of the hole and found the two pups looking at her expectantly.

Sara could barely carry both pups but didn't want to take the chance one would run off while she brought the first to the wagon. She made her way back to the wagon and fed the hungry pups a bit of beef broth until she was sure they could stomach meat.

Her dad had been more than a bit angry when Sara showed up with two wolves in her arms. He got over his anger quickly, however, when the white wolf Sara would name Winter crawled into his lap, curled around her full tummy, and fell asleep. Sara named the pup for her snow-white coat and icy-colored eyes.

The two pups had been Sara's almost constant companions ever since. She had learned how to take care of them, mostly by trial and error, and with the patient love of a farm girl. She trained them to be obedient and to track an animal or a person. She had also trained them how to protect her parents' small herd of milk cows and to bring them into the barn for milking or bad weather.

Sara's reputation for skill in taking care of her wolves spread through the community. In her second year with Thunder and Winter, a neighbor brought a small, sickly smoke-colored wolf pup to her. The pup had been found close to death, wandering the prairie not far from town.

Sara took the pup from the neighbor's wagon bed. "She's the color of a smoky fire," she said. She nursed the pup back to health, and in time, Smoke became the mother of four pups of her own, fathered by Thunder. Sara now had a pack of seven wolves. Well, eight if you counted Sara in the mix, which the pack clearly did.

Sara threw the bedclothes back and sat up, surveying her small bedroom. She swept her long braid to her back as she looked around her small room. Sara lived in this house all her life and knew every log and board by heart. Her father built the house before marrying her mother, but his family lived on the land for generations.

They were mostly wheat farmers and planted almost five hundred acres. They also raised milk cows, that Sara took care of. Sara could smell the bread her mother was baking in the front room, which was a combination kitchen and sitting room. She quickly dressed for the day and went out to greet her mother and father.

The house was small enough to be heated by the big cookstove in the front kitchen and the fireplace on the back wall. She found her mother slipping loaves of bread out of the oven and grabbed the unbaked biscuits that were on the table beside it. Ellie, her mother, stepped out of the way, and Sara slipped the biscuits in before closing the door.

Her mother was very proud of that stove. It was cast of iron, very big and very heavy. It was one of the first woodburning cook-stoves brought out from the east coast after the villagers there started making them to sell. The stove was a wedding present from Sara's father. Ellie supplemented their income with it ever since, making breads, muffins, cakes, and pies that she would sell to the cafes in the village.

"Do you want oatmeal with your tea this morning, Sara?" Ellie asked her daughter.

"Please, Mother, I'll go let the pups out of the kennel and be right back."

Sara's wolves followed her out the door, and she latched it behind her. She walked through the yard to the long, low kennel at the side of the barn. Her other five wolves heard her coming and spoke to her in low, muffled woofs.

"I'm coming, guys," she said as she unlatched the gate around the fenced work yard to let the wolves roam the yard. They bounded out and greeted Sara, Thunder, and Winter in turn, before all seven of them ran off to carouse around the yard. Smoke had four pups, fathered by Thunder. There were two males and two females. First was a black-and-tan male Sara named Summer. His brother was the color of smoke and named Dusk. The first female to be born was also a black-and-tan that Sara named Spring. She started hopping around the whelping box as soon as she found her feet and hadn't slowed yet. Last to be born was a completely black little girl Sara called Midnight, or simply Night for short.

Soon after Smoke had the wolf pups, Sara's dad built her a long, low kennel building in the yard next to the barn. It was made of logs, and the packed dirt floor was dug out about three feet. It was just tall enough that Sara could stand up without hitting her head on the low ceiling. The overhead was covered with small round saplings and topped with a thick layer of prairie dirt and grasses. Sara worked the whole of seven days to collect the sod for the roof from a spot close to the house. She dug it up a wheelbarrow at a time and placed each piece carefully.

Sara left the yard gate open as she walked back to the house. She'd trained each of the wolves since they were pups and knew they might leave the work yard but wouldn't go any farther than the front of the house, unless told different by Sara.

"Has Dad gone to the village, Mom?" she asked as she picked up her tea and took it to the kitchen table, where her mother had placed a bowl of steaming oatmeal for each of them.

"No, honey, he's taken the wagon to the Donnelly's farm. They had a cow go into labor last night, and she's having a hard time. They're going to have to pull the calf or lose it. Not likely they'll let that happen."

They ate together and discussed their plans for the day ahead. Sara was planning on working the dogs today, while her mother and father would go into the village to drop off baked goods, butter, and eggs and other products they were selling.

Sara explained to her mother, "Thunder and I are going to work on tracking a bit more, and Smoke and Winter will as well. Now that the grass is up, they should have a better time of it. The pups need to be worked on their leash manners as well as starting to learn to bring the milk cows in without running them ragged. They're at the age when they can do it themselves, but they sometimes get too excited. I'll run Smoke out there with the younger ones a time or two, and she'll teach them."

After breakfast, Sara talked her mother into helping with tracking practice. Having helped with the tracking training many times before, Ellie walked out into the woods near the house. She walked into a small creek in the woods and up the middle of the creek for a few minutes. Stepping out of the water and onto a flat rock, she allowed her feet to dry and then walked over the rocks on the creek bank until she found a cottonwood tree with low, drooping branches.

She carefully climbed high up into the tree and hid between the branches, covered by the new growth of emerging leaves.

Ellie sat and waited for her daughter and Thunder. Soon she saw them approaching the wood over the newly planted alfalfa. Thunder was on a twenty-foot leather lead, but the wolf was walking about ten feet in front of Sara. He had his nose down, intently following the exact path Ellie had taken. Rarely did Sara use the leather lead. It was something she had been playing with of late, to get the wolves used to the idea of being attached to something.

Sara's attention was focused intently on the wolf. She had given him the command to "Track" and pointed out where her mother dropped her hat just outside the house. She watched the wolf's back, head and tail, as well as the way he moved over the grass. This was her favorite part of the exercise, being able to watch his progression on the track. She could see the decisions he made as he headed through the field and toward the woods.

Thunder entered the wood and headed directly for the stream. He stopped at the water's edge and went first right, then left down the bank. Sara could tell he found no track in either direction, so she stood with the lead in her hand, watching him figure out his next step.

The wolf crossed the stream and again cast right and left at the water's edge. Finding nothing, he walked slowly out to the end of the lead and walked in an arch, with his nose to the ground. Thunder suddenly stopped and sniffed the ground back and forth in an area about two paces wide. Sara knew he was back on track when his tail wagged just a bit, and he continued into the deeper woods.

Sara felt the slight breeze blowing from her left and realized Thunder was walking just to the right of the path her mother had taken. The slight disturbance she made in passing lifted just enough scent from the forest floor to give the wolf something to smell. Along with her mother's smell, it was almost too easy, once Thunder realized what was expected of him. After a few turns right and left and one complete circle around a tree, he came to a sudden stop at the base of a large cottonwood. He went to the right and to the left and then circled the tree once around. He sat under the tree and, looking up into the branches, woofed once softly.

Sara looked up into the branches and told her mother, "Be careful coming down, Mom. I think we're done here."

Thunder barked once more as Ellie told him, "Good job, Thunder! You are a very good tracker!"

Sara let him off the lead as her mother made her way down to the ground. The wolf greeted her with a nuzzle as she stroked and praised him, and the three companions headed out of the woods.

Ellie struck up a conversation with her daughter on the way to the house.

"The training is going very well with all of the wolves, Sara. You would get a good price for any of them if you were to take them to gather."

"Mom, these are not wolves to be sold, they are my companions and family. I could no more sell them than I could you or father. The time will come when I do offer wolves to trade, but none of these. Each of them, even the pups, have taught me so much more than I have them. They've taught me about the woods, the movement of the animals that make a home in the woods, and about myself.

"Don't worry, I will make this a profitable concern. I know you and Father are worried about that. Remember I've traded what I have learned when I taught the Donnelly's dogs to guard and herd their milk cows."

"Sara," her mother said, "I never worry that you won't have success in something you start. It's just that spring will be over before you know it, then summer, and the fall gather will be here. I was thinking you might want to have something to trade."

"Thunder and Winter will both be with us at gather this year. When people see how well they're trained, I believe I'll have many requests to train farm dogs or hunters. Once the pups are grown, I can see about getting one more female to breed a few litters as well."

Sara saw the look on her mother's face and smiled, adding, "For trade, Mother, for trade."

Sara's father was just turning the wagon into the yard when she and her mother got home. She filled two water buckets and sat them in front of the horses when they were stopped.

"Should I remove the harness, Dad?"

"No, Sara, let's have some lunch," he said. "Then we'll ride into town and do the business your mother has planned."

"I won't be going to town, Father. I want to work the pups on bringing the cows to the barn. They're just a little flighty yet. If I set Smoke out with them a few more times, they should be right with it."

"All right, well, let's eat, just the same. I want to get started into town before the day gets too late."

They sat down to chicken pot pie just out of the oven. After the noon meal, Sara's mom and dad took the wagon into town, and she headed for the cow pasture gate with all seven wolves scampering around her.

Elk in a Meadow

Don, Bren's uncle, had been a teacher to Bren since he could remember. He taught him how to fish, to make fire with flint and steel. He taught him to catch and clean the small animals that a young boy would hunt. He taught him how to prepare the hides, scraping and stretching them to dry on willow hoops. Don was a good teacher.

Bren owed his uncle Don his reputation as one of the finest trappers and hunters in their village. His hides always brought among the highest of prices at the gather, and he was fast becoming famous for the expert craftsmanship and attention to detail of his finished hides. He tanned a few of his hides himself, and his sister finished the rest. She was, he had to admit, better at the final processes than he was himself.

"Eat fast, Bren, we want to move soon. We have a lot of ground to cover today."

"I know, Uncle," Bren answered. "The hunting camp is another two full days' ride from here, if the children and the elders move fast. My bedroll is ready, and my horse will be, in a moment."

"I'd like to get camp set and have a day at least to scout before the rest of the village arrives. I need a few more elk before the fall meeting."

Although there were always several women who accompanied the first group, most of them came with the supporting group in the wagons that followed the hunters more slowly. They knew it would be a good chance to ride leisurely and gather herbs, onions, turnips, and other foods they would find along the way. The people had made this trip enough to know where the choicest foods and herbs the woodlands and the prairies had to offer.

The hunters cleaned up the camp quickly and mounted their waiting horses. The miles melted behind them. Horse and rider once again fell into the rhythm of the trail. They were now coming upon the higher grass and green tree lines that told them they were entering the big horn basin. They would have to be careful to follow all the rules established by the ancestors who set up this shared hunting area. They wouldn't kill what they couldn't carry out for food. Their camps would be carefully cleaned, and most importantly, their fires would be buried and hidden before they continued. This was prime buffalo hunting space and guarded by the laws of the agreements of all the plains peoples and those who visited here to hunt.

Bren was already seeing the signs here and there of small herds, off in the distance. The group knew better than to go after these, though. The smaller herds were just a forecast of what they would soon see. They were careful now to travel quietly, in case they come upon a large herd and warn the animals of their presence.

Ben decided, as the hunt leader, to continue on the trail through the noon meal. They had made very good time on this second day of the trip. They stopped again after dark and settled quickly around the comfort of the small cook fires.

After the evening meal, the elder hunters gathered around one of the cooking fires to choose scouts. These scouts were sent out first, on the last day of travel, to choose the best campsite and look for signs of buffalo. Bren hoped he would be chosen. The day of scouting would give him a good chance to set his mind to the tasks ahead and hopefully get first shot at a good-looking elk or two.

He sat out of the way of the elders around the council fire along with the rest of the young men. They listened to the words of their fathers as they spoke of the candidates for scouting. He heard his name mentioned quietly several times and noticed Airik, Jamie, and the others looking in his direction frequently. They knew he was the most likely choice as scout. Bren's reputation was known through the village as a skilled hunter and a hard worker, and he was well-liked by all the people. No one seemed to mind that his name was mentioned most.

Bren had skipped a hot evening meal. Instead he would find some coffee and maybe some fruit to eat when he returned. Earlier he rode toward a high hill to see what he could in the distance, before the light was gone. He sat and chewed thick elk jerky as he watched the surrounding country. He memorized as much as he could so he was prepared to give a detailed account of what would be found ahead.

Now he looked past the fire and into the dark, running a picture through his mind of the path he would take. He had seen a forest hundreds of acres wide and deep. He thought this old growth forest would be prime for holding elk or deer.

He was called to the main fire circle along with Daniel, Airik, and four others. The young men were told to prepare to leave early next morning. They would scout ahead for buffalo.

"Bren, I saw you leave camp earlier. What did you see?" asked Don. He was Bren's uncle and one of the elder hunters with a reputation for knowing the movements of the game they were looking for.

"I haven't seen sign of buffalo, other than in single, older bulls or small groups. I did see a place I would check for elk. I had a good spot where I could see for a distance over the prairie, but there was no sign."

"Well then, Bren will go to the northwest with Airik. Two will go north, and two will go north and east. The camp will follow, and we'll meet on a line as we have been traveling. If a herd is sighted, one of the team will find the rest of us, and we will leave sign for the wagons to follow. Don't stay out more than three days and you will send one of your group back after two days to report your progress."

Bren and Airik left before daybreak the next morning. They each trailed a packhorse to carry gear in case they came upon an elk or other game. The young men followed the trail that Bren had mapped. They moved toward the foothills and the forest that started on the west side of a large feeder stream winding toward the Yellowstone country.

They were alert for any sign of buffalo, although neither of them felt they would see such sign until after they cleared the far side of the forest. The trees were thick from the edge of the wood and stayed that way as they continued through them. A buffalo herd of any size would stay away from such thick wood, preferring the open prairie for ease of movement. The horses followed game trails that led them easily through the trees. An hour later, they climbed a short grade that opened onto a large meadow stretching toward the east. They paused and sat for a moment, watching the clearing and the tree line at its edge. The sun was barely above the trees and just at the place where light melted into the woods. Bren caught a movement from the corner of his eye. He pointed to the spot with his chin and froze, waiting. Airik slowly and quietly slipped from his saddle to the ground, straining to see what might be there. After a moment, a shape formed into a body and moved soundlessly into the dappled light under the trees at the edge of the meadow.

They saw the dark golden brown and white of a young adult and very large bull elk. He moved slowly, hesitantly through the thick chest-high grass. His ears moved right to left, casting for sound. His head was elevated just a little as he scanned the woods with his nose.

Bren guessed the distance to the bull at sixty yards. The wind was in his face, so unless the breeze changed as he neared the clearing, the animal would have no scent of him before he was close enough to use his bow. The problem would be in closing the distance to the wary bull without being seen or sensed.

He solved that problem by leaving Stone Foot and the pack-horse with Airik. He could tell by the look on his friend's face that this decision didn't sit well. Airik realized, however, this bull was Bren's, and he would do well to follow his lead.

The young hunter walked, with painfully slow steps, without sound through the trees toward the rock outcropping at the north end of the meadow. He picked every footstep carefully as he maneuvered through the leaves and grass on the forest floor. He stayed well into the tree line to prevent any movement giving him away. However young he was, this bull didn't come to such great size by being careless.

He carried two arrows with his bow, as well as his belt knife. He was dressed in a simple deer hide shirt with long sleeves. His hide pants were of thick elk to protect him from the sage brush and small trees, in case he had to run his horse. He felt the excitement begin to flow through his heart, out the tips of his fingers as he neared the target. He felt the sun warm his skin through the dappled shadows as it shined between the leaves. He moved soundless through the trees.

Bren loved this moment in the hunt, when his senses seemed to sharpen. He could taste the forest in the slight breeze against his face. He heard the almost imperceptible, soft brush of the leaves under his moccasins and felt the air brush against every tiny hair on his skin as he moved through it. The trees seamed to speak to him in their soft, shushing whisper from overhead. Bren believed he could begin to smell the bull's musk as he closed the distance now, to within about forty yards. His blood rushed through his veins. He had to be careful not to let the fever take him over. He knew if he didn't concentrate, his vision could narrow. He would begin to shake and most probably make a sloppy shot. He stopped and took a deep, slow breath. This was his bull, not one Airik would be able to tell stories about showing its back side after hearing him coming.

Bren came to an area in the trees where his progress was impeded by a large rounded boulder dropped by a glacier sometime in the dim echoes of seasons long past. If he scrambled over the boulder, he was likely to make a slight noise as the surface abraded his clothing. Even breaking the shape of the stone could alert the elk to his presence. If he went around the obstacle, he knew it would take some time, and the animal may move farther across the meadow and out of killing range of his bow.

At the rock, the woods met the clearing, forming a bowl that dipped down into the sunlit area. This gave Bren twenty yards to cross from cover to cover. He decided this was his only option.

He watched the elk drop his muzzle into the high grass. Knocking an arrow on the bowstring, he kept it down at his side. Slowly he crept around the boulder and to the edge of the tree line. He moved as if he were walking through deep water, feeling for the bottom. Suddenly, the bull raised his head and stared straight at the hunter. Bren froze in his tracks. He looked down at his hands, concentrating on the position of both. His bow ready, with an arrow knocked in place. He dared not look at the elk, for fear their eyes would meet and the animal would recognize his danger.

He watched only the shape of the bull from his peripheral vision. He had done this many times as a young hunter with rabbits and other small game but had never tried the ruse with something as wary, as formidable as this big bull. He felt the last of the shade on his back and the warmth of the sun on his face and chest as he stood in the transition between wood and open meadow. He stood still as the stone. He felt an almost imperceptible breeze waft over his face and knew the bull would not smell him, for a few moments at least.

The elk slowly relaxed his position and resumed cropping the grass. Bren was thirty yards from him now and knew, if he were going to make the shot, he would have to do it from where he stood. He could not take another step without spooking the elk into flight.

Bren carefully raised his right arm up the front of his shirt to a point on his chest between the center of the breastbone and the armpit. A cloud drifted over the sun and brought the whole meadow into shadow. He stayed in that position while he moved his left hand, with the bow and the arrow held in their positions, almost casually up to meet the right.

Every fiber in him seemed to ache with tension. It seemed to him the stars would shine in the sky before he was in position to take his shot. He relaxed there for a moment and forced himself to breathe. He watched the elk from the corner of his eye, not daring to look directly at him. When he felt he had allowed sufficient time to pass, he slowly placed the fingers of his right hand against the bow-string and began to push the bow away from him with his left. He pulled with his right as he pushed with his left, bringing the knocked arrow toward a position next to his right ear.

It seemed to take forever to Airik, as he watched from the depths of the shadowed forest floor. He couldn't believe the animal was still standing quietly. Bren finally brought his right hand up to his face in full position to release the arrow. His arms ached from the strain of holding tension on the bow. He allowed himself, at last, to take a good look at the elk that stood just yards away, still calmly crop-ping the tall meadow grass. He measured the girth of the bull in his mind. He marveled at the immense stretch of his rack and the play of the muscles in his neck and shoulders as he stood pulling at the grass. Ben had taught him this ritual to honor his kill. He was sure the breeze would change and give him away before he could make the shot.

He took a short breath, released a bit of it, and let go of the shaft. The elk heard the twang of the bow, and his body twitched as his head came up. Bren felt as if time and his heart had both stopped. He saw the arrow leave the bow and wobble side to side as it began to spin clockwise with the fletching. The energy in the arrow traveled up the shaft to the point before it straightened and seemed to gather speed. The fletching feathers spun less than a turn before stabilizing.

Bren saw the whole of it in slow motion. After an interminable flight, the arrow reached its target and buried almost to the feathers. It had struck above and back just a bit from where the right front leg met the massive chest and rib cage. The bull turned half away from Bren and paused before dropping to his front legs. He rolled onto his side with a soft thud, made one last effort to fill his lungs, and lay still in the grass. Bren stood stock-still and, after a moment, had to remind himself to breathe.

The hunter waited a moment more then started forward toward the big bull. Bren said a silent prayer as he moved, thanking the elk for his sacrifice. He heard a whoop from Airik and drew his belt knife as he closed the distance across the meadow. He checked for vital signs from the bull as he walked. He looked for breathing, the nostrils flaring, or the twitch of a hoof. Reaching the bull, he tapped an eyebrow with the tip of his bow, looking for any reaction. Finding none, he made a cut deep across the bull's throat, allowing it to bleed out as much as possible.

Airik brought the horses to a stop in the grass where Bren stood admiring the big bull.

"That was the most excellent shot I've ever seen. Look at the placement. Exactly where it should be for a quick kill. It went right into the heart muscle. I was waiting for him to run every time you moved. How did you know he wouldn't?"

"I didn't," Bren said. "I wanted to get as close as I could, and I couldn't get a good shot from the trees. If you listened and watched Don better, you would be able to do the same."

"I would not. I don't believe I have the skills you do. In fact, I think there is something more than skill involved. I watched you during that whole time of stalking. You moved as if you were in a different place. It seemed to me you were not you but one of the elk. It was a bit frightening, actually. There are things some are meant to accomplish that others can't.

"I have to say, even if we hadn't been friends from birth, I would seek your company. The teachers tell us in every couple of generations, people are born that stand above the rest. They are touched by the magic of the true human path, the red road. I've always thought you one of these people. I'm glad I can call you friend."

"Airik, patience and practice aren't magic. I killed an elk, that's all." Bren grinned before he continued. "It was a fine shot, though."

Bren and Airik worked mostly in silence to skin and quarter the animal. Bren placed his fists between the skin and flesh of the body and pushed and pulled to remove the hide, preventing the knife cuts that could score the hide, decreasing its value as a finished piece for clothing.

Under a Mountain

After quartering the elk, the two young hunters wrapped the meat into the hide. Bren brought the antlers, still attached to the head, and tied them to his packhorse along with the hide and half the meat. Airik took the other half. They would be used for making knife handles, spoons, and other tools. The brain would be used to tan the skin into a soft and flexible hide for clothing. The bones could also be cleaned and made into utensils, game pieces, and other items. The people had learned to use most of the animals they took for food, much in the way their ancestors did. Bren's sister still liked to use the sinew from the back strap and shoulders, as well as the legs, in many of her sewing projects.

The two scouts took a few minutes to wander around the woods near the area of the meadow where Bren had taken the elk. Not far from the first meadow, they found a large flat area with a few trees. This second meadow was blocked from view by a tremendous face of granite soaring straight up from the valley floor to a height they estimated at almost a hundred feet. The access to the meadow was a trail little more than a wagon width from one side of the wall to the far side. The second meadow was hidden from the first by a deep growth of forest. This old growth forest was thin enough that many lodges could be set among the trees. Lodges placed here would be protected from the worst of the wind and the snow of deepest winter. They would also be hidden from view of anyone who didn't know where to look. There was ample deadwood lying about, and some of the oldest trees had died upright. The larger meadow was big enough to hold and feed twice the village herd, but not so large that the horses could not be easily gathered and find shelter in the trees.

The wood mostly consisted of thin high lodge pole pine and bigger sap-filled pine. After a mile or so into the wood, over the old, well-used game trail, the trees turned to a mix of pine with aspen. There were even several groups of very large cottonwood trees along the creek, at the end of the meadow. There was sign of game everywhere on the trails that constantly crossed one another.

At the far end of the meadow, Bren saw a fissure had opened in the granite of a huge wall of stone. The wall continued to rise, almost straight up the mountain. The clean granite rock was smooth and straight on each side of the fissure. A clear, deep spring welled from within the rock. The water arced out and down in a ten-foot drop, into a natural basin forty feet across. It spilled over the rock into a wide, knee-deep stream that ran through the middle of the meadow and into the trees. Several smaller feeder springs ran into the stream from somewhere up the mountain.

The friends dismounted and walked around the park, breathing deep of the air scented with pine and wildflowers. Bren thought this place could not be any better if someone had built it specifically for a winter camp. It was just outside the area set aside for only hunting, so the people would be able to use it as they liked. He and Airik laid out the village in their heads as they walked. In their minds, they placed the lodges of the elders in the spots closest to the wall's edge. They saw the large communal meeting house in the center of the camp. They drew a floor plan in the dirt of a communal kitchen that would be close to the meetinghouse. They outlined a cold storage cellar that could be cut into the earth below the mountain and a smokehouse close by. There was still room for plenty of space between the lodges. Privacy was important in the winter months, when tempers could be shortened by inactivity and the cold. Bren didn't know if the elders would be interested in this area, but he felt it was a good enough candidate for winter quarters to speak to them. Airik agreed with him. Bren marked the trail well in his mind. He cut four notches in a tree at every intersection of trails, on the way out of the woods.

They left the trail they had taken into the wood and took another that led them west of where they entered. They turned north after a while, on still another well-used game trail, in the general direction the hunting party would take. The ancient growth of forest continued for another five miles before thinning out gradually onto a point looking down over a wide area of undulating prairie floor. The grass before them waved in the breeze as it rolled over the hillocks for what seemed like days.

The rich green of the grasses was broken here and there by the blue of water from a pond or a stream. The streams and rivers were marked by tree lines that meandered through the country like an old grazing buffalo. The green mats of grass folded over the banks and into the water. The deep red ochre soil stood out against the grass in spots. In others it was bleached pale pink by the sun. The blue sky appeared like an ocean turned upside down. To the northwest were the Bighorn Mountains. The snowcaps shined as if lighted from within. They marched away north, toward a cold, windy country still days away that few of Bren's people had memory of.

Below them on the prairie, they both noticed something that made them sit high in their saddles and carefully scan the grassy rolls. The grass was matted smooth in places and trampled everywhere else. There were buffalo droppings scattered about, and the color of it, even from their distance, told them what they were seeing was as recent as last night. They rode down the slope to confirm this area had been used by a very large herd as an overnight bedding spot. Being early in the afternoon, the herd should not be far away. There was no sign of a hurried departure.

The companions' hunting habits took over, and they dismounted to walk their horses through the low spots between the hills. No words were spoken between the two. Speech wasn't necessary in the moment. They knew each other well enough to anticipate the other's every thought. They were careful to see what was ahead of them, trying not to give themselves away. Two miles from the bedding site, they followed a dry streambed around a large hill and saw the herd a quarter mile to their front. Bren estimated its size at more than four thousand animals. The sound of the herd was astounding.

The lowing of cows, the high plaintive call of calves separated from mothers, and the bull's bass notes from everywhere in the herd. This was a sea of buffalo.

They were grazing around a large clear pool of water at the end of the streambed. Some were standing in the water to their bellies. Bren pointed out several cows he thought might be in the water to take a break from their nursing young. He could see several first-year calves standing very near the water, calling for their mothers. He was glad to see the many buffalo calves born this year and the yearlings as well. This herd was doing very well indeed.

Airik and Bren stood for a few moments, taking in what they were seeing.

"I'm always awed when I see this," said Airik. "The size of the herds amaze me, after what the teachers said our ancestors once did to them. I have a hard time believing they could come back from so few to so many in such a short time."

"There've been eight or more generations of the people since the devastation, Airik. That's a long time for nature to right a wrong. They look strong and healthy though, don't they? That's all that is important now. The herds are well, and there's plenty of grass to go around. I feel sorry for the town dwellers in the east, who still live on cow and pig meat."

"A well-roasted pig makes a fine meal, Bren. I've seen you fill your belly with it more than a time or two." Bren smiled at his friend. "I'm not saying it's an altogether bad meal, but I would get tired of the taste of cow and pig meat after a time, wouldn't you?"

"Yeah, you're right," Airik said, and a smile crept over his sun-browned face. "But you know, along with that farm-raised dinner comes the wine they make in the west. I could find a spot for a skin of that tonight."

"I'm looking forward to fall. The gather is coming at summer's end. There will be wine enough to go around."

Airik said, "Everyone knows you're looking forward to fall, Bren. Everyone knows why as well."

Bren let the remark slide.

The men made small talk while they appraised the herd and what would be the best course of action for the hunt. They made a plan of approach if the herd continued in the direction they were presently grazing. Bren figured, from the condition of the surrounding grasses, the animals had stayed close to the watering hole for most of the week. This spoke well for the weather and available water in the area.

They decided this herd wouldn't travel far during the night. The animals were hidden well enough they could take their time getting the news back to the hunting group. They stayed well downwind from the herd so their smell wouldn't spook them and traveled several miles before again dismounting. This time, on the highest hill they could find, they built a small fire of dried sticks and piled green sage on top. The smoke they made was a signal the others would understand. The main traveling body would stop and wait, as there were scouts coming in with news all should hear. They let the fire burn out and scattered it well, to make sure it was dead before continuing.

Airik and Bren made no attempt to hide themselves now. The wind was blowing at their backs. They were away from the herd and wanted to make good time back to camp. They had fresh buffalo horses with the main herd, so they traveled quickly, being careful not to overburden these mounts but in a hurry to share their news.

Airik was first to spot the smoke of the main group. In the distance, it appeared as a slight tendril and could have been missed very easily. This was a signaling fire as well. It would tell any scouts near enough to see it where the main body was located.

With an hour of steady riding, they came into camp an hour before dusk. There were more and more fires starting up as dinner preparations began. They shared the story about the location of the buffalo herd and were told that one of the other scouting groups had also found a herd. Plans were made to split the hunters early the next morning and start each group for a hunt. They would make better time traveling in smaller groups and were likely to get more meat and hides without depleting either herd overmuch.

With the business of the hunt planning out of the way, Airik sat down by the fire and began the story of Bren's elk hunt. While he told the story, steaks broiled on the fire, and coffee perked in a steel pot. He let slip he had a story to tell when they entered camp, despite the looks Bren shot his way. The younger members of the party had been at him to tell it. Airik told in great detail about the stalking of the bull and the way Bren entered the clearing in full view of the animal. The hunters listened with rapt attention. The younger boys stared at Bren in awe. Some of the older hunters were looking at him with envy and a few in disbelief.

Bren's dad spoke, "Don has taught you well, Bren. This is why you're chosen as a scout so often. The younger boys will do well to learn your methods. It is sometimes not enough to be a good shot or to know the life patterns of the animal you hunt. There's something else much harder to achieve. You must become as close to the land as you can. We are but one of the animals that live here. This is one of the things the ancestors forgot, and look what it led them to. They are gone, along with all their ways. We're here to make sure we walk the proper road. You'll be a good teacher, I'd wager. Now let's eat some of that elk before it cooks too much."

The elk was spitted on sticks and roasted over the open cook fires. The sticks were run into the ground at the edge of the fire. Several roasts had been cut, and steaks were being placed in pans as well. There were large kettles of venison stew with onions, potatoes, carrots, and turnips.

The whole group was laying around the area of the camp kitchen. They were planning the hunt that would take place over the next several days while checking their tools and weapons. Here and there a pipe glowed, lighting the craggy face of an elder. This was a good time. The people were together, working toward a common goal of feeding their village through the coming seasons.

A Sea of Buffalo

A messenger had been sent out to inform the trailing camp of the plan. They would need to prepare a camp close enough to both herds that the meat could be easily transported from each hunt by the wagons they would send out once they arrived.

Bren sat on his buffalo robe, sharpening his knife, and made sure the sling on his quiver was strong. He adjusted the strap so it hung off his back at the correct angle when he was mounted. He made sure he had plenty of arrows and that the feathering was tightly wrapped with sinew. He'd been taught sinew was the best wrap for arrows. The sinew was more resilient to wear and more easily repaired in the field than other threads obtained from the traders. The glue boiled down from the bones and tendons of the animals had a tendency to destroy thread but kept the sinew strong through longer hunts.

Earlier in the evening, the horses had been tended to. They were brushed with handfuls of sage and wooden brushes with hair from pigs. Their hooves were cleaned and dressed. Of all the equipment the hunter used, his horse received the most attention. If the horse's feet were sore, he would not run well. If he took a fall in the midst of a pursuit, he could cripple or kill himself or his rider.

These thoughts came to Bren's mind as he made himself ready. He ran his hands slowly over Stone Foot's body, feeling for too much heat that would signal a strained muscle. He went over everything he had been taught, ticking off the lists and checking again. He wanted to be sure when he started after meat, he need only concentrate on the movement of the horse and the buffalo as they raced across the grassy ground.

Bren took his bedroll and moved away from the group earlier than most. He found a spot under a group of Aspen trees for the night. He wrapped himself in his summer robe and went quickly to sleep. He wanted to be well rested and ready to hunt.

Bren woke in the night. Keeping his eyes closed, he felt the pressure of tiny feet across his chest and knew he was being visited. The field mouse stopped on his chest as he sensed Bren was aware. They sat that way for a few moments, until the mouse's panic subsided. He slowly crept up to Bren's chin, and Bren could feel the tiny rapid breathing as the mouse sniffed. Then turning, he hopped into the dark. Bren faded off again, wondering if the visit had truly happened or was only dreamed.

He was awakened by a kick to his heel. Opening his eyes, he saw Airik grinning down at him.

"Get up, you bone bag, everyone else is ready to ride and waiting for the lazy ones."

Bren knew this wasn't true but let Airik have his moment. He couldn't hear the bustle around the camp that went with preparation for such an important event. He was surprised, however, that Airik was up before him.

He saw the last few stars in the sky and the spreading of a deep cerulean blue as the coming sun streaked the eastern horizon. He sat up and pulled on new moccasins he had unpacked the night before. Dressing quickly, he made for his horse. Today's trip would call for only one horse. The dun-colored runner had been chosen the day they left the village for his speed and sure-footed stride. The horse nickered at him from the dawn mist. Bren grabbed his bridle and went to the herd. He slipped the harness over the horse's head and led him back toward where his father had picketed his own favorite hunter.

Bren led both horses to where his father and Airik were quietly talking. They sat around the fire and sipped coffee between bites of bread and elk left over from last night's meal. They learned from Mika that the wagons had been contacted last evening and were not far from the camp. Mika had ridden out soon after the scouts finished their reports, to contact the rear group. They would be here in plenty of time to help with the first of the meat.

They were soon joined by more of the hunters, until everyone in their group was gathered. The men split up into two hunting groups. With last-minute wagers and wishes for a safe hunt, they mounted and made their way out into the waking prairie. The sun was just coming full over the horizon as Bren's group rode up the hillside that hid the camp from the wider grasslands.

The horses were showing signs of life now. They had been through this many times before and knew what the early day portended. Soon they would be running alongside thousands of tons of buffalo. They pranced and hopped, the excitement infectious. Ben smiled at his son with obvious affection. He was as ready to run as the horses. This was truly the most natural way to live, Bren thought as he looked over at Ben. It made his heart big to ride beside his father.

They rode for a half hour before the first sighting of the herd. The scouts to the front had seen the animals from a high ridge. Now was the time for the hunt to begin. The elder hunters decided the best way to approach was the old way. They brought buffalo robes with them for this purpose. They would leave the horses to the rear and slowly approach the herd from the downwind side. The younger hunters would hold the horses, following closely so they could bring them up quickly when they were needed. As they got closer, the hunters would cover themselves with the robes, to appear as much like a buffalo as possible. The eyesight of these huge beasts was not the best, and this trick had worked for many hunts. As long as the wind stayed favorable, their trick should work.

The stalk was slow and careful work but worse for the young ones delegated to hold the horses. They watched the luckier hunters slip away through the grass and tensed every muscle with the waiting. If this was done right, the group should be able to kill many nice cows before the herd noticed. A change in the wind, however, could ruin the hunt. It could become dangerous in seconds if the herd was spooked enough to stampede into the men on foot. The last hundred yards was covered at a crawl, with the right and left flanks of the group moving in unison, at times waiting for an individual to catch up with the line. Patience was key to a good outcome.

Luck was working in their favor today, as the herd was strung out on the side they were approaching. The animals were separated by enough distance that it would be easier to get a shot and hope for a quick kill. At last the line was within bow range. The hunters stopped and assumed sitting or kneeling positions with their robes pulled loosely over their heads. Bren brought one knee to the ground and brought his bow into position as he scanned the herd for a target. He laid two arrows against his leg in case he might need a second or third shot. Slowly the hunters drew their bows. Thirty men held their breaths. Bows began to sing, and arrows crossed the distance to unsuspecting targets. Bren heard at least two arrows fly before he let go of his. He watched the spin of the arching shaft as it flew.

The cow he had chosen turned her head as she was struck and tried to bite at the spot where feathers were now sticking out of her hide. She took a step, stopped, and appeared to concentrate on moving. Her front legs quivered at the command to run. The knees buckled, and the animal fell.

From the corner of his eye, Bren saw several bulls and cows had taken less accurate shots and were trotting off. Within eyeshot, several more buffalo were now laying as his was. He knocked another arrow as he quickly looked for his second target. He thought how lucky this hunt was starting out and that this would be a time his people would remember in stories around fires when snow was deep and cold.

Bren chose, but the cow was too far away to risk a shot. He got to hands and knees, moving forward once again. He saw many of the group in the same posture. Airik had struck his mark, but not with a killing shot. Bren watched as his friend carefully let fly another arrow that did the job. She was not able to rise but had not died quickly enough.

When he was close enough, Bren raised carefully to his knees and took his second shot. The cow that he chose turned as the shaft was released and the arrow penetrated to the hilt too far back to be a killing shot. Bren knocked another and took quick, careful aim at the retreating cow. She turned her side to him to avoid colliding with a bull, and he took the shot. This second shot hit its mark. The cow went down, rolled over her shoulder, and was still.

Bren looked up to see his friends stop moving forward. The herd was quickly trotting to the northeast. They appeared to be looking around them for the presence of animals other than themselves, but they were not showing signs of panic yet. Many buffalo were down behind him. Now that the arrows weren't immediately needed, the hunters would leave them in their kills to identify the owner.

The helpers brought the horses quickly up to the kill site, where they would assist with the processing. The wagons would soon come forward, and they would begin the butchering process. A few of the wagons would load what they could and make their way back to camp, where the hard work of smoking and drying and preparation of the hides would begin in earnest. All day long, as long as the hunt continued, the wagons would move back and forth from camp. They would repeat the process until the light left them, if they were lucky.

Bren went to the first cow and soon had it gutted, ready to go to the wagon. Her hide was in good shape and would make a nice winter robe. The hides that were not in such good shape would be used by the village or traded for use as a lodge panel, coat, or other covering. He left his arrow folded within the hide as a marker of ownership.

The men mounted and began to gather behind the rise of a hill where they could check the direction of the herd. They would hunt on horseback for the rest of this day. They let the herd move without harassment for the time being and so had time to check that the horses were ready for a running hunt.

The cow Bren brought down second was round and fat for so early in the spring. She looked to be in her prime. This hide would bring a very good price after Aria tanned it. The hunters passed around handfuls of jerked meat and ate as they discussed the movement of the buffalo herd and the best approach. They finished eating as the last of the wagons rolled up to the group and the first rolled away toward camp.

The men greeted their families and filled them in on news of the last few days. They took little time catching up on the news. They were here to hunt and anxious to follow the herd again. The young men, feeling unfortunate to have been chosen for horse holders, were rewarded by being allowed to ride out first and scout the herd. They were first given strict instruction as to their manner of approach and report. This was a fairly safe introduction to scouting. Their faces shone as they wheeled their horses and trotted after the herd. The trail was not hard to follow since the ground had been churned by thousands of hooves.

The main group continued in quiet, good-natured conversation to follow the path of the herd. This day was turning out to be very productive. Over thirty buffalo had been taken and no one as much as scratched in the process. Each person took stock of their weapons as they rode, because the next stage in the hunt would be intense. Now would come the chase. Every one of the mounted hunters would bear down on more than five hundred buffalo and ride among them as they took aim with bow and arrow. It was not unusual to have at least one horse gored, or one rider thrown from his horse, if the herd panicked.

The young scouts were not long finding the herd. They came racing back along the churned path and skidded to a halt in front of the leader. "They are no more than a mile ahead. They ran hardly at all. We found a draw we can walk the horses through to a point fifty yards from their flank. From there we can mount and charge."

"So, Nic, I allow you to scout for the herd and you take over my hunt? I'm going to have to watch you."

This came from Don, who grinned as he spoke. The young man grinned back.

"A suggestion only. It's your decision, of course."

"Good work, all of you. Now show us this path to meat, and you can lead the approach."

The scouts made a show of stalking to the point nearest where they last saw the herd. They dismounted, walking their horses carefully to the point where the near flank could be seen. Bren took note to compliment them on an excellent job, when the hunt was over.

This was proof they had been paying attention to all their teachers. Once more the excitement became a palpable thing. The hunters were nervously making last-minute checks on their mounts, their weapons, and one another. Bren could almost smell the adrenaline pumping through the group. He centered himself, slowly breathing and relaxing into the place where he could shut out the nerves. The hunters mounted after a moment and were ready to ride. The scouts were in front, and the rest of the group fit where they could in the narrow draw. Bren's horse pranced and snorted in anticipation. He could feel the tense, steely strength of the buffalo pony under him.

They started from the cover of the low grassy hill at an easy trot so as not to panic the herd. They knew they would begin to run soon enough. Each rider encouraged his horse to the best position.

Sensing their approach, the herd began to move, and the race was on. Within a few yards, they were at full speed. The riders began to fan out along the right flank of the herd. The horses were working themselves as close as they could get to the thundering dust cloud. Bren chose a cow and moved the dun toward her. She looked full grown but didn't appear to have a calf. She would be young and her meat tender. His hands held bow and arrow while the horse was controlled with pressure from his knees and feet. The dun was working almost from instinct now.

Bren needed little correction to get the position he needed for the shot. His eyes stung with the dust. His body canting just slightly right and left with the horses running. The terrain they covered was mostly flat, but the dun was running through scrub brush, affecting his balance. Hair whipped Bren's eyes, making it difficult to focus. He pulled the short bow to full draw, set the arrow on the target as best he could, and released. The cow toppled head over heels in a cloud that obscured her from view. The dun ran.

He had already dismissed the cow and began selecting a new animal to chase. This was wonderful sport to him, but to run with the buffalo was a dangerous game. Bren found a bull to his front and pushed his hunter to catch up. He saw he had chosen an old bull and edged his sprinting pony past, to a target worth the chase. The older the bull, the tougher the meat and the hide would probably be scarred. Bren saw a huge cow in the group just yards ahead of them. He urged his horse on and carefully cut into the herd behind the cow.

Being inside the herd was not the safest position, but the chance was also part of the thrill of the game. In their panic, the buffalo paid little attention to the horse and rider that were among them. They could easily damage the small pony with a turn of the head, and if rider and horse went down in this tumult, it meant almost certain death for both.

The dun quickly caught the cow and matched its pace. Bren leaned to his left and began to shout at the few animals that were between his horse and the open grass. They moved to put distance between themselves and the strange noise, and Bren sat ready. He quickly aimed at the rib cage exposed to his bow and let fly the shaft. The dun heard the twang of the release and pulled hard to his right. Bren held to the mane to keep from being pulled off and under the churning feet. The animals behind continued to surge around him like a dark frothing flood of hair and horn, as the horse pulled up and slowed, reacting to Bren's gentle leg pressure.

The horse was trained well and ran a large arc across the grass, turning back toward the herd. First it slowed to a gallop then a trot before coming to a stop at Bren's slight pressures. There was empty grass around them now, and they stood watching. The huge mass of the running herd continued past. Both animal and rider slumped slightly where they were, breathing hard. Bren's legs hung loosely and moved with the rhythm of the horse's heaving sides.

He felt the calm return to them both. He was sure he had seen the arrow hit its mark but hadn't seen the cow go down. He looked back along the trail. The brown bodies of the fallen buffalo lay on the churned prairie like stepping stones in a rocky stream. The cow was there lying on her side, where she had died as she dropped. The shaft of Bren's arrow barely protruded above the hide, halfway up on her right shoulder. Not his best placement, but a killing shot nonetheless.

He looked around the hunting ground and saw that few of his fellows were still in the chase. Two or three young ones still followed at a trot, watching the direction the herd had taken. The majority were sitting as he was, surveying the aftermath on the broken ground of the prairie. Several hunters farther back in the field were already opening their kills and removing the liver, heart, and other organs considered to be delicacies. A small group of young hunters had taken the liver from a young cow and were sprinkling the yellow contents of the gallbladder on the organ before taking bites and passing it around.

Bren saw most were still mounted, but Mika was not. One of the younger hunters, he was on his feet at his gelding's side. Mika was running his hands gently over the horse's left flank and appeared to be speaking to the animal in soothing tones. The horse stood still but quivered at his touch. Bren trotted Stone Foot to him and dismounted. He saw what he expected to. The horse had been gored by the turn of a buffalo's head. Mika had also not been able to resist the temptation to run inside the herd.

Bren examined the injury and reassured Mika that it didn't look too bad. "Hold steady now, Mika. It's not as bad as it looks." He called for a passing rider to find Lanis, the village healer. The wound was not very deep, although he was sure it would be much worse if inflicted on a man. He thought it best to have it tended to where the horse stood rather than walking the animal several dusty miles back to the wagons.

Lanis arrived at a dead run. Stopping her horse several yards from the injured animal, she flung herself off before it had come to a stop. Mika stood cradling his gelding's head. She gave the young man a cold, knowing stare as she walked stiffly up to him. She had read the sign on the animal and in the guilt on the young hunter's face.

Lanis knew full well what side the hunters had made their charge from and surmised the cause of the wound. She didn't hold with abusing the trust of these animals for the thrill of the chase. Mika said nothing. He turned his face from her with a pained expression.

Lanis gently washed the wound with a cleansing liquid mixed with crushed herbs. Next, she applied a thick, pungent salve that numbed the area. The horse's relief was visible and immediate. His whole body shuddered and began to relax. Lanis took a curved metal needle and thick sinew thread from her bag and began suturing the wound. She gave Mika terse instruction on care of the wound and a small pot of salve for later use. She rode away cursing hotheaded men in general.

Mika stood bewildered and shaken. Bren realized how much he cared for his animals and so let him chastise himself. Besides, he thought to himself, he had done the same thing. It was only by the luck of the hunt that the roles weren't reversed. Mika made arrangements with Don to take care of his meat and started on the walk back to base camp, leading his injured buffalo pony. Only time would tell if the horse would become shy of the chase after this day.

Bren began to prepare his kills for the wagons and the butchering. He left the meat wrapped in the hides to protect it during the move back to base camp. Bren and Don rode out to find the wagons. They helped load the buffalo carcasses, now cut to manageable pieces, onto the flat wagon beds. The two and four horse teams were well trained and walked from one buffalo to the next. They needed little correction as they stopped with the wagon beds' rear section as close as possible to the fallen animals.

Camp dogs were being used to pull travois loaded with meat. Bren thought, what an excellent group this was. The people would hunt for another day, or several, if the weather held fair, and the herd didn't move too far. Everyone from the head elders to the camp dogs were doing their part to make sure the people had sufficient supplies for the coming summer season.

On the ride back to base camp, Bren reflected on the events of the day and how proud he was to be a part of this village. His people worked well together this day. He hadn't seen anyone need to ask for help from another. If there was a job to be done, someone stepped in and helped until it was completed.

Halfway back to camp, Bren was hailed by three young men running their horses toward himself, his father, and Airik. They stopped short of the group and beckoned Bren to follow.

"Bren, you have to come see this! You won't believe what we've found."

They left their heavily laden packhorses with one of the young hunters and trotted after the two. The young men had been scouting the trail and led them between two small hills. Soon they looked down into a small green valley. Bren saw a herd of buffalo and immediately noticed what the young men were pointing out. There, at the edge of two huge willow trees, stood four white buffalo calves. As he watched, the calves wandered for a moment then settled, laying down in the deep green grass, about four horse lengths apart. These calves weren't light tan or an off-white shade. They appeared to be as white as new snow.

Bren couldn't pull his eyes from what he was seeing. "Go get Don, please. And bring Lanis as well. They need to see this," he said to one of the young men. "Father, do you see what I'm seeing?" Bren quietly asked.

"Yes," he answered. "They've lain across from each other, in what appears to be the four cardinal directions. It's as if they send a message. They are facing inward, looking at one another. The rest of the herd is milling about quietly eating. Not a single animal has entered the circle. See how the four cows stand very near to each white calf. They must be the mothers."

Shortly Don and Lanis trotted up on their horses. Don sat still and watched. Lanis gasped and jumped down from her mount. She took three or four quick steps from the group before she stopped and stood looking.

"Look how they lay, Don. Have you ever seen such a thing?"

"No, Lanis," he answered her. "In my lifetime, I have never seen the like of this. I believe no one has."

"But these are fascinating times," Ben added. "A new age is upon us, I believe. I've heard such events as this being foretold. We need to send riders to the villages who hunt this area. We must do everything we can to ensure these white buffalo calves are not hunted. They need to be watched to see what becomes of them, or rather, what they become."

They sat quietly watching for a bit, before Ben said, "We'll send riders as soon as we get back to camp. Let's go back to the hunt party and spread the word now. We can only do what we can do, but at least we can pass the word. There is something very special here." He glanced at Lanis, who was wiping tears from her welling eyes.

They sent riders in all directions to contact each village as far as they could ride in four days' time. They were to tell what was seen, but not too much of where the white calves could be found. The riders were also told to say that the white buffalo calves were under the protection of the plains villagers, and Ben's family of the elk dreamer clan, in particular. Those riding the message trails had instructions to begin their return after four days, without fail.

The riders would trade their mounts for fresh horses in each village. They would be taking time only to eat as they told their story. They would sleep for a few hours when they must, then swap their riding gear to a fresh horse and be away. They knew their succession of mounts would be waiting for their return all along the trail, so that each village would get their same horse on the return trip. The rider would return home with the horse he started on. It was considered an honorable thing to allow the rider to have your best horse. In this manner, news had been spread reliably across the plains back through the generations.

When the hunting party reached the camp, they saw the other party had done well also. Everyone was busy cutting meat to be placed on the drying or smoking racks. Others were preparing hides or cooking in groups. Word spread quickly of the four white buffalo calves. Preparations were made for the two young hunters who had first seen them to take a small party back to view them next morning.

Bren got to work on his share of the animals as soon as he saw to his horses.

He looked around as he worked, watching the industry of the people.

They worked happily and, for the most part, complained little unless it was in good-natured jesting. He saw skills today that he knew would rival any on the plains. He saw the first of the stars overhead, as the sun had gone down while they worked. He felt the coolness of the evening breeze in his face. He smelled the sweet perfume of sage and the high grasslands at sunset. He watched all this and knew beyond doubt, he had been born in the right time, in the right place, and to the right people. For Bren Redhorse, there was no better time to be.

He spoke to the elders at the base camp the night of the first hunt. He and Airik told them about the meadows they had found. The elders were interested in seeing them after the hunt, on the way back to the spring village site. Bren and Airik would guide a few of the elders to the spot for an inspection of its possibilities as a winter camp.

The work was done at the hunt camp to get the meat ready for storage. Racks for drying and smoking were scattered everywhere around camp. They took a good number of animals, and no one had been injured. The base camp support group and the hunters had to send back to the village for more wagons and packhorses to transport the meat. Every wagon would make more than one trip to take the meat from the fields. The group would stay at the hunt campsite for a week or more in order to complete the processes and package the meat so it wasn't spoiled on the trip back.

The hunters stayed in camp a full two days eating and visiting. They repaired and cleaned their equipment and rested their horses and themselves. Mika's gelding was doing much better under his careful ministrations. He had stayed with the horse since the injury, keeping him hobbled next to his small hunting shelter in order to keep him away from the herd. Lanis checked on them every morning and was even beginning to speak to Mika without the venom that had been evident in her voice earlier on the hunting field.

The next morning, Bren was awake again at first light. He stayed in his mother's hunting lodge since the hunt camp group had arrived. The rising sun shined through the door and cast a golden glow inside the small lodge. He smelled the odors of morning in the camp. Oats were cooking on the fire, and the coffee smelled strong. There was meat and fruit and bread for those who would get out of the sleeping furs before the children ate it all. Most of the youngest had stayed in the village with caretakers, but those who were of age to help had been brought for that purpose. They could eat a hunting camp down to empty plates in a hurry, and Bren didn't want to be left with no breakfast. He got up and washed at the nearby creek then joined his family for the morning meal. He ate while they talked about the hunt, the possible winter camp that Bren had found, and also the coming of the fall gather.

"You should do well this year with the traders, Bren. I've seen your hides, and they're all top quality. Aria has been working hard to get the elk tanned. In fact, she's finished with that one and has almost finished scraping the buffalo. I hope you don't forget her when you're trading."

"I won't, Mother. She worked hard, and I'll make sure I bring a buying list for her, as well as myself. If she would prefer credits, I can arrange that also. I'll talk to her and see which way she wants to be paid. I've been thinking about my list, and I'm not sure what I want to include. I've listed the basic needs, of course, but I don't think that will take up even half what I expect to earn. I want to make sure the remainder is spent well."

"I have no doubt you'll be smart about it, Bren. Remember the long winter ahead of you and what you might want to accomplish when the spring comes. I'm sure your list will grow accordingly. Now eat and get ready to move. This morning you have to leave to show the elders your campsite."

Bren ran his mother's comment through his mind as he walked toward his horse.

"What I might want to accomplish in the spring, what could she have meant by that?"

"Bren," his mother called. "Make sure you pick a nice spot for our lodge. We'll need plenty of free space around it!"

She waved at him as he looked back.

A Wintering Place

Bren rode with his father and Airik. Some of the elders who were on the hunt rode along also. Their packs were full of fresh buffalo jerky, fruit, and bread from the hunting camp. They thought they would at least have an extra outing. It would be good to get away from the drudgery of camp, even if it turned out the place Bren was showing them was not adequate for this winter.

A few of the village council members were already expressing their doubts about the location of the camp spot. Bren had no problem with that. He knew there were always scoffers in any group. He'd already made up his mind. If the council didn't choose to stay in the spot he and Airik showed them, he wouldn't be bothered.

They moved at a leisurely pace toward the mountain meadow where Bren killed his elk. The sun was getting high, and the clouds were white and full. They floated slowly through a bright blue sky. He saw a hawk hanging motionless above the prairie grasses, intent on the patch of ground below. Its muted red tail twitched slightly with a subtle change of wind.

Bren's father told him the council had been thinking about a new winter camp for several months, well before he announced what he and Airik had found. Their old winter camp had been used for several years, and the available wood supply was fairly depleted. Without cutting down existing timber, they would have to haul a good deal of firewood before winter.

Besides the lack of firewood, the place had been used for such a long time it was showing a good deal of wear. The people thought they might leave it for a season or two, allowing time and new growth to erase as much of their presence as possible.

The small band of travelers found themselves at the forest edge by dusk. They decided to make camp at a clear deep stream where it came out from the woods. Ben had surprised a white-tailed deer earlier, so they had fresh meat for the fire. He stuck each of the rumps on two sticks to roast, slowly dripping fat into the small fire. He wrapped the remaining meat in the hide and hung it in a tree to keep overnight. The small group sat comfortably fed and warm around a single fire as the stars appeared in the sky. They talked well into the rising moon about past camps, the place they would visit tomorrow, and what was expected of a winter camp.

Bren loved nights such as these. Every time he sat at the fire of elder folk, he learned something new about his people. He listened to the old stories and learned lessons about the woods or the world. He looked around the fire as he sat surrounded by people he'd known since birth. He watched the play of light and shadow on each face and realized again how lucky he was to live this life.

At Kennon's urging, Bren explained the stream where they camped flowed from the mountain they were headed to. He told again of how the deep woods backed up to the face of a towering cliff. He explained how the spring flowed from the rock, emptied into a pool, and became the deep, clear stream. By his recollection, they were a short morning ride from that spot now.

The group unrolled their beds and settled in a circle near the fire. Sleep found Bren quickly. During the night, he dreamed of a dark and quiet night in a place unfamiliar to him. He walked alone through dark woods as a huge ghostly shape loomed in front of him. He heard the breathing of the creature and smelled the dank musk of it on his face. He was struck in the side of the head and knocked semiconscious to the ground.

Bren sat up with a start. Another dream, but he was awake now. He smelled the smoldering fire and saw the orange glow of the coals under a thin layer of ash. He raised his head to see the familiar shape of his father sleeping next to him. Straining into the blackness surrounding the camp, Bren neither heard nor saw a thing. He felt the sweat cooling on his face. After a few minutes listening, he got up, put a few sticks on the fire, and went back to his bedroll.

Bren was awake at dawn the next morning. He wondered about the dream as he slipped on his moccasins. Was it a bear he dreamed of? Why would he dream of such a one, at a time like this? He searched the camp and surrounding woods for sign of a bear visiting during the night. It wouldn't be the first time a camp was awakened by a nocturnal wanderer. He found no sign and asked the other men if they had seen or heard anything in the night. Each answered they had not. Bren decided it was nothing more than a dream, a misheard sound in an unfamiliar place, interpreted incorrectly in the fog of sleep.

They broke camp quickly after the morning meal and headed deeper into the wood. Bren was again struck by the quiet of the place. It was as if he and Airik were the first people ever to find it. The game trail they were using now was the same one by which they had left the woods on their earlier visit. It was easily broad enough for two horses riding abreast to be comfortable, which was unusual for a game trail.

The forest alternated here between stands of oak widely spaced, lodge pole pine, and the paper-thin white bark of the aspen tree. The oaks took up large areas, with their branches spread like open arms. The grass under these forest elders was scattered with lupine where the sun shined through. The knee-high white blooms of the bear grass plant appeared here and there, like a beautiful afterthought. In the clearings where the trees hadn't grown, the blue of lupine was complemented with the red of flax and columbine in shades of purple and lavender. The hillsides were shared by the grasses and the sage, along with a multitude of herbs and vegetables that were native to these hills since time began. He smelled wild onion and garlic bulbs. Bren thought perhaps he was wrong and people had been here before. Surely, he was not the first to think of living in these woods.

He began to feel the presence of an ancient people here. He knew this was a good place to be. He looked around, seeing the same thoughts echo from the smiling faces of his friends. Several elders acknowledged him with a nod of the head as they rode among the trees.

At last they came to the place where the trail crossed the creek. The water was deep, fast, and well over the fetlock on the horses. Bren recognized the place where they had tied their hunters when he and Airik were last here. He dismounted, and the others followed. As they walked, Bren pointed out the spots he and Airik had chosen to place the various buildings and lodges. They followed the stream toward the rock cliff face, until they came to the pool. The water covered an area at least sixty feet across. Bren saw it bubbling up from under the rock face, as well as through seems in the rock. A man could stand and be covered to his chest almost anywhere in the pool. There was a ledge that hung the width of the pool, thirty feet above its surface. The ledge was no more than a foot or two wide. It was thickly covered with ferns and vines hanging into the water. The pool disappeared behind this green curtain. Bren could see darkness, an opening behind the ferns. He made a mental note to explore that possibility.

Don and the other elders in the group decided to set a quick camp and explore the area at length. Airik, Ben, Bren, and his father chose to explore together. Airik showed them the meadow where Bren had taken the elk. They saw sign of more elk and deer everywhere. There were porcupines in the woods, as evidenced by the freshly exposed soil where the prickly creatures dug for their favorite grubs and roots. These would be appreciated by the ladies of the village. Aria and others worked with the quills and guard hair of this animal to decorate clothing and other items used by the people.

The small group inspected the woods and plotted the grassy clearings where they would set their family lodges. They picked the places for the log meeting lodge and the storage and smoke houses. Bren was pleased the places they picked were almost exactly as he and Airik had seen them.

They were exploring the wall of the cliff, when the group came upon an unexpected discovery. There was a small family of aspens set tightly against the wall of the cliff face. Behind the aspens they could see a large black void in the rock. They pushed and squeezed their way through the trees until they found themselves looking at the dark mouth of a cave. It was an opening big enough to ride two horses through side by side, with a smooth dirt floor that faded into deepest shadow in the space of a footstep or two.

Bren had borrowed two tin candle lamps from his mother. He retrieved them from his pack and brought out candles to fit both. The candles they lit from the fire that had been started to prepare the morning meal, and they were ready to begin exploring. Airik held a lamp and entered the opening first. The amber light cast against a wall to his front. He turned to his left, to see the cave made an immediate left turn and opened into a modestly sized cavern. He took several steps into the cavern. He was about to tell the men crowding behind him this was the limit of the interior, when he caught a glimpse of what appeared to be a hallway at the edge of the lamplight.

From behind, Bren urged them forward. As he walked into the cavern, he noticed an irregularity in the floor at the approximate center of the room. He walked toward it and sat his light down on a large rock. It was one of several arranged in a circular pattern in the room. The center of the circle was covered with gray ash, black charcoal, and small bits of half-burned wood. Bren stood amazed as he realized he was looking at what was left of an ancient fire circle, unused for unimaginable eons.

At the edges of the hearth were two wooden stakes set into the ground in what appeared to be the remains of a cook fire. He examined the floor around the fireplace and saw no footprints in the soil. He thought there should have been some sign of the people who had cooked their food around this fire, if it had been anytime in the measurable past. He looked up toward the ceiling of the cavern and was barely able to see where the rock loomed over their heads in irregular, jagged chunks. He guessed the ceiling to be at least eighty feet from the floor. He examined the walls of the cavern and found small pictures of recognizable animals there, painted in black, red, white, and yellow pigments. There were dogs, antelope, elk, and bear. There were also a few animals Bren didn't recognize. One had a long nose that curled at the end and long teeth that extended from either side of the mouth, some as long as the nose.

He called the others over to inspect the fireplace and pictographs. They wondered aloud how the fire could be used in this closed space, without the smoke suffocating the people using it. They answered their own question with a quick test. Airik removed the cover to the lamp he carried and exposed it directly to the air in the cavern. The flame bent very slightly, as if drawn toward the opening of the cavern. It was clear to the observers the flame was being gently pushed by air currents from deeper inside the cavern. There must be another entrance to the cavern.

They began to follow the current to its source. Airik found a low opening at the end of the cavern farthest from the door. They had to stoop a bit to keep from hitting their heads, but the ceiling opened up a few paces into the hallway. Bren and his father could easily walk side by side down the path. It continued for yard after yard, without a turn. Airik counted over a hundred paces to himself before the hallway turned once right, then left, and finally right again and opened into a second chamber.

This second chamber was larger than the first and dimly lighted from the outside. There was a stronger breeze coming from the area where the light originated. They walked to the light and pushed aside the vines to find they were standing on the back side of the pool they had discovered outside. Bren could see the green of the ferns and vines wave in the breeze as they hung over the opening.

The pool was fed by a trickling stream of water falling from above, at the same time a spring on the floor of the cavern filled the pool. The force of the water falling from the cliff face above was causing the air to circulate into the cavern and down the hall. The opening was sixty feet across, it was tallest where the stream pored over the lip of the cave and narrowed down to a foot or less on each end. The opening allowed enough light into the chamber to look around without the lamps. They found several more, smaller openings in the rock walls of the chamber. Two of them carried the slight smell of a chemical that was familiar to the group. No one could put a name to it yet, but they knew they had smelled it before. The water bubbling up from the ground was warm and caused a slightly visible, slightly damp fog within the room.

Airik was sure, being smallest in frame of the explorers present, he could squeeze through a few of the openings. The hunters decided against further exploration for the moment. They had found more than enough to make compelling conversation around the fire tonight.

They made their way to the cave opening with some haste. Don voiced his concern aloud, being last in the group. He could not help but feel a twinge of apprehension in the darkness at his back. His was a life lived on the open plains, surrounded almost constantly by the sound of the wind, the light of the sun, or the sparkling of the stars.

They all squinted at the light as they walked through the doorway and into the more familiar green and white of the aspen grove. Ben and Don, almost in perfect unison, echoed what several voices had repeated in the different settings of the park they were exploring. "This will be a good place for a winter home."

The hunters sat as a group around the fire and spoke of what they found in their explorations of the day. Wil and his group found grass in several large meadows. Each had enough thick green grass to hold a herd of horses twice as large as the village herd. They had also found more than one cave farther around the mountain that were a perfect a size for keeping provisions. Several of the caves were deep enough for the cold storage of meat through the hottest of summer months. They could be stocked with ice in winter and easily hold the cold.

A young hunter named Jamie found and mapped stands of lodge pole pine, which had grown so close together they were tall and straight. There were no limbs at all on the first forty feet of the trees. These would make perfect lodge poles. Nothing, however, matched the story that was told by Don, of the exploration of the caves Bren's group found. The party sat openmouthed as he went over in detail what they found in the cavern. They had already made plans for further exploration into the cavern the next day.

The question of using the woods for winter quarters had been answered. Next was only to plan the how and get construction underway. There were enough elders in this group to make the decision official, but they decided to send runners for the whole council of elders. With their help and that of their families, the work of gathering the material and overseeing the start of the project would go much more smoothly. There was a lot to be done before the beginning of winter, keeping in mind the fall gather was at the end of summer.

Ben was put in charge of gathering tools for the construction of the buildings. He and a few others would take several of the village wagons and travel to neighboring villages to buy or borrow the needed saws, hammers, and other tools that a nomadic village kept few of but in short supply. Don would oversee the day-to-day operations at the new site. He and a few selected elders had the final say on the placement of buildings and their design.

A Bear in the Night

Bren's mother and sister arrived early in the afternoon of the third day. They put up two lodges, Bren's smaller lodge and the family lodge, next to each other. Bren and Airik were to pack light for travel. They would start for the spring camp early in the morning. Once there, they would help with the packing of the village for the winter move and guide the rest of the village back to this new spot.

The mood was light and cheerful around the fires that night. Stories were told over again as people from the hunting group found their way to the new camp. Several young riders had been charged with camping on the plain near the new trail and directing the hunting party who had followed the sign to the new camp.

The people scattered to their separate lodgings where they talked into the night of what this place held for them. They had a lot of work ahead, with the coming of the deep summer and then the cold, long winter months. Bren wandered from place to place and visited with the people he hadn't been able to speak to during the afternoon. He heard the people calling this village in the woods Bren's Place more than once as he walked from fire to fire. He advised them each time to remember Airik had done as much as he had toward the discovery of the new camp, but the name was beginning to stick.

Bren allowed his neighbors to fill and refill his cup several times with the dark red wine that was his favorite drink at such occasions. He usually didn't drink much at all, but he knew there was plenty of work ahead of him in the next few weeks. He looked forward to the ride home with Airik. They wouldn't be in too much of a hurry, as the slow-moving wagons would not be hard to find. He believed his people would be pleased with their new winter home.

By the time Bren made his way to the farthest of the small fires, the warmth of the wine was working in his blood and on his bladder. He backed into the dark and made his way down the trail toward the place where it crossed the creek. He relieved himself at a discreet distance from the camp and was making his way back toward the light of the fires, when he sensed movement in the darkened woods to his right.

A huge dark shape loomed out of the night woods. It was in front of him in an instant, cutting him off from the light of the fires. He felt immediately alone and reached for the knife at his side. His hand closed on the horn handle of the battered old knife and pulled it free, almost without thought. He moved as if in a dream. Part of his mind wondered if he was not asleep and dreaming of the bear again. This was a bear, for sure, and no dream. He realized this was the biggest bear he had ever seen, in the brief second he had been able to assess its size. The bear had come upon him as if he were waiting specifically for Bren.

Out of the dark he came, with no warning, until he was so close Bren could smell the pungent musky odor of the damp fur. He could taste the moist breath of the animal, and it made him gag, as it closed the last step between them. Bren felt, more than saw, the swing of the enormous right arm of the beast. He ducked and brought his own left arm up in a defensive attempt to avoid the strike. He thought this would be the last fight of his life. Bren was determined not to go easily. If this were his last fight, he wouldn't go down without making his mark. This bear would know he fought a warrior of the people.

He felt the knife strike and bury deep into the flesh of the bear as he jabbed hard and upward. At the same time, he felt and heard the metal at the tang of the weapon give, in a sharp popping protest. He knew he was holding only the bone handle in his hand and dropped its useless weight to the ground. As he did, he ducked under the shadowy right side of the form and to a position behind the massive shoulder of the bear. He reached for the smaller but razor-sharp eating knife he kept at his left hip. The cross draw took slightly more time, but the bear had taken a moment to roar his loud and angry rage to the stars and sky.

Fear welled in him for an instant, as the noise seemed to physically rattle his body. Even the trees began to quake. Bren knew fear was a killer and fought to keep his wits about him. He felt the satisfaction of knowing he had marked this beast. These thoughts went through his mind as he moved. He found an opening and swung his body around to the animal's massive humped back.

He grabbed a hand full of fur at the crown of the head and reached for the throat. He slashed with the small sharp blade at the arteries carrying life to the brain. He was thrown with a tremendous force over the bear's head. His back hit the ground with such impact he felt strength ebb from him. His breath left his lungs in a whoosh. He saw tiny points of light spinning before him and knew he was losing consciousness. Would this be how he died? He thought it strange as he faded into blackness how warm death was. The coolness of the evening was completely swept away, and he was blanketed in warmth that surrounded him like a suffocating weight.

The camp heard the roar and knew something was fighting in the trees. Thinking it was a horse they were about to lose, they grabbed weapons and torches and ran toward the sounds. Mika was the first to arrive and recoiled in horror as he took in the scene before him. He saw the largest grizzly bear he had ever seen and recognized the quill work on the pants sticking out from under the animal's massive body. Bren and the bear had fallen in such a position that Mika, at first, thought the bear was in the process of devouring the man. Then his eyes focused in the dim light. He realized the bear didn't move, even at the approach of the whole camp.

He saw the huge beast was dead and so shouted for help from the crowd. They rolled the massive form from atop their friend. It took six of them. As they rolled and pushed, they saw the body of Bren was drenched in blood. Airik cradled the slack form in his arms and saw his friend's chest begin to heave in a spastic fight for air.

Airik shook him, and the eyes popped open. Bren's arms flailed about him, trying to ward off the next blow from the huge paws.

Airik carried Bren gently to the center of the creek and set him carefully in the water. He was trying to find the injuries he knew must be there, in order to stem the bleeding. Airik shouted for Lanis the healer, and a young man ripped down the path to fetch her with her bag of medicines.

He sat with Bren in the water, submerging them both to the shoulders. Bren struggled with the shock, as Airik slowly ran his hands over the body of his friend, trying to scrub away the blood that was hiding his wounds. He yelled for light, as Ben leaped into the water at recognition of his son and the scene he had come upon.

With Ben's help, Airik lifted Bren up to the light of torches the people held. He tore away the shirt his friend was wearing. A quick inspection showed only a small wound on the exposed rib cage. It had been caused by the grazing of the knife Bren stuck deep into the chest of the bear, as the lumbering beast had collapsed in death over the body of his final foe. So it was in dying the bear had wounded the man with the very weapon that had taken his life.

Airik stood dumbstruck as the picture of this scene unraveled in his mind's eye. Seeing his childhood friend fallen before him, the size and weight of this beast from the forest, and putting together the pieces of this oddly dreamlike puzzle had rooted him to the ground where he stood. He looked around him now. Finding his voice, he said to his half-conscious friend, "I've told you this before, brother. There are things some are meant to accomplish that others can't." He turned and spoke to the crowd. "You see before you people, one who walks the path of a true human being. Here is one who has been delivered to us to accomplish feats of magic, in a time of magic. This man walks with spirits to guide him. This is truly a time when dreams come to life."

Ben took Bren's hand and arm to help raise him to his feet. He spoke quietly to his son. "Your friend may be speaking more truth than he himself realizes, son. Last night you dreamed of the bear, and here he lays. This is a spirit thing."

"He fell on my knife, Father. This water is cold. Let's get out of it and to a fire."

"You're bleeding, son, there may be other injury. Stand a moment and mind your body well."

"I'm bleeding from a scratch made by my own knife. A knife given to me by my father's father and one that lays broken in two pieces now."

Ben comforted his son. "That knife was made and handed down to you for use on this night. It has come to its proper end and knew well the time. The knife you choose to replace it must be chosen wisely and handed down again. This is the way with legend, Bren Redhorse. Get used to it, son. I'm starting to see a pattern in the path you walk."

As they stepped from the water, Bren's mother took his other side to help him back toward their family fire. Bren told them both, "Let me walk on my own, please, or everyone will think I'm a helpless boy."

His mother told him, "There is a very big, very dead bear laying on the ground that argues the opposite, son."

They both let him go nonetheless. Each of them walking close to his side, to assure they could help if needed.

They passed by the bear, and Bren got a good look at it for the first time, in the light of the burning torches. It was a massive dark-cinnamon grizzly. The size of it made Bren weak again. He asked Airik to take care of the carcass, and the young man immediately began to prepare the animal. Several of the younger men in camp turned to the task as well. The hide would make a fine rug for the floor of Bren's lodge. He saw the eyes of the crowd follow him as he walked away with his father and mother. "Airik talks too much," he said under his breath.

Ben laughed gently. "He did sometimes, however there are times when your friend is smarter than anyone gives him credit for. Giving voice to a momentous event sometimes gives glory to the speaker, as much as the event itself. Airik is a good friend to you."

"Father, this was a bear that sneaked up on me from the dark, when I went to pee. I was lucky enough to kill it before it killed me. That should be the end of the story."

Bren's father laughed again but said, "People say you make your own luck. You trained for meetings like that one since your birth. I don't doubt that you were lucky, but you perform as you practice. Let's go get warm."

Ben took Bren to the small lodge beside his parents' to strip off his wet clothing and get him into dry blankets. He took his time, and the longer it took, the more Bren's muscles felt the effects of the battle. Adrenaline was draining from his muscles as he stood. The whole event had taken no more than two minutes, but Bren felt as if he had been fighting for hours. He told his father he needed to rest.

"Are you all right, son?" Ben asked as he added wood to the fire.

"I've been better, but I think I'm all right. I'm sore and tired, that's all. I have to leave early in the morning, and I've had enough to eat and drink tonight."

"I understand, but I'll send Lanis over to look at that scratch on your ribs. There's no sense taking chances with infection. I'm also going to get someone else to ride out to the village in the morning. You'll be in no shape to ride. You think you're sore now, wait until tomorrow."

Ben made sure the fire was going well enough to warm the lodge, and his mother brought several candle lanterns to give extra light for Lanis's healing handiwork. Bren dropped carefully to his furs as the healer unceremoniously and without announcing herself pulled back the hide door cover and ducked in.

"What kind of trouble have you gotten yourself into this time, Bren?"

He knew full well she'd been given a full report on the way to his lodge. She had probably been to the woods to see the bear and read the signs on the ground as well. He thought about the bear, and the blood of the beast that had drenched his body. Without ceremony, she rolled the young man front to back and left to right, searching for wounds with cold, hard hands. His mother held the lantern close.

Bren had been bathed in the blood of the bear and he felt sure that blood had mingled with his own.

Lanis knelt at Bren's side and examined his ribs. The wound was only a few inches long and not deep enough to need stitching. She slowly ran her hands over the rest of his body to assure herself there were no broken bones or other injuries under the skin. She spoke quietly to Bren, asking him where it hurt as she gently, carefully bent his joints and pressed on his bones, all the while looking into his eyes for sign of pain the movement might produce.

After a rather undignified inspection, the healer mixed a powder with a small cup of warm water. "Drink this all now. I could mix it in wine, but I think you've had your share for this night! The powder will help you sleep soundly through 'til morning. I'd bet you will be too sore to move for a few days, but the wound is small, and I see no others. You're lucky that fat thing didn't crush your ribs when he fell on you. I'll leave you another powder for the morning. Mix the whole thing in water, not coffee."

Bren drained the cup and lay back into his sleeping furs. He watched the stern woman gather her things into the bag that was always with her.

"Thank you, Lanis, I'm glad we have you to heal us," he told her.

She gave him a withering look as she said, "Walk carefully through the woods at night, Bren Redhorse, and be careful where you pee! That's all the thanks I need from you!" She smiled widely at Thora as she gathered the last of her things. Thora laid a hand on the healer's arm in silent thanks.

Bren relaxed into the warmth that overcame him, as Lanis quietly left the lodge. "I'll never hear the last of that, will I?" he said out loud. He heard Lanis chuckle as she walked away. Bren watched the golden light of the small fire flicker on the hide walls as he closed his eyes and drifted into tomorrow.

Bren didn't realize that Aria slept the night in his lodge. Neither did he know the young girl checked her brother closely many times. He didn't wake when his mother dropped by in the night to check on him as well or add wood to the fire. He didn't feel the lamp in his eyes when Lanis knelt over him in the small hours, to inspect the wound at his side and check for signs of infection.

Sara sat by her family's fire with Thunder's muzzle over one foot. Winter was lying at her other side. The purple evening sank around them and her family as she listened to the life of the farm. Suddenly she raised her head, staring into the distant west. Something felt wrong, but she couldn't put her finger on it.

"Sara, what's wrong?" her mother asked.

"I don't know, Mom. I just had a feeling of something happening far away."

"I'm sure it's nothing. At least, nothing we can do anything about now," her mother said.

Sara, apprehensive, stared into the fire and thought of Bren.

He was surprised at the amount of light entering the lodge when he awoke. He remembered vaguely being awakened by several people during the morning as they looked in on him. When he moved, the night came back to him with every painful twinge of muscle. He could breathe without pain if he took air in slowly, but that was the extent of it. Every other movement caused his body to complain strenuously. He groaned at his father when he opened the door flap. "Get up" was all he said.

It took a long while and several fumbling tries, but he finally managed that simple task. He carefully rolled to his hands and knees and slowly stood on his aching legs. Dressing was a different problem. He hurt from the tips of his toes to the top of his head. Even his hair was sore. Slow and careful were going to be his favorite words for several days.

He saw someone had laid out one of his new hide shirts and a pair of pants and moccasins to match. It took him a very long, slow time to get dressed. The softness of the smoked hides felt good against his skin, and he began to feel he might live.

The morning sun shined on the trees as he pushed back the door flap and stepped into the warming morning air. He walked as if he'd been tied to boards all night. His father, Airik, Mika, and everyone within eyesight of him smiled, or laughed out loud, as he gingerly walked, stiff legged, into the thin morning sunshine.

"I'm glad to see I'm entertaining you all," he said as he helped himself to coffee, then remembered Lanis's words. His mother handed him a cup of slightly warm water.

"It's already mixed in the water, just drink it all. You should begin to feel better shortly," she told him. "Stay on your feet! Move around a little, it'll help!"

He thanked his mother and downed the water in one go. "I apologize to you, Airik. I should have been up hours ago. I suppose Lanis's potion worked a bit too well."

"I slept late myself, Bren," Airik said through a wide grin. "I thought you might need a little extra rest. You drank quite a lot of wine last night. Your father found several young men more than happy to take our chore from us, and they are ready to start for the spring camp."

Bren grinned. "So it was the wine that did this to me? In that case, I swear off the stuff here and now."

"No need to be hasty, brother, it wasn't just the wine that brought you to this," Airik said, pointing.

Bren saw the bearskin already stretched on a frame and leaning against nearby lodge poles. The skin was intact, except for where the knife had entered, and it was even more imposing in its size. Airik asked one of the younger hunters to begin the process of tanning the hide. The young man was scraping the fat and bits of flesh off the inside. Aria would apply a thick layer of brain to the flesh side after the membrane was scraped away, and the process would be repeated, working the oils and enzymes into the hide to turn it to a soft, useful skin as it was worked dry.

Bren talked to his friends as his mother traded him Lanis's potion cup for a mug of tea. He ate warm bread his mother passed to him. Most everyone in camp had seen him removed from under the bear the previous night. Many of them asked after his comfort as they walked by on their morning tasks. He felt uncomfortable as the center of so much attention and told Airik it was time he moved around a bit.

Airik read his thoughts. "I took the liberty of loading your packhorse and saddling your hunter while you were sleeping away the day. Since we won't need the packhorse, I'll go unpack that."

Bren stopped Airik as he walked and addressed both him and his father, "Thanks for looking out for me, but right now I think being out on the trail for a few days will do me good. I can't shirk my duty every time I have an injury."

Airik spoke as Bren finished his breakfast. "Bren, you may as well get used to some attention. You will be getting more of it as you go through life. The price of fame, my friend, is that everyone knows who you are. I will gladly relieve you of as much of it as I can in the coming years. For your benefit, of course."

Bren excused himself from the fire. He went to say goodbye and to ask his sister and mother to take care of his lodge and bed furs. Bren could feel himself becoming moody and stared through his friend as they got ready to mount. "This will be a fun trip," Airik said under his breath. "It's not my fault, you know. I'm just telling you what has been obvious to everyone but you for some time."

Lanis came to them as they were leaving and forced Bren to drink another concoction of herbs, saying, "This will help the sore muscles. Make sure to get down off that horse and walk often, or you'll regret it at end of day." Bren thanked her and reminded her she left a powder in his lodge last night. He assured her he just finished it with his breakfast. "This is a different mix," she told him as she held it out to him and stood patiently. Seeing she wouldn't relent, he took the cup and drank it down quickly. He knew it was futile to argue with the healer. She asked Bren to slowly raise his arms as she checked his ribs and looked him over briefly for bruises and swellings. She must have been in a better mood, he thought, because she worked gingerly. By the time she was done, Bren had to pee.

Ride to Spring Camp

Bren and his companion rode southeast, letting their horses set the pace. His bones ached less the more miles they put behind them. He had promised Lanis he would keep the bandage clean and change it every night. The sun was warm, and the sky was clear. They passed the time in quiet thought, studying the terrain for sign of a wagon train at every high ridge.

The first day passed without sign, with little conversation between the travelers.

They were both in their element now. They were on horseback and alone on the plains. Bren preferred the mountains, with a little less wind and a lot more cover, but the high plains was a beautiful place to be. Riding through the grass, with the never-ending sky above them, they were satisfied just to be in the moment. This was an almost religious experience for them both.

They chose a group of cottonwoods that lined a small clear creek for their camp the first night. The grass made a thick cushion on the sandy bank, and Bren and Airik rolled out their bed furs on it. The horses had plenty of grass on the meadow above the creek, and they were happy to be hobbled there to eat. The creek pooled at the cottonwoods, and Airik found more trout than they could eat for dinner. This reminded the young men of one of their many trips onto the plains in their younger days. They were free to come and go as they pleased, with no one to answer to. Bren thought out loud that those days were coming to an end.

"It's true, isn't it," Airik said. "The older we are, the more we have to look forward to, the more freedom we have. At the same time, the more we have to do, the less time we have to get it done. That's why we need to have as much fun as possible when these opportunities present themselves." He flopped himself down in the grass as he was talking. He had just finished weaving a grill made of cottonwood limbs. He placed two fat fish on it, high over a small and smoky fire. The fish would be ready in a short time.

They watched the few white puffs of cloud turn to pink then darker colors of purple as they waited for their dinner. They talked about the day, deciding to sleep early and start before dawn. Both were anxious to get on to the village. The sooner they accomplished these tasks, the sooner they would get back to the new camp, to see what progress had been made in their absence. They watered and checked the horses then ate. They were in their bedrolls before the sun was completely gone.

Bren lay on the ground realizing he felt less muscle soreness than he thought he would. He was always surprised how much good it did him to ride the plains on the back of a horse. He felt relaxed and at home under the huge sky. The rolling of the hills and the movement of the clouds and water soothed him.

They had made several miles before the sun was above the horizon. That day was like the one before. They found a good camp in the late afternoon and were up again before the sun. On the morning of the third day, they saw a line of smoke rising in the sky to their east. They could make out the village wagons a mile before they got there. The train had stopped for the night near one of the many creeks winding its way out of the mountains.

Bren allowed Airik to explain their coming. He did a good job keeping the incident with the bear to an abbreviated version of the story. He went into more detail on what they found around the camp and in the caverns. His obvious excitement filled the listeners with the same exuberance being shown at the new camp. They were ready to break camp and be underway before the story was complete.

Bren's aunt Jemma and the people in charge of the train were attempting to restrain the enthusiasm of the party. Jemma gently reminded them all that they had the charge of safe delivery of almost the entire spring and summer meat supply. This was much too important a load to be running off with, without properly securing it.

The two messengers ate stew with Jemma and the wagon crew. They sat with the crew for a while then filled their traveling pouches with some of the jerked meat the train was carrying. Bren was fond of the jerky meat his village was noted for. They also carried pemmican, the dried meat was pounded and mixed with berries and fat. Formed into cakes that were easy to carry, it lasted forever on the trail. Bren and Airik finished their meals, said goodbye, and rode for the village.

Bren was moving much better now, so the two young men made good time. They decided to see how fast they could make it back to camp. They rode their best hunters, leaving their packhorses with the wagon train. They each carried a bedroll and food sack. They stayed to the lowest-lying landforms to conserve the horses as much as possible. They didn't have to look for a sign this time. They knew exactly what they were looking for and what heading should take them directly to it. This was a game they had played many times while growing up. They would find themselves on the plains or in the mountains and want to get home in a hurry, either because of commitments made or for the fun of the challenge. This kind of game honed their directional skills and the physical condition of the horses they rode.

They worked the horses at a moderate pace, putting the miles behind them quickly. They stopped to let the horses rest only twice during the day. Before dark, they were in familiar territory and decided to continue until they arrived. As a sliver of moon rose over the plains, the campfires of their village could be seen. They sped up their pace until they were all but racing the horses over the last two miles into camp. Toren and Faith met them at the northern entrance into the village. Toren took the horses and said to them both, "I was about to raise the alarm until I recognized the horses. You're lucky the elders are away or already in their beds. Otherwise, you'd be plucking arrows from your hides as we speak."

"Toren, you're lucky we're not bandits, or we would have been on you before you could raise the alarm. I was less than a quarter mile out before I saw any movement at all. If you would please treat these horses well, I would be grateful. They've worked hard today and deserve your best care."

Bren and Airik went directly to the lodge of Airik's uncle Davan, who was the elder left in charge of the village. They sat at Davan's fire, and he brought out his pipe. This was an ancient ceremonial pipe made of red pipestone. This stone had been quarried since time began, in one location only, a quarry that was shared by all the first nation people in peace. Davan followed the oldest ceremonial ways of their ancestors when it came to the pipe. He filled it from the tobacco pouch he carried with the pipe. He lighted the pipe with an ember taken from the fire. Holding it to the heavens, he offered the smoke here first then to the earth and the four directions. They passed the pipe between them in a clockwise manner, until the bowl was empty. Davan then tapped the ash into his palm and placed it in the coals of the fire. This done, Airik was allowed to fill him in on what had happened on the hunt from the time they left to the ride into the village tonight.

Davan asked them both questions as they came up. He had Airik clarify and expand on several points. He was specifically interested in the dream of the bear and the subsequent battle. He'd been spiritual counselor to the village for many years and teacher to both men on different aspects of village life. Davan's wife, Kasa, became concerned with Bren's wound and demanded to inspect it at once. She cleaned it with her gentle hands and applied a soothing salve. Satisfied he would live through the night, she allowed the conversation to continue.

Davan asked for a detailed description of the dream Bren had of the bear. He remembered more than he thought he would, under the old man's gentle prodding. At the conclusion of the story, Davan asked Bren to interpret the dream and the attack of the bear so shortly after. Bren's only answer was that he must have heard the bear in or around camp the night of the dream, recognized it in his sleep, and brought it into his dream.

Davan nodded his head and pursed his lips in silent thought. He sat for such a long time that Bren thought the old man had drifted into sleep. Davan moved to fill the pipe a second time and began to speak as he worked.

"In the time before the white people came to this place, there were people who lived much as we live. They made the plains and the mountains their home. They studied the animals and the plants around them and even the earth herself. They came to understand the world in a way that few people ever will. They understood every living thing has a spirit. They understood even the rocks, the water, and the wind have a spirit and a message. All we need do is listen to what the spirit has to say. There is knowledge in their voices and power too."

Davan talked as he passed the pipe and allowed the gray-blue cloud to seep from him, slowly encircling his head before it spiraled up and out the smoke hole atop the lodge.

"The old ones believed an animal spirit would sometimes see a person in need of help and give a part of himself to that person so he might accomplish this thing or that thing that needed doing. The animal would guide the person and protect him. He would look over the shoulder of that person and allow his spirit to mingle with that of the person for all of time. The ancestors believed this was a great gift to receive, that a spirit would sacrifice a part of itself to benefit a man. This is why our people today hold all living things in reverence. This is why we say the prayer of thanks when we take the life of a buffalo or an elk or even a fish.

"I'm getting to be an old man, young Redhorse, and I've sat at many winter fires thinking about such things. This bear that you fought, he was a very powerful spirit. I can see that he has influenced you already. Do me this favor, and you will make an old man happy. Think about these things we spoke of tonight. I know some of what you hear from me is hard to understand as you sit at this fire, but listen to your heart. This spirit will help you many times in your life, if you allow it to happen."

The slow silver tone of the old man's quiet voice lulled Bren to a peaceful, thoughtful place. He sat for some time with Davan and Airik. He was unsure of how much time had passed, but he was aware of the filling of the pipe and the smoke billowing from their mouths through the smoke hole into the sky. Bren realized he'd not been so relaxed for a long time. He thought how much he missed these quiet times with Davan and was embarrassed he'd spent so little time with him in the past few months. He loved this man as if he were not just an elder teacher but his closest family.

Davan tapped the pipe into his palm one last time and took the bowl from the stem. This was a sign their talk had come to its end. "Now go to sleep, young sons, but do it in someone else's lodge. You'll be up too early, and I intend to sleep in as much as this old back will let me."

Bren and Airik got slowly to their feet, and saying good night to Davan and Kasa, they left the lodge. They made their way to the lodge of Airik's elder brother, Jon, and his wife, Tam. Jon was one of the newest of the village shirt wearers and so was chosen to stay behind and help with the daily chores of the village. He was a man in good standing with everyone in the village and an accomplished hunter.

Bren liked Jon very much, although, being several years senior to Airik, the brothers did not always see eye to eye. Bren quickly filled Jon in on the details of the hunt, giving him the abbreviated version because of the late hour. At the end of the story, Jon asked Bren, "You're not telling me about this fight with the bear. The whole village says it was the biggest bear ever. The ones, that is, who are not saying it was just the wine and a vicious tree limb you fought with."

Bren found it hard to believe how quickly this story had spread through the people.

Airik opened his mouth to defend his friend, but Bren said quickly, "There will be time for the telling of that story another day. Now it's time for us to sleep. I want to get started as early as possible in the morning. If we could take space at your fire tonight?"

Bren and Airik threw their bedrolls next to the door of Jon's lodge and were asleep before their heads hit the blankets. Bren slept without dreams and awoke feeling less sore than he thought he would. The cut at his ribs pulled at the surrounding skin but was only a minor inconvenience. The remaining villagers spoke to him or waved as he made his way to the meadow where the horses were being kept. Logan met him there, with the hunter already watered, fed, and ready to ride. "Thank you, Logan, as usual you've done a good job, and I owe you."

"It's my pleasure, Bren, I'm glad for the chance to help. I'm also glad to see you walking so well this morning. That bear gave us a scare," he said as he took the horses. The young man looked up at the hunter with undisguised admiration. Bren told himself to remember the boy sometime in the future.

It took only a few hours to get the village ready to move. Somehow word had spread, and preparations for the move began before Bren and Airik arrived. A lot of the belongings had gone with the hunters and the wagons that had followed them. Somehow too the village had been told stories of the new winter camp. Everyone was anxious to get there and get settled before it was time to travel to the gather.

Finally, they set out for their new home. Bren realized he was a little torn at this leaving. He looked forward to this place every time they came here, since childhood. Now he thought it may be some time before he returned. The thought startled him because it came on him suddenly, and he could not explain why. Nonetheless, his spirit was light as they came down from the low mountains and onto the high grass prairie. The people were laughing and sharing the good feeling of a productive hunt and the security of knowing their winter camp was waiting for them a few days distant. The wagons were loaded down, and the packhorses carried the rest on top of the two-pole travois they dragged easily behind them. The camp dogs hopped and barked at the feet of the horse herd, carefully shying away as the occasional hoof shot out in their direction.

The days passed quickly, and soon Bren was directing the group toward the spot where he and Airik had first seen the trail into the woods. There were still two young men sitting their horses on the plain, in anticipation of their arrival. They wound their way toward the north side of the forested hills, to the wider road that had been cleared a bit more in his absence.

Bren was amazed at the progress that had been made in such a short time. Ben had completed the trip too, from their neighbors to the south. He brought saws, adzes, and other tools to work the trees for the great house where elders would meet, as well as other village buildings. There were the beginnings of a whole village set up among the trees, just as Bren had envisioned it. Many lodges were set up in the meadows, to allow for more workspace and the clearing of the cabin sites.

The caverns had been explored a bit more, and a massive wooden door was being built in place at the opening where the aspens had been cleared away. Don gave Bren a tour, showing him where lamps were now set into the rock walls. Don took Bren and Airik down a new corridor past the pools. They had removed a rock wall, at one of the smaller openings, and found it continued into several more chambers.

Several chambers contained pools of hot water that drained off and into what was thought to be an underground aqueduct somewhere in the heart of the mountain. These pools were what had been producing the strange smell they had noticed on their first visits. Don called them sulfur springs and said the people were using them for bathing. There were wooden platforms on the ground and benches built near the pools. Bren was amazed at the progress with this place. The lamps on the walls lit the interior like a lodge on a summer night. The pools appeared comfortable enough, but Bren could tell it would take some getting used to.

Don explained how the chambers were still being explored. Some of the people were already talking about making this a permanent village and actually living in the caverns. Bren had heard of people doing this, in the mountains to the east and in some places to the west. Bren began to feel closed in, at the thought, and headed for the doors. This would make a fine place for a meeting hall. He found himself thinking as he came once again to the bigger, first chamber.

He mounted his horse and went for a ride around the outer perimeter of the village. He saw several teams of horses pulling borrowed mowing wagons through the grassy fields. With any luck, they could harvest enough of the grass to feed the whole herd for the winter. They built three pole barns with the beginnings of roofs, but no sides, in which to stack the hay and preserve it from the snow and rain. Another group of teams were in the lodge pole pines, where they were busy selecting and cutting trees, then dragging them the short distance to where the workers were cutting them to length, and preparing them for the main meeting hall and the smaller log outbuildings.

The foundation for the meeting hall was laid from river rock, mortared into place to the height of a man's knees. The floor was excavated into the earth that same distance, and the log walls were added atop the rock. Things were going very well, indeed, and it was good for him to see the people were happy with his choice.

The next few weeks would pass with the busy work of making the place in the woods into a village. Buildings would be erected, and many people were in the process of planning where they would stand and cutting the logs, far from the village grove of trees. Many cabin sights had been dug into the ground several feet, in the old style that saved from the need to stack the logs too high. The interior was still a good eight feet from floor to ceiling and would be watertight as well as warm, often with a firepit at both ends. Two log smokehouses had been erected close to the main meetinghouse and were already in use. The people were finding many white-tailed deer in the area, and fish were thick in the streams and creeks.

Bren's Cabin

Bren had decided to build a log cabin of his own at the edge of the woods, facing the meadow where the horses were kept. He had lived his whole life in a hide lodge and knew he would continue to do so from time to time, but he'd been thinking of a cabin made of thick, sturdy logs for several years. The location he picked sat at the edge of a large meadow. It had a perfect view of the mountain that hid the caves and the wall that hid most of their village from the prairie.

He began by clearing a spot on a small rise, leveling enough of the topmost portion to footprint the cabin. It still left a sizeable flat spot for a yard. He borrowed a wagon and brought the largest stones he could carry from the nearby streams to build a foundation. Airik and several young men from the village helped with the foundation and mortaring the stones together so the logs had a solid rock base to sit on. They went about picking logs out of the surrounding lodge pole forest. The logs needed to be the very straightest available. He took trees far enough away from the village sight so as not to deplete the forest of cover. He was being picky, so this took some time.

After the trees were cut down, they were carefully limbed with hand saws, axes, and hatchets and peeled of bark with draw knives. They allowed the peeled logs to sit stacked in the sun while other logs were gathered and the foundation cured. After several weeks of cutting and peeling, the first course was ready to be laid atop the foundation of cured stone and mortar. The base logs were shaved on bottom and roughed with an adze then mortared to the foundation.

Each additional log was carefully shaved and notched to fit on top of the preceding log without gaps. This would prevent the logs from needing any kind of chinking or barrier between them and make for a stronger, more draft-free home.

Bren and his friends reveled in the hard work and began to take satisfaction in the woodworking as the logs grew into a cabin. He fitted interior log walls toward the rear of the structure so that the finished product would have three separate main rooms. He cut enough logs to add a smaller, separate room attached to the main structure. This would attach to the main cabin and be his bedroom. He built two fireplaces from the stones gathered at the rivers, one on each end of the building. Two stacks of stone for fireplaces seemed like a lot to him, but he wanted to have a separate fireplace in his sleeping room.

He was joined from time to time by young men and older villagers wandering by to help him lift logs into place or place the heaviest of stones. He often stopped to hear advice from many of the elders of the village that had built log structures before and was always glad to listen.

After weeks of cutting and peeling logs, fitting and stacking them for walls, the huge crown log was settled into place. It took the effort of a dozen or so friends, but once set, Bren could begin closing in the roof. He cut and placed rafters and many smaller lodge poles. Last came the painstaking task of splitting shingles to waterproof the finished interior.

The doors were made from boards that Airik helped split and shaved with a drawknife and hung with wooden hinges carved by Bren's father. The windows were covered with oiled deer hides scraped very thin by Aria, that could be rolled up in the warmest weather to allow the breeze in. They could also be closed entirely by wooden shutters to be swung into place and latched securely from inside.

He heard from one of the villagers that there would be a trader at this fall's gather who was making windows of glass. He carefully recorded measurements of each of his window openings, in hopes that he would be able to fill them with glass he bought at gather.

The most difficult job, in Bren's mind, was cutting and fitting the floor. Each log not only had to be cut to the proper length but had also to be shaved with the draw knives to be flat on each side so they formed a level and almost seamless surface.

Bren moved his lodge to the trees at the rear of the cabin. Most days he could barely drag himself to his furs, usually just after dark each night. After eight weeks of constant hard labor, he and his friends, who helped more and more as the cabin took shape, ended up with a structure that was quite impressive. It would keep out the rain and the snow and hopefully the critters that lived in the woods.

He spent some of his time making a table and chairs, even log beds for the two bedrooms. Everyone that passed by the finished cabin made sure to tell him how impressed they were. Bren eagerly allowed everyone who came by to inspect the build and give advice as to where this should go or where to put that.

Next, he went to work on an outbuilding for Sara's wolves. She called it a kennel and had described it to him in detail at last year's gather. He dug a hole in the ground, away from the cabin. He made it twelve feet long, eight feet wide, and three feet deep. Then he built a small structure on top of the hole that matched the cabin. He put a door on both ends and roofed the top with logs and sod. Once finished, it would be comfortable for the dogs through the roughest winter and cool enough in the summer when the doors at each end could be opened for a breeze to flow. He also built a smaller building to be used for a smokehouse. Now, all he had left to do was build a corral and a small shed for the horses he wanted to keep close to the house.

He promised himself next summer he would build a larger barn to house the horses and maybe some chickens through the cold wet months. Such a strange thing, this village taking shape. Bren had been to permanent villages before, but he'd never lived in one. He looked around at the buildings going up within the woods and at the edges of the meadows. Bren realized this place was becoming the first village his people would live in, at least for as long as he could remember. He felt he would always need to wander the plains, but this place was a good home to come back to. This would be a comfortable place to make a future and to build his family.

During the cabin build, Bren had forced himself to get used to bathing in the caverns. His sister and Lanis repeatedly urged him. So did everyone else in the village who tried them. He soon decided it was very much better than a cold stream. Bren had to admit his wound seemed to feel much better after a soaking in the warm mineral water, and it healed very quickly. Besides, he was always relaxed after a soak in the pools.

As twilight fell, Bren was cleaning up construction scraps around his cabin. Over the days he built a respectable pile of both kindling and split firewood to use on the winter fires. It struck him that he hadn't been paying too much attention to what was going on in the rest of the village. He finished his task as the stars were coming out and decided to take a walk through the trees toward the caves. As he walked down the well-traveled path through the trees, he noticed there were now many lodges setting off the path among the trees. There were even a few log cabins in various stages of construction. There were torches and oil lamps and small cooking fires scattered round the eighty-acre woodland that lent a pleasant glow to a beautiful scene of peaceful village life.

He was greeted by name at every lodge and stopped at many as he walked. He saw Aria sitting with a group of her friends around a small fire next to a buffalo hide lodge, and he spoke to his sister.

"Good evening, Aria, I feel as if I've been neglecting you and our parents. Do you know if they're at home?"

"You have, and they are, Bren," she said, and her friends giggled at the slight, although there was no malice in her tone. Bren was shocked at her answer, and it must have been apparent by his expression, because she stood and took his arm in both her hands, patting him as they walked. "We all know you've been working very hard on your cabin, Bren, and everyone understands. Come with me. Let's go see them together. I have something to show you anyway." She waved goodbye to her friends, and she and Bren turned down the path to the edge of the village. They could see the lodge of their parents glowing warmly from the fire within.

As they approached, their father stepped out of the lodge and spoke to them both.

"Bren, how is the cabin coming?" his father asked him.

"Just cleaning up the last little chores. I felt like it's been too long since I visited you all, so I stopped and came to see you."

"We know you've been working very hard to get things done, son. I was just telling your mother I feel bad that I haven't helped more."

"You've come every time I asked. That's more than enough," Bren told him.

"Let's go inside and say hi to your mother. She has a buffalo stew bubbling, and I can't wait to try it. I was just coming to find Aria for dinner."

Bren sat and accepted the stew his mother dished up for him. He realized he couldn't remember the last time he sat in his mother's lodge and shared a meal with his family. He promised himself he would make every effort to change that in the future.

After dinner, Aria showed him the new pants and shirt she had made for him from the bull elk he killed before the spring buffalo hunt. They were smoked a rich golden-brown color and decorated with the most beautiful and intricate quillwork he had ever seen her produce. The shoulders and sleeve strips were done in red and white, and there was a bear paw symbol in brown on each side of the chest, between the collarbone and the curve of the shoulder.

She also showed him the four finished buffalo robes he'd taken in the spring hunt. Bren was very pleased with the result. Aria saved the best for last. She left the lodge for a few minutes, and when she returned, she opened a bundle she had been storing at their aunt's lodge. It was wrapped in a winter elk robe, still covered with thick, soft hair for warmth during the cold months.

Bren spread the package open and saw it contained a winter coat made from the hide of the bear. She had tanned it with the head on and sewn the head into a hood to protect him from the winter wind. The hood was lined with a soft black felted material. Bren stood and tried on the coat. It fitted him perfectly, and he told his sister.

"Of course, it does, Bren. This isn't the first time I've sewn clothing for you," she said this with a proud smile.

The coat not only fit him perfectly but it felt soft and warm where it touched his skin. It covered his arms just past the wrist and hung down to his knees in front and back. The back was split partway up, so he could wear it comfortably mounted on a horse.

The hide had dressed out big enough for her to also make him a pair of winter boots to go with the outfit. She had sewn them with the fur on the outside and lined them with the same thick felt as the hood, to keep his feet warm and dry during the winter months. The soles were made very thick with several layers of heavy hide from an old lodge cover. Bren looked at the new clothes and hugged his sister to him.

"I won't be able to trade enough to pay you back for these things, Aria," he said.

"Wear them around the village and to gather," she told him. "Maybe someone else will have me make some clothing for them as well."

"When word of who has made such wonderful things gets around, you'll be much too busy to make my clothing anymore. You'll be spending all your time making clothing for your husband and all of his family as well," Bren said, teasing her.

"It has to happen sometime, brother," she answered him. "I am old enough, you know."

"You'll be old enough when I say you're old enough," their mother interrupted them. She looked pointedly at her son as she continued. "Let's not hurry you out of the lodge too quickly, Aria. Your brother has just left. I would appreciate if you wouldn't put such thoughts into your sister's head. She's difficult enough as it is.

"Don't think I don't see that young Airik, as well as your other friends, looking at her. You would do well to tell your friends that I carry a skinning knife and know very well how to use it."

"I'm sorry, Mother," Bren said, throwing up his hands to ward off the assault. "I was only trying to thank her for the wonderful things she's taken the time to make for me. You must admit she's learned very well," Bren said, intentionally tossing the compliment in his mother's direction. "I've noticed that many of the village women are asking to copy her patterns, and some are bringing their daughters to Aria for teaching. I think she would do well if she were to hold classes this winter and charge a fair fee. That would keep her busy and help her to earn her keep as well!" Bren paused, grinning at his sister. "And each of my friends is well aware of your skill with a skinning knife."

"She has surpassed my skill, hasn't she?" Thora said with obvious pride. "This one will earn a lot of marks at the gather, with all the things she's made this past year. If, that is, she doesn't trade it all away for beads and needles to make more things."

The family made small talk together for several hours that night. It was a rare occasion these days that they were able to get together long enough to share each other's time and company.

Ben left after dinner to attend a meeting of the elders. Some of the people were talking about moving into the caverns on a permanent basis. There were people living in caves in many places on the continent, some in large complexes, others in small pockets big enough for a family and no more. Bren was getting used to the idea of using the caves but didn't see much of an advantage to permanent residence. His people had lived in their lodges for many generations in winter cold and summer heat, and they had prospered. Bren felt that the cabins and the caverns for occasional use were enough of a compromise from the old ways. He had made his opinion known and now would let the elders decide.

Bren kept a running total of the hides he collected during the summer hunts and found he was well off, to say the least. Not only had he taken four buffalo in the summer hunt, but he had seventeen other prime buffalo robes from other, smaller hunts. He had taken a dozen elk, fourteen white-tailed deer, and three moose. The moose had been a surprise to him. His father found them very early in the spring and took him to the high mountain lake where they appeared to have spent a majority of the winter. Not in many years could anyone remember seeing these biggest members of the deer family this far south. There were seven of them together, living around the large marshy lake. His father limited the kill to three, allowing his son to take all three. They were big males and in prime condition. Their large hides had smoked to a rich dark-brown color, and the texture was butter soft, thanks again to his sister's skills.

He gave one of the finished hides to Don, as a gift for the knowledge his uncle shared with him. He tried to give one to Aria, as a gift for the tanning. His sister refused the offer, saying she preferred the lighter weight of the antelope for her summer clothing and the elk for winter. Bren had also taken another dozen antelope and gave Aria her choice of the finished product. She quickly accepted this offer, choosing two, then another four, after her brother goaded her into taking more.

They made a good team, he thought. He would miss her skill and her company when it was time for one of them to marry and for her to move from their mother's lodge. He vowed to do everything he could to keep her close to their village.

He was grateful for the closeness they shared, he thought. They got along much better than most of the brothers and sisters he knew. When they were growing up, they would work hard on their daily tasks in order to run into the hills or across the prairie for a time. They spent many hours climbing a tree to sit back-to-back and discuss the world. Their close friendship was cherished by them both.

Bren decided early on this was due to the way their mother and father treated the both of them and how they treated one another. He never did see his mother and father fight. There were times of disagreement in the past, but they never became cross or heated. They always treated each other and their children with respect and equal affection.

Bren and Aria had always been allowed to develop their own personalities and interests from an early age. They were given the freedom to learn the skills they found enjoyable. Their parents only gently urged them to perform well at whatever tasks they chose and always, always to finish what they started. This was the way with most of the people of their village. Because of this freedom to choose, their village was noted for the skill of their young people as hunters, crafters, and for their intelligence and kindness.

Bren's thoughts were interrupted by his father as he stepped into the lodge. He only now realized how curious he was to hear the outcome of the meeting. Ben sat and took the coffee offered to him. He looked into the expectant eyes waiting for him to report, and he grinned.

"A few of the people were upset. They believe these caverns are going to be a new beginning for the people, and we should take full advantage of them. I think that's probably so, and said as much, but I still believe their advantage will be limited to special use like storage and the baths, not full-time residence. Wil Horn was so angry for a while, he was ready to split the village and start his own within the caverns. Kennon pointed out to him that young Bren here and Airik had discovered the caverns and by rights had first call. Wil didn't like the thought of needing to barter either of the young ones out of their share. He soon calmed down."

"I hope this isn't going to be a problem for the village, Father," Bren said. "I didn't intend for this place to split the people. If I'd thought that would happen, I would have sworn Airik to silence and moved on."

"Son, there are always a few who disagree with the majority. That's how new ideas are born. It was a fun meeting for a change, that's all. Wil realizes the advantage he has here with our people. He would not risk that for a few holes in a mountain. He's a stubborn man, but a good one. Bren, more than a few people asked your whereabouts at this night's meeting. You're going to have to start taking a bigger part in the decision process in future. It's expected."

Bren thought about that for a while. He wasn't sure how to take that statement, but his father let the message sink in and changed the subject.

"I think we need to discuss what we're going to take to the gather. We leave in weeks now, you know. We spoke at the meeting about who would go and who would stay. We are at a place in the construction of the village that we can leave just a few here to continue the building. Everyone has worked very well together, and we deserve the break!

"This will be the best gather in a long while, with people from the eastern coast, the north, and the south bringing trade goods. The mountain people as well as the forest people and many of the plains villages will be coming. We'll have opportunity to meet many different folks, see some new things, and maybe even get some new ideas on what can be done with these caverns of ours. I'm planning that we all four go, of course, and that we stay at least two weeks, maybe longer. I think we should leave this lodge here and carry the new one with us. We will have to take most of the wagons anyway, to carry the trade goods back and forth. Our family may as well be prepared to represent our village well."

Thora knew something was afoot. Ben was already smiling. "What do you mean the new lodge, husband? I didn't know we had an old lodge. What's wrong with this one anyway? The seams are strong, and it is easily large enough for the four of us."

"I took the liberty of having Don speak to his friend Lee, in the pine ridge village. His wife makes some very good lodges, and I wanted to surprise you. I know you've been busy with the hunt and the gather that's coming. I was very specific on detail and material. She will use fourteen strong buffalo cowhides for the skin, and I was very specific about the strength of the seams. It will be painted in a red-and-blue pattern that I saw last year in the north. There will not be another one like it at gather, I'm sure! It will be delivered in two days. If you aren't satisfied, we'll return it and take the old one to gather. I know this lodge is new this past spring, but I thought soon we may be wanting to give it away."

Thora smiled at him. "My happiness isn't centered on how new my lodge is, Husband, but on who I share it with. I've seen Corin's workmanship, and I'm sure it will be wonderful. You do always think of me."

Bren was invited to spend the night in his mother's lodge. He awakened so late the next morning that he had the whole lodge to himself while he dressed for the day. By noon, he had his bails of robes and furs packed and ready for the trip to gather. He stashed them in his cabin to wait for gather. He spent the rest of the afternoon and early evening preparing the horses he would take. It was always best to take two saddle horses on a long journey, if possible. He could switch from one to the other during the trip and prevent the wearing down of the mounts. He chose the high-spirited Paint and Stone Foot, his favorite buffalo hunter, as always.

He took Stone Foot out for a ride in the afternoon, both to exercise the horse and to find meat for the evening meal. Bren rode several miles west into the mountains and passed up several young animals on the way. He was surprised that he was able to pick and choose his game, after all, the village had been here for some time now. He stopped on a hill to rest the horse, while he sat on a rock overlooking a wide oval meadow. It wasn't long before he was able to take a shot at a good-sized yearling cow elk that wandered within a long bow shot of where he sat. It was more than sufficient for his needs. He dressed the meat, wrapped it in the hide, and was back in camp well before nightfall. He had the roasts cut, seasoned, and over the fire before his parents made their way back to the lodge.

The next afternoon the new lodge came, and it was just as his father had promised. Bigger than the present lodge, it measured a full twenty feet from front to back. The cover was decorated with blue-painted circles to represent hail stones at the top and a series of red triangles around the bottom. It was an ancient design from the people of the northern plains, from where his mother's people had come years ago.

Bren spent a few days cleaning up his new cabin. The main work was finished, so all he needed to do was add a few shelves and last-minute details. Several people from the village brought by small gifts, lamps, dishes, and the like. He woke up one morning to find four very fine wooden chairs on the front porch. At last he moved his personal items in. It was a fine thing to know he'd built this place himself, excepting of course, for the help of many friends.

The day came when they were packed and ready to leave for the gather. Bren was up before dawn. His horses were packed and his trade goods bailed and ready before the first of the morning fires. A surprising number of people had decided to stay behind and work on the village and so had given lists of what was needed to relatives.

Gather

The village started out before the sun was up. Many wagons were filled with trade goods. There were another forty pack animals in trains of five animals, each train with a young man to lead and care for the group. With a group this size, they hoped to keep the rest stops to a minimum, making good time. Three days out of the village, they met with the group from the southern plains village and traveled with them. This was the village where Ben had gone to borrow some of the tools they were using to build their new village. This was also the village where Don had ordered the lodge for Ben and Thora. Bren's parents found Corin and thanked her for the lodge cover. Ben had agreed on the price of a saddle-trained horse for the work done and let Corin take her pick of the five saddle mares he brought to trade.

Late in the evening, the two groups set up camp. They picked a small stream near which a group of cottonwoods were growing, draped like a curtain down over the water. The travelers set up several fires and cooked their meals in large family groups. After the meals were done and camp was put away in anticipation of tomorrow's early departure, they sat around the fire and caught up on the news they had missed. Many of these people hadn't seen one another since the last gather.

They sat into the night, talking about family times past and people they had known. They also spoke about times to come. Everyone was talking about what was expected at this gather, as well as what they had brought and what they would be looking to buy.

The days of travel passed this way in comfortable, pleasant companionship. The people moved across the high grass prairie as they had done for hundreds of years. They stopped at the places their fathers and grandfathers had camped before them. Kennon told many stories of the places where they built their campfires in times gone by. Although he was aged, he was still an impressive figure sitting on his short tan saddle horse. The patriarch of the village with close to eighty years behind him, he was still able to ride these many miles across his country.

The people closed the distance between themselves and the gather site on wide, flat pathways the teachers said had been used by the machines of the ancestors. The machines, as with most of the ancient people's tools and buildings, were no more than legend now. The prairie had reclaimed most of the land, leaving little trace of what was.

Days rolled by, and after almost two weeks of travel from Bren's village, the friends crested a mounded, rolling bluff. The grassy plateau approached the bluff like waves on an ocean, dipping quickly down to a widespread grassy field sloping gently half a mile distant to a wide dark river. The temporary village could be seen in the trees at the river's edge and spilling out onto the boulder-strewn meadow. The grass-covered ground trampled flat by the passing of wagons, horses, and herds of farm animals. The trading village followed the river for almost a half mile and bulged out into the prairie a considerable amount.

There were barges on both sides of the river, conveying wagons full of goods across the strong current to gather. Bren and Aria sat their horses with Airik and their families, taking in the sights and sounds before them. Bren could hear the village sounds floating up to him on the gentle, persistent breeze.

The murmur of conversations, laughter, and the leaves in the cottonwoods brought a smile to Bren's face. The lilting sweetness of a group of flutes accompanied by violins, sitting under a canopy of three giant white oak trees floated to his ears. He smelled the tang of wood smoke and the mingled aromas of many foods in the air. The earthy smell of the animals mixed with everything else brought back the memory of the past years for Bren. All this was a picture engraved upon his heart.

The city of gather was growing by the moment. Set out on the rolling grass meadows were several hundred lodges. Among these were placed many more of the square tents the eastern people used, both for temporary dwellings and for selling at gather. The camping or living area was set aside from the trader's stores. Bren could see the main trading park closer to the river's edge. Here, the early arrivals were already gathered to display their goods and barter or buy.

The trading area was a huge half-moon shape with each end touching the river's edge. The crescent itself was set up as two double rows of tents, separated by an avenue down the center. This center roadway was wide enough to pull two wagons side by side. The merchants could unload their goods from the wagons, and the buyers could pick up their newly purchased goods without getting in the way of the rest of the tents.

On the inside portion of the huge curved space stood the many food tents where every kind of tasty bit of fair was sold. Wine merchants and butchers, cafés and bakers had their tables filled from morning to night with every conceivable treat to keep the traders happy and full.

Everyone was in the best of moods for gather. The center of the crescent was a place for music, food, and fun. Drums and flutes, violins and guitars, and every kind of musical instrument were played nonstop.

Dances were held every evening of the gather, where young and old could get together and spend time talking of the year past. Many people would reunite with family that had spread out across the continent or make new friendships.

New friendships. Bren's heart skipped as he remembered the first time he had seen Sara, at last year's gather. She was standing at one of the craft tents watching her mother barter for a bolt of cloth. She was dressed simply in a long, flowing pale-blue dress with white lace. Her golden hair was gathered at her neck in a thick braid hanging to her waist. Her beautiful smile shone like the sun through her eyes and took his breath away.

Stone Foot sidestepped and bounced Bren from his reverie. The young man looked out over the living area trying to pick out the tents of the people he most wanted to see at this celebration. He looked for the wagons and tents of the grain growers. Bren said a silent prayer asking that Arden and Ellie Bjornssen had brought their daughter to the gather. He had been looking forward to seeing Sara, the girl with the wolves, since the day they rode from gather a year ago. They had promised one another they would sit and walk and tell each other what had happened in their lives during the year that passed between gathers. He could make out where there were people walking around the tents with the familiar golden wheat banner. What worried him was, he hadn't been able to spot the tiny girl with the long honey-blond hair.

Ben rode up to him and read the expression on his face. "I see a familiar banner by the cottonwood grove, Bren. Shall we see if we can find a spot close by those trees? Remember, we have a camp to set before we can do any trading or visiting." He smiled at his son.

"I remember, Father," Bren said, not taking his eyes from examining the camp. The wheat banner was blowing gently near the lodge. "I don't intend to trade until I have a chance to look at everything anyway."

The two villages found a place large enough to set up camp as one. They set their lodges in a circular pattern, forming a shared area in the center to prepare food or talk about their day. Ben and Thora hung the banner of their village. It displayed the ancient, stylistic pictograph drawing of the elk dreamer on a golden-brown field. A simple stick figure bull elk with four jagged lines radiating forward, out of its forehead, was at the center.

Bren was looking in the direction of the wheat banner as his was unfurled. He saw the unmistakable fall of golden hair, as Sara poked her head out of her parents' tent. As always, his breath caught in his chest at first sight of her. She stepped out of the door and looked in his direction. She caught sight of Bren and waved. He waved back and heard his sister giggle at his back. Bren went quickly inside and took out his new elk hide clothing, with his sister's beautiful quill-work. Feeling just a bit foolish, he changed quickly and made sure everything was right.

He checked with his father to make sure nothing else needed doing then walked toward the wheat banner. As he approached the lodge, he was met by Thunder and Winter. The huge black-and-tan male and the tall white female wolf were Sara's constant companions. Thunder approached him with a fixed stare, but Winter was all bounce and wag as she danced around him in enthusiastic greeting.

Thunder's legs appeared to be too long for the huge, muscular body. His legs were a little stiff, Bren noticed. His head held low in the classic stocking challenge of his breed. The male stopped only a few feet from Bren, and they confronted one another. Bren went to one knee and looked directly into the animal's eyes. He knew, at least everyone said, this is not the proper course of action when meeting a strange dog, or wolf in this case. He wanted to make this test short and to the point. Bren wanted to convey that he had no intention of harming the wolf's family. Nor did he intend to be scared away. He knew beyond doubt he was being judged and was not about to fail. There was no menace in the canine's amber-eyed stare. There was only the calm confidence of a warrior.

With no warning and without looking back to see if Bren followed, the wolves turned and trotted toward the tents. He had only taken a few steps when the lodge flap opened, and Sara stepped out. She smiled at Bren, and he forgot to breathe. The beautiful young girl with the golden braid simply said to him, "Let's take a walk."

Bren felt as if they had left each other only hours before instead of so many long months ago. He was overpowered by the smell of flowers from her shining hair. She was a slim girl but carried herself with the same confidence as the wolves. Her glacier green eyes held the assurance that she knew what she was doing at any given moment. Her long, tanned, and muscled legs carried her with the solid but somehow delicate strides of an athlete.

A Walk-Through Gather

"Wait one moment, please," he said to her, "Is your father in the camp? I'd like him to know you're with me."

She smiled up at him as she told him, "He's gone to speak to a man about wheat, and my mother is with him. They intend to visit around the camps before returning. He knows I'll be with you, Bren, and has given his permission. Besides, I have my wolves. He knows I'm perfectly safe. You, however"—and her smile grew wider—"need to tread carefully in their presence!"

Bren looked to her and saw the laughter in her eyes. He felt the same thrill he felt every time he came within sight of this lovely girl. His face flushed. He felt as if his spirit rose from him and followed along above. She walked close to him, with Thunder on her left. Winter chose to walk at Bren's right side, and the wolf ducked her head under his hand so it rested gently on her shoulder. They made their way across the prairie meadow toward the gathering place.

Bren was speechless for a moment. He finally looked down at her and simply said, "I've missed you." She laughed, holding his eyes for a moment, and Bren melted into her smile. *She is completely relaxed*, he thought, *and I can't remember my name.*

Her hair was the color of golden honey, lightened in streaks by the sun. It parted in the middle and fell to her waist in straight waves of morning light. Her eyes were the green of the pools in the high mountains that collected the glacier's cold, clean water. They held tiny golden specks sparkling with the light from the shining sun. Her skin was golden too, smooth and shiny, fresh and perfect. Her nose was tiny and turned slightly up at the end. The line of her jaw was clean and curved into a chin that was, well, she was perfect. Her body was strong and slim and took his breath away. He felt insignificant in her presence and wondered why this girl, who could obviously have any man she fancied, chose to walk with him.

"You seem to have grown taller, and your hair is longer than I remembered. Otherwise you are the same," she said to him.

"Well…thank you? I think. I…" Bren looked down at her quickly. His eyes widened in pleasant wonder. "You're wearing buckskins I see. They're very nice." Bren remembered last year. He had teased her for always wearing the cotton that was so prominent in the farming areas where she lived, but not the most practical choice for a life on the plains. He had explained to her that cotton was so much more fragile than the skins he wore.

She was dressed in very light-colored, loose-fitting pants and a tunic that showed just a touch of the color of smoke. The top was loosely cut and decorated at the throat with small sky-blue glass beads that formed an upside-down triangle. The boots she wore appeared to be sheepskin.

Around her waist she wore a thickly woven cotton belt matching the beads perfectly. Bren wondered if she had dressed for him. The outfit appeared to be new and never worn before.

She asked him "Where is your bear skin?" as she looked over his outfit. She saw the wary look in his eye and said, "Yes, I've heard the story, Bren. Everyone was talking about you when we arrived at gather. They say the bear was the largest anyone has seen for many years." She slipped her hand into his as she continued. Bren felt a tingling thrill shoot up his arm at her touch. He could feel the firm coolness of her fingers fitting into his perfectly. His nervousness vanished. She told him, "I was afraid for you when I heard what happened. I couldn't find anyone who had actually seen you since the attack. Some said you'd been horribly scarred, while others said you weren't touched by the beast. We arrived yesterday, and I found it hard to sleep, worrying for you."

"I left the bear skin at my family's camp. Aria has made a very fine winter coat and a pair of boots from it. It's too heavy for such pleasant weather, but I will show it off to you later if you want to see it."

She stepped in front of him and stopped. Spreading her legs slightly, she put her hands on her hips and, with the scrutiny of a merchant buying hides, looked him over slowly. "You don't appear to be damaged." She paused, still looking. "You will tell me the story, won't you?" she demanded.

"I will…First thing first, if you please. I see the food booths under that group of oaks, in the center of the trading area. Let's go find the sausages and cheese and some bread. I've been thinking of those sausages for a year. Then we can sit for a while, if you will."

"Sausages, you've been thinking of sausages for a year?" She acted crestfallen. This time it was Bren's turn to tease. He looked at her with raised eyebrows and a crooked smile.

They walked to the open tents of the food vendors and looked over each one until they found some of the large boudins, or buffalo sausages, that Bren loved to eat. He wisely bought two extra, one each for Thunder and Winter. They were served in warm, soft sourdough bread. Bren bought some mild white cheese to go with them, and they made their way toward the massive oak.

They soon found a table under a deeply shaded portion of the tree canopy, suitably removed from the traffic of the tents. He set the food carefully at the feet of the wolves, and they looked up intently at Sara. "Eat, babies," she said quietly, and the wolves made short work of the sausages, bread and all. Sara thanked Ben as Thunder folded himself at her feet, and Winter lay down under the tree, at its base. The gentle breeze flowed over them as they ate and talked of the trip to gather. Bren felt completely relaxed. He couldn't keep his eyes off her hair or her eyes or the way the light played against her skin as she spoke. He was enthralled by the way the breeze blew a strand of hair out of her face. There was magic framed in her perfect smile.

"You will begin now, bear hunter! Tell me the truth of this story!" Sara said, as they finished their food. Bren took a deep breath and told her the story of the bear, from front to back. He did not leave out any of the detail he remembered, including the wine that he had consumed and the reason for the walk into the trees. She laughed at this part and closed her eyes tightly when he told of his thoughts as the bear landed atop him.

"I'm sorry," he said as he saw the look on her face. "I could have left that part out."

"No, nor should you have. I asked for the whole story and didn't want anything less. I didn't live the thing as you did. I can hear it from you as it happened, at least. I will expect always for you to tell me exactly the truth and nothing less." Her words shocked him with portent, but they also reassured him. He heard in her tone that she expected to talk to him of many things through a lifetime of stories.

He told her of the way the people had looked at him in the days following the killing of the bear and the talk he had with Kennon. He told her of the village site he and Airik found and the wonderful feeling it gave him for the future of the people. He found himself telling her of things that had been only on the edge of his conscious thoughts. Things that he was vaguely aware of feeling but that he hadn't put into words yet to himself. He could speak to her more easily than he could to any other person. He noticed that, during some point in the story, the wolves had turned and began watching him. It seemed Sara's friends were listening to the story as it was told.

When Bren began to speak of his talk with Kennon, Thunder lifted his head and appeared to look directly into his eyes. They finished their meal and decided to walk through the traders' booths.

Bren was happy to follow Sara through the booths and tents as she pointed out clothing, kitchen tools, and farming implements. He couldn't help but notice the glances sent Sara's way. The men, young and old, furtively and often blatantly stared at her beauty. Young girls gawked at her in awe and young ladies sometimes in jealous disbelief. Sara didn't seem to notice. That made him all the more interested in her and proud to walk beside her. He wondered if she was hearing his thoughts, because she reached out to him with a smile and once more took his hand in hers.

As he walked beside this beautiful young girl, he knew beyond any doubt he was deeply in love with this farmer's daughter who friended wolves. He would soon ask and only dared to hope she would consent to spend her life with him.

They walked through the entire trade area, commenting on one thing or another. They were looking at gifts for their parents, for their friends, and for themselves. It was Bren's practice at gather to look over every item that was offered, sometimes for several days before making a purchase.

Sara didn't seem to notice the wide path the other patrons took around the wolves, even though Winter's demeanor was pleasant and playful. Bren could see her watching the movement of the crowd. A time or two he saw her free hand make small, quick signals. These movements seemed to be without thought, but the dogs reacted instantly to her unspoken commands. He remarked to her, "They listen well to you. You don't have to speak aloud."

She answered, "They're my friends and constant companions. We trust one another. We're family."

Bren first looked at the booths that sold the hardware he needed. He found beautiful knives and a flint and steel kit packaged compactly in a small round tin container that would be perfect for him to carry on hunting trips. He looked at finely tooled leather saddles that were a cross between the heavy working saddles the sheep and cattle ranchers used and the lightweight saddles the message carriers preferred.

These message carriers were young men in the plains villages that were paid for taking letters from one community to the next or across the continent by relay. They were usually the smallest and lightest for their age and rode very hard many miles at a time. They changed horses at villages spread over the course of their journey. Their saddles were light but sturdy, and Aria had been coveting them since she first saw one pass through their village. Although he preferred only a small hide or wool pad between himself and his horse, he was thinking of such a saddle for his sister, who had pointed out this very tent to him at last year's gather.

At another booth, Bren stood and watched intently as a metalworker heated iron with his coal forge. The muscular man pounded the glowing metal into shapes of knives, forks, and spoons for use at the dinner table. Bren was fascinated by the way the man took a bar of iron and bent it into the shape of a horse's shoe. He watched another man in the tent next to the blacksmith take the cooled shoes and affix them to the foot of a horse, tied to the back of his wagon. The man first shaped each hoof then fitted the shoe and nailed it to the foot of the horse. Bren had seen shod horses before but had never seen the process. He vowed to himself he would return with Stone Foot and all his other horses to have these shoes fit to their feet.

While he was watching, he caught the smell of roasting coffee from somewhere close.

"Smell that," he said to Sara as he looked for the source of the aroma. "Let's find the roaster!"

Winter twitched her nose and trotted down the aisle. She waited at a spot where two aisles intersected and looked back at the couple. Sara looked up at Bren with a grin and told him, "Follow the wolf."

Two turns later, they were standing in front of a tent with light fragrant smoke billowing out of a stovepipe into the afternoon sky. A young woman with long red hair was standing at a table in front and pouring dark-amber liquid into small ceramic cups. She was looking down at the white wolf and smiling softly. "She drinks coffee, does she?" she asked as Sara and Bren caught up to her. Thunder stuck his head between the two. "Oh my, what beautiful friends you have." she told the pair.

"They don't drink coffee." Bren smiled. "But I'm beginning to think they speak our language better than I speak theirs."

"Have no doubt, sir. I have a…smaller pair myself, and I'm quite sure they know my words far better than I can understand theirs, try as I might. Taste this coffee and give me an honest opinion, if you will. This is a dark roast I just took from the roaster."

Bren and Sara both took the offered cups and inhaled the aroma before they drank. "How much are you asking for this, by the pound?" Bren asked the proprietor.

"This coffee will be getting a ten coin for five pounds. I'll grind it for free, if you have the time to wait."

Bren raised an eyebrow as he thought for a moment. "I'll take twenty pounds. Whole bean would suit me well, and I'd like one of those grinders I see behind you, if you please." He pointed to a row of wooden boxes with cast-iron workings.

"The grinder is a ten coin as well. Very fine craftsmanship from the northeast coast," she told him.

"Could I pick it all up tomorrow?" Bren placed the coins on the table and slid them toward the red-haired girl.

"It will be packaged and ready for you come the morning." She smiled. "Would you prefer it packaged as a whole or by the pound?"

"By the pound, if you would please," Bren said.

They moved on and soon came to a booth that had some nicely tanned shirts and pants hung out for inspection. Right away, Bren thought of his sister. The hides were of very good quality. Bren could tell the Taylor was expert at his craft, but the art that Aria put into her work was missing here. He was noticing a jacket that hung on the corner of the booth, when the proprietor was drawn to Bren's outfit. "I see a plainsman at my tent," he said, noticing Bren's quilled outfit. "Beads are sometimes hard to find in the west, but that quill-work is beautifully done. The moose is perfectly tanned. I do prefer the darker smoke on a moose hide. If you don't mind, who did this beautiful work for you, young man?"

"This is my sister's work. Her name is Aria. She's the best tanner in our village and by far the best quill worker I have ever seen. She is here at gather and has brought many beautiful things. I would guess she might trade, for the right payment. I can't promise she has not sold all of her best by now."

"Tell her, if you would please. Tell her I've asked for her to bring her goods and see trader Jameson before she sells a thing. She is a fine an artist! I would be willing to pay her top marks for what she has, if the quality of the rest of her work is comparable to what you wear. Don't forget my banner," he said as he pointed out the forest-green square of cloth, trimmed in gold threads, atop his booth. Bren liked the pleasant little man, with his bowl-shaped haircut sitting on top of a full graying beard.

"I'll be sure to tell her, sir."

"What is your family name young man, so I will know her when she comes to call?"

"My family is Redhorse, sir. I'm called Bren."

The man took a step backward and his hands splayed out to his sides. His jaw dropped slightly as he gaped at Bren. "I should have known you. You're the bear killer everyone is talking about. The clothing surely fits." Bren noticed the crowd within earshot of the old man had stopped and turned to look, as they heard his words. The wolves noticed the attention as well and turned their backs to the booth, to stare intently at the people who stopped to watch the conversation. Bren felt warm and uncomfortable, so he urged Sara on and away from the gawking folks. Trader Jameson smiled at their backs as they left. "Don't forget my banner, Bear Killer." He raised his voice to be heard by all within earshot. "The best marks, you know! If her quality matches what you wear!" he called after the couple. The eyes of the crowd followed them away.

"That was fun!" said Sara with a mischievous smile. "I like walking with someone as famous as you, Bear Killer! I wonder if he heard about the reason for your visit to the woods as well." Sara's dimples showed when she laughed, flustering Bren more than a little. "You'd think people would have something better to do than spread stories about folks they don't know."

They spent the next few hours wandering through the tents and booths, comparing items for trade. They talked about what they needed and what they wanted. Sara stopped at a tent with several cast-iron stoves sitting on display. She explained to Bren about the stove her mother used every day. Down the way a bit, she showed him a sled the dogs could pull and the harness that went with it.

"This," she told him, "will be my job for the coming winter. Smoke's pups are getting to the age when they will soon be able to learn to pull this sled. I want to have the whole team learn. It sounds like great fun and a convenient way to get around in winter, don't you think?"

"I think it would be very much fun and come in very handy for winter travel," he admitted. "Do you know how to train for it?"

"I've been speaking to an old man in the village close to our home. He's seen my wolves and used to have a team of smaller dogs that pulled a sled for him. He thinks it can be done, with careful teaching and with time."

"I'm sure," Bren said to her, "that if anyone can do it, Sara of the wolves, it will be you."

Bren and Sara had started toward the living areas to see if they might be free to go to dinner together. They had just entered a large grouping of lodges, when they heard a voice call out, "Young man, what is your name?"

Bren stopped and looked in the direction of the voice.

"Yes, I'm speaking to you!"

Bren saw the owner of the voice was a small ancient, man with very white hair and a very old style of plains clothing. He was sitting in front of a lodge that was bigger and as new as his mother's. The man appeared to be looking right at him, although his eyes were clouded with age, and he appeared to be sightless.

"Yes, young man. You, with the new moose hide clothing. The first time you wore them, I judge," the man said this with his nose in the air. He reminded Bren of the camp dogs that searched the air when a visitor approached.

"Please, bring the girl and come sit with me for a moment. Sit here, if you would." He indicated the buffalo robe he was seated on by patting with a spotted, wrinkled hand. "I believe you might be courting, as she wears new buckskin also. She has washed her hair, not many hours ago. Tell me your name, young man, so I will know if I speak to who I seek."

"Grandfather," Bren used the ancient honorific, in respect for the one he spoke to, "if you need something, ask and I'll bring it for you. You shouldn't have been left alone, if I might say. But I fear I'm not the person you seek. We have never—"

"I am never alone these days, young man. Tell me your name" was the elder's quiet, insistent reply.

"I am Bren, Grandfather. Bren—"

"Redhorse," the man finished the sentence for him, nodding his head as he did. "The bear killer. You are the one who was spoken of, true enough. Please sit and speak with me. I'll promise not to take too much of your courting time, Bren Redhorse."

Bren's eyes met Sara's as he said, "Who are you, Grandfather, and how do you know me?" He crossed his feet as he sat on the robe in front of the man. Sara sat beside him. She was looking at the man in amused puzzlement. Thunder walked up next to the old man and lay down, his shoulder touching the man's leg. Winter lay down on his other side and placed her head gently in the man's lap. His wrinkled hand went directly to the huge head, the bony joints caressing the crown between her ears. The wolf accepted the caress with half-lidded eyes, as if from an old friend.

Sara was amazed and speechless. She had never seen Thunder make friends with anyone so quickly, but he appeared to be at ease. The old man sat looking at them both, with an expression of self-satisfaction. "I am called Joseph Red Star. I was born and have lived on the lands at Turtle Creek for all of my life. I am called a medicine man, or one who sees things, an old one. I am, in truth, nothing more than an old man who listens. I have little else to do, as you can see." The man made a sweeping gesture toward his milky, clouded eyes with both hands. When he did this, his hands touched a small bell hanging over his heart, which made a small tinkling noise.

A young woman came from inside the lodge. She walked with upright dignity, wearing her night-black hair straight and loose down her back. She appeared to be no more than Aria's age but projected a regal confidence. She held a ceramic pot of tea and three small matching cups. The cups were beautifully polished and inscribed with several ancient pictographic designs. Bren recognized his father's own elk dreamer symbol among them. The slight girl sat the tray of tea down on the fur at the man's left side, serving the old man first, Sara next, and Bren last. Sara said thank you to the graceful young woman before she stood and disappeared into the darkness of the lodge without speaking a word.

"Young woman, before we get started, I have your young man's name and you know mine, but I don't know what you are called?"

Sara said, "I'm Sara Bjornssen, Grandfather, and my wolves, at least I think they're still mine, are Thunder at your left and Winter has her head in your lap."

Winter opened one eye to peek at Sara.

111

The old man tasted the tea and smiled again. "You can drink, you know. My granddaughter makes it for me. She picks the herbs herself. Or are you both too full of sausages?"

Bren looked at Sara as she laughed. Her dimples popping again. He was not sure why he had come to meet this man, but he was beginning to like him, and he tasted the tea. "Grandfather," Bren asked the old man, "how do you know these things about us? Why would you be waiting for me?"

The old man smiled as he addressed Sara, "Dear one, I'm sorry you've found such a simple man. He is polite though, and sometimes that's enough." Sara laughed again as Bren turned red, and the man continued. "Sometimes we don't need eyes to see. Along with my youth, I have almost lost the sight of mine. Although it is truly inconvenient at times, it's opened my vision in ways I hadn't before considered. We carry shadows with us our eyes can't see. Not only in the bright light of day, but always. These shadows don't go away in darkness but only change substance. They are always with us. We carry with us the touch, the influence of the people who came before. They quietly influence our lives and speak to us through teaching and spirit left behind after they die.

"When you approached, I smelled the fresh smoke on your skins that only come from the thick smoke of the tanning tent. The girls were tanned by a different person than yours. They still smell of the brain, and yours have the special musk of the moose. The girl's hair is fresh from washing, again the smell. Her buckskins smell more strongly of the brain tanning, and I would guess that they are lightly smoked because of this. The sausage smell comes from both of you and the wolves." Thunder licked his mouth in remembrance.

"You've been through the crowd at the fair. I smell the coffee, the meats and breads, as well as the furs and hides that are sold there. I hear the difference in the sounds of your clothing as you walk. The moose is a thicker hide. The fibers are thicker and more loosely connected due to the excellent workmanship of the tanner. The lady wears the hide of a young deer or antelope. The fibers are tighter and thinner and make a different sound as she moves.

"You need only listen to the world to know. Most people concentrate so much on what their vision has to tell them they forget their other senses almost completely."

Bren began as the man paused, "Grandfather, you still haven't told me how you come to know us and why we are stopped at your lodge."

"I've spoken to Kennon, who watched you grow since your birth. The story I have for you is full of words. It will take some time and some trust. Let's move into the lodge and out of the sun. I'm told it isn't good for my thin old skin, and we will be more comfortable in the shade." Bren took the old man's arm as he got to his feet, and Sara followed with the tray. She spoke a single quiet word to the wolves. Winter gave a short wag of her tail without opening her eyes.

The interior of the lodge was colorful and very well done in the most tasteful of the old plains style. The grass floor was covered with several layers of buffalo hides, which cushioned their feet nicely. The walls were covered waist high with a liner of buffalo skins. They helped to keep out the cold of the winter wind and provided shade from the sun. This liner was decorated at its top edge with a line of porcupine quill work that rivaled his sister's best. Bren marveled at the time and care this must have taken.

There were willow rod back rests set on the hides opposite the door. In front of the center of the three stood a beautiful pipestone tobacco pipe on a base of carved elk antler. The stem of the pipe was decorated in woven porcupine quills in an intricate design of a running elk and a beautiful bald eagle. Suspended from each end of the stem, at the attachment point of the bowl and at the mouthpiece, were a set of four golden eagle feathers fanned out. The bowl itself was an effigy of a magnificent bull Elk in full rack. He appeared to be standing and bugling to the tree that was the bowl of the pipe. The carver of this pipe was a true master of the art, who understood the oldest ways of the people. Laid at the feet of the pipe stand was a smoked and tanned pipe bag easily four feet long. The bag was covered from bottom to top in deep red, purple, and white quill embroidery, with the elk dreamer symbol sewn in browns, golden yellow, and purest white.

Suspended from racks and tripods near what Bren recognized as the sleeping furs of the old man were his ancient bow and its quiver, as well as a shield, a war club, and other pieces of a man's personal arsenal. The shield showed the elk dreamer sign, and Bren counted sixteen golden eagle feathers attached to the outside rim. Hanging from the lodge poles directly opposite the door and above the sleeping furs was a buffalo skull, its mouth and eyes stuffed with sweetgrass in the ancient way.

The old man's granddaughter sat at the small fire as they stepped through the door. She moved quickly to take Bren's place at her grandfather's arm and seat him in his place. Once seated, the girl sat the pipe in his hand and a very old tobacco cutting board in his lap. The center of the board was worn almost through to the back from the cutting of the tobacco leaf on its surface. Once she knew the old one was comfortable, she took the tray from Sara and put it to one side of the lodge.

Joseph prepared tobacco carefully and lit the pipe. The lighting of the pipe was exactly the same as Bren had been taught by Kennon. He passed it to Bren, who found himself very conscious of the presence of Sara during this ceremony. The smoke was offered to the cardinal directions, as well as the earth and sky. He handed the pipe back to the old man, who looked at Sara and handed it to her. Bren was shocked once more, as Sara took the pipe and drew the smoke into her mouth. As she exhaled, she spread the smoke over her chest and head, in the ancient prayer way. They smoked in silence, as the blue-gray smoke once again swirled from their mouths to the heavens through the lodge vent hole. Joseph tapped the pipe four times on his palm. He placed the ash on the cutting board and set the board aside. The girl quietly took the pipe from him, placing it reverently on the stand near his feet.

"Bren Redhorse, what I have to say to you will take all the faith in you to believe. I have been chosen as the storyteller for the generations of our people that have come and gone before this time. I speak not only for the first nations, but for all the races of the world living and gone. When the people first came to be here, they lived within a circle created by the great mystery of life. The animals, the trees, the rocks, the soil, and the water all lived together as one complete world.

"This world started to change almost from the beginning. There were people who began not to think of the world as a place to live within but as a place to own and to use as they wanted. The circle of life unraveled small bits at a time, until the great change occurred. Some say that the spirits looked at what the people did to the earth mother and brought their vengeance down upon them. Others say this happened because the people who lived here simply became too greedy. They stopped caring for one another and for their world.

"Which is the right answer has been debated since even before the great cataclysm brought the old world to an end. Maybe it was both. In any case, when the people that remained saw they had a second chance, they vowed not to make the mistakes they had made in the past, and the circle began to heal.

"There is an ancient prophecy that the second coming of the buffalo will signal the healing of the circle. The people will begin again to walk their land in a true and sacred manner. Many of the old ones like myself have seen the signs that times are changing in very… unusual ways. We believe this is a result of the healing. The bringing together of the ends of the circle. The ways of the old, ancient earth mother are being reborn. They awaken from where they laid dormant, in sleep like the bear for untold winters. The teachers and the elders have kept these prophecies, legends, and teachings alive as best we could while this healing process was carried out. We have also taken the vow to see, as best we can, that these changes are for the benefit of the earth and of the people.

"Some of the old ways are set solidly in the fabric of our lives, and some of them are still to be learned or learned again. We are told that a group of the people will return to the very old ways and teach the people to once again see the true spirit of our world. We feel we may be living in that time today, when one people will take the forefront. When the people will begin once more to walk the red road back to the healing ways. These people will need the strength of all the beings, truly, of all the spirits of the earth. They will need a leader to take them back into the ancient ways and, in so doing, take them ahead into tomorrow.

"There are people who would upset the healing of the circle in these days, not by evil intent, but by a lack of understanding of what has happened and is happening to our world. We who are left need the help of the young people who are living through this change as well. We need the help of the people whose world this will be. We are entering the beginning days of the fourth world.

"When the bear came to you, I believe he was giving you some of the power you will need to finish your journey. You will have other helpers on the road, if you are able to see their power. Some will walk as we do, some will not. I don't know other than this."

Bren sat without speaking. Sara had, at some time into this dialogue, slipped her hand into his. She squeezed it now with a gentle pressure to remind him of her presence.

Bren spoke, "Kennon spoke to me of this not long ago. I don't know if I am the one you think I am. I'm an ordinary person. I have no special gifts or powers. What makes you think I am the chosen one you speak of?"

"You are correct. You have no special powers or magic. You're a person like any other, but, young man, we have waited for you for a long, long time."

"You are simply a leader of people. That's all the power you will need for this journey. I would ask only that you look into your heart and remember your blood is the blood of an ancient people. Search yourself as the ancients did, in the purification rituals of the sweat lodge and the vision quest. If you don't find the answers to the questions you have been asking yourself, then you need not continue along this path."

"I would do anything I can for my people," Bren said. "I hope I will have the spirit within me to help. What would you have me do, and when must this quest begin?"

"For now, there is no hurry. Enjoy the gather, some of the answers you seek are here. One of those answers is sitting at your side. When the time comes, look for Kennon and he'll guide you through the preparation. I have something for you, to remind you of our visit."

Joseph produced a piece of hide from inside his shirt. Wrapped in the hide was a necklace on a chord of braided horse mane. The necklace was made of two eagle claws, placed tip to tip, forming a crescent pointing down as they hung. The claws were attached at their joints to a sky-blue beaded hide wrap, or medicine bag.

"This is a very old piece. It is said to contain much power from the old world, before the European people took away the buffalo." Joseph gestured for Bren to lean forward, and he placed the talisman over his head. "It will provide assistance at some time in your life, guard it well."

Joseph leaned back and, for the first time, rested against the willow rods. Joseph's granddaughter moved from the fire to his side. For the first time since their meeting, she spoke to Bren and Sara.

"It's time for him to rest. Your visit is finished. Thank you for speaking to my grandfather."

"Thank you, Grandfather, you've given me much today. I believe you've helped me on a path I've been traveling for a while."

"One last thing for both of you. From this day, you will please call me Joseph. All this 'grandfather' talk is very polite, but it makes me feel like an old man."

Bren, Sara, and White Calf smiled at each other as the young lady bustled around the lodge. "We'll see you soon, I believe," White Calf said to them as they left the lodge.

Bren and Sara stepped outside Joseph's lodge. They looked at each other without words for a long moment. The sky was turning toward evening. In the west, the clouds were changing from the last soft pinks and purples, to the colors of twilight. Sara slipped her hand back into Bren's and spoke softly to Thunder and Winter as the wolves joined them to walk away.

They found themselves walking through the trader's booths once again. The day had turned to evening as they took the path, and the traffic was light. The tents were illuminated by candle lamps and small fires in shallow metal pots. Traders were closing their shops for the night, to begin their rounds of the more personal dealing at the campfires. Each trader knew he need only tie his tent flaps closed. The woodland village that was hosting this gather would post guards to make certain all the goods now present would be untouched come morning. This was one of the easiest of jobs at a gather. Rarely was there a need for the guards to perform tasks other than to carry a lantern for one who had consumed too much woodland red wine.

Bren and Sara soon found themselves at the benches where they had eaten earlier in the day. Bren straddled the bench, and Sara sat between his legs, her back to him, with her head resting on his chest. He wrapped his arms around the girl and felt their warmth mingle between them. They watched the last vestige of light fade from the twilight sky and the first of the stars awaken. He marveled at the fit of the girl next to him, as if they were made to be together.

She said to him quietly, "Bren, I haven't felt this way ever in my life. The feeling I have for you. It's as if we've known each other for a lifetime and longer, though it's been for only a few months this summer past and the time we were away from one another this winter.

"There were times during the winter months that I thought you were a dream I had, or worse, you would not remember me when we met at gather. I know I will sound very forward to you, but I need to say these things. If something is to happen to you on this journey you are about to take, I want it to happen to me as well. I have loved you since the moment I first saw you. I couldn't live through another winter not knowing where you are or what bear you are fighting in the dark. When this gather is over, I will go to visit my grandmother at the place where the big river turns to the west. After that, I would come to you if I were asked...nicely."

She sat very still, fearful he might think her words too forward. His forehead brushed her hair, and he breathed in the scent of her for a long moment. When he spoke, his breath gently brushed her left cheek.

He wrapped his arms more tightly around her and said, "I've never been more certain of anything than I am of my love for you. It comes from a place in me that holds room for little else. But, Sara, I don't know what the future has in store. You've seen what people are telling me is my future today and know as well as I that it is uncertain. What kind of man would I be for you if I were to bring you into this uncertain life that awaits me? When gather is over, we'll see what is to be. I hope that you will, from this day forward, be a partner in my life. I would share my heart and my life with no other.

"So I have no choice but to ask you, no, to plead with you to come to my village as soon as you can. I would go with you if I could, but I have a different path to take, as you do, for now. Soon though and for the rest of our days in this world, our paths will be the same. Sara, would you spend your life with me and be my wife?"

Sara turned to him, her features melting into a soft glowing smile as their mouths sought one another. He felt her heart beating beneath the warm, soft hide of her tunic and knew this was right. They sat together under the oaks and kissed until the moon rose, large and shining in the night. They spoke softly of the events of the day, trying to discover the import of the things happening to them.

Finally, Sara posed the question that was on her mind. "What about children, Bren? Do you see children in your life? I honestly don't know where my heart lies with this question. My wolves, and now you, are enough for me for the moment."

Bren turned Sara fully around on their bench to face him and looked into her clear and shining eyes. He placed his hands on her shoulders and slid them down to her waist as he spoke quietly. "This life, this body are yours alone, Sara. The choice is yours to have children or not and when. I'll be with you either way. I would be honored to be the father of your children and would be just as honored to walk alone with you for the rest of our lives. I only ask that you talk to me about it when the time comes for you."

Sara's eyes grew wet with tears as she wrapped her arms around him. Their mouths met once again in a long, soft kiss.

At last Thunder rose and looked pointedly in the direction of the family tent, then over his shoulder at the entwined couple. Sara giggled as she said, "Thunder says it's time to go, and he is never wrong." Winter sat and watched them go, until Sara finally turned to her and said, "Come along, young lady, there will be plenty of time for us to sit together and look into the sky."

They walked the distance back to Sara's family tent in silence, reveling in the closeness they shared. She stopped a short distance from the front of the tent and turned to him. Taking the eagle claw talisman gently in her fingers, she felt a warmth emanate from it.

Sara looked at her young man, and Bren saw the moon shining again in her eyes. "This is strange, this thing that is happening to us. I can't hide from you, Bren, that I'm frightened. I'm frightened for you and for us both. At the same time, I am very proud that you would do this thing, whatever it might be, for the people. I'm prouder that we will be together when it is done. Say good night to me here." Sara smiled at him, and her face glowed in the soft moonlight. "It will be better for you to greet my parents by the light of day."

Bren felt a wet muzzle on his hand and said to Winter as she looked up at him, "I thank you for your company today, I hope this means we're friends now."

The wolf looked directly into his eyes for a moment and trotted away to lay down at the door of the tent. Thunder chuffed quietly and trotted off after his sister.

He kissed Sara lightly on the mouth, knowing full well they were being watched from the shadow of the wagons near the tent. He heard a small gasp, as proof of the spy.

"I'll come calling in the morning. I'd like you to come trading with me, if you will."

"I'll ask Mother if she has plans for me," she told him. "Don't come too early though, I want to sleep in for a change. Now that I know my bear killer is safe."

"I love you, Sara of the wolves," he said, and Sara said to him, "I love you, Bren Redhorse. Healer of the circle." She smiled and turned, slipping quietly into the glowing interior of the tent.

Halfway back to his parents' camp, he met his father on the path. "Come with me," His father said. "We're on our way to a meeting of the elders, and they wish to speak with you."

Bren was taken aback by this announcement and asked what the meeting would be about. "They've heard stories about you during the spring and summer and want to hear the truth of it from you."

Bren followed his father to a large canvas tent near the trading grounds. The tent was lighted by oil lanterns inside and out. They entered the opened door, and Bren saw a large table at the center. Men and women from every part of the continent were seated around the table. They all followed Bren and Ben with their eyes to two empty seats.

Bren sat next to his father and was addressed by a woman who sat opposite them across the table. "Welcome, Bren Redhorse. My name is Ashlen. We at the table have heard many stories of your busy year and wondered which ones are true." Bren noticed Joseph sitting near the woman and inclined his head toward him.

Bren answered with all the confidence he could muster. "Probably none of them are completely true. The stories have changed a bit every time I've heard them so far. If you are speaking of the bear, I went to the woods to...relieve myself and was caught unaware. I broke my grandfather's knife off in him and got lucky. That's the truth of it." The people around the table grinned and chuckled as Bren finished speaking.

"Joseph tells us," Ashlen continued, "there is much promise in you. We have faith in what Joseph sees. He has spoken truth to us many times over his long years. Tell us, young Redhorse, have you had a chance to think on what Joseph told you in your meeting at his lodge?"

Bren looked around, into each face at the table. They returned his gaze expectantly. "I don't know what to think about what I am told by Joseph. I have no doubt of his truth or wisdom. Why I would be chosen to perform an important task for my people is beyond me. I'm a simple man of the plains, no more. I wish only to hunt and ride and build a life with my people. To continue to learn to be a true human being is all I've asked."

"Well spoken," Ashlen interjected. "What Joseph tells us is you have a part to play in the healing of the circle. What we want to hear is assurance you are ready to play that part."

"I mean no disrespect to the people seated at this table, but I must speak the truth I see. I can give you no assurance. How am I to know I'm ready for a task when I know nothing of what that task might be? I tell you only this. I am a son of the people of the plains. If I'm given the opportunity to help my people, I will do everything within my power to provide that help. I would do this thing only if it's the right thing to do, not because it's expected of me."

The table sat in silence for several minutes after Bren spoke. He looked around the table once again and saw Joseph smile as he leaned in to speak to Ashlen. Several other heads were bent together in quiet whispers as well. He was beginning to think he might have done harm to his family's reputation when Ashlen spoke again.

"You speak well for a young man, Bren. You do your family proud, as expected from one raised by Ben and Thora Redhorse. Know that whatever is to come, you have the trust of this council. If you should ever want to sit at this table, let it be known, and we'll make room for you."

Bren spoke as he stood. "I thank you all for that confidence, and I hope I will earn it. Tonight, what I want more than anything is a good sleep. I have trading to do tomorrow." He looked at Joseph and saw the old man smile directly at him, nodding his head. With that, he left the tent. His father stayed seated.

Bren walked the distance to his mother's new lodge lost in thoughts of the long day and this very strange evening. He was sure Joseph told him the truth as the old man saw it, but he was unsure of the meaning behind what had been said. He felt unbalanced for a moment and didn't know where to turn. He thought a good night's sleep would help more than anything to clear his head.

The fire was low and casting an orange glow over the inside of the circle of lodges. He saw his mother and sister were still away. He lit two lanterns, hanging one outside and the other inside the lodge before laying on his furs. He let his thoughts wander for a while and didn't remember going to sleep.

Trading Day

Bren awoke the next morning to the sounds and smells of his mother's cooking. He sat up, and Aria thrust a coffee mug at him. "I'm rich," she said with a gleam in her eye and a smile that lit her face. "I spoke to an acquaintance of yours last evening. He said you happened by his booth earlier, and he was admiring your clothing. It didn't hurt that he seems to think you're famous. He offered to buy all I have. Mother and I agreed it was a most generous price.

"He sought me out at Don and Seela's lodge, where he saw the quilled pipe bag and a few other things I made for them. Father will take me to the traders' tent later to deliver my things and collect the marks. I told you if you wore my hides it would do some good for me."

Bren sipped from the proffered mug before answering his sister. "I'm happy for you, little sister. So happy in fact that I will only charge you a small fee for getting this deal started. Because of me, you'll soon be famous throughout the plains. The people of the eastern farmlands and the ocean shores will be ordering clothing from you. You won't have a moment's time to spare. You will be working constantly. For the right price, I'll sell you my spare hides from time to time."

Aria stepped on his foot, with purpose, as she passed. "You won't make me mad today, brother. I'm rich, and I can take your teasing all day, while I count marks!"

"I'm really happy for you, Aria. I knew it was only a matter of time before your skill would be discovered far and wide. Skill like yours will always be in demand. I'm glad Father is going with you, because I have deals of my own to make."

Bren thanked his mother for the food and sat to eat with them. He took the morning's leisure time to catch up with his family. Don and Kennon stopped by and invited them to a meal at Kennon's camp in the evening. Bren said he would be there and asked if he could bring a guest. He endured a bit of teasing, although he knew without doubt his family knew just what was happening between him and Sara. He was sure they were informed by everyone in the gather village.

They left camp to continue their trading two hours before noon. Bren made his way to Sara's camp, hoping he wasn't too early. He needed both his horses and a borrowed one from his father to carry his hides for trade. He was greeted by Thunder and Winter both while still a good distance from the tent. This time, the wolves trotted in front of him good-naturedly and stood at the door of her family tent. Thunder woofed once softly, and Sara's smiling face appeared as she drew back the canvas door.

"Good morning, Sara, it appears I have been accepted," he said, looking at the wolves.

"Good morning, I'll be right out," she answered.

Bren waited outside the lodge, with Thunder casually leaning against his leg. The wolf did seem to tolerate him and even seek his company now. It seemed they had come to an understanding Bren should be aware of.

He saw Sara's father approaching and was suddenly unsure of his welcome. He felt a sudden intense need to run. Realizing there was nowhere to go, he stood resolute and waited for the inevitable. His name was Arden Bjornson, and he was a huge man. His face was fair and bearded, and he always looked happy and friendly. This gave Bren no relief though, as the big man approached. Arden smiled absently as he sat and offered Bren a seat at the fire circle.

"I've heard a lot of talk about you at this gather, Bren. They're all good words, of course. They tell a story of how you were attacked by a bear and won the contest. The story is told several different ways, but I am sure one is correct. They are not far off, one from the other.

"I've also heard the elders say you're involved in the changes being spoken of. This concerns me, because my daughter has made it clear you are very close to the center of her world. She speaks of you more than she speaks of the wolves now, and that is truly something.

"I'll tell you that you have a responsibility to her. You will keep her safe, and you will keep her from being hurt by what's going on around you. I have every confidence this will happen. I've watched you for the while that we've known you. I believe I can trust your judgment, or you wouldn't be spending even a moment with our Sara. Your family is well respected on the plains and in the mountain communities. I've asked. We will visit your village before the winter begins. I hear your new site holds much promise for your people and you've found some very interesting caves, with pools. Sara's mother doesn't want her to go from us at such a young age, but we'll see what will be."

"You must know that I love Sara more than my life," Bren said. "I'm not sure what is happening in our world. I'm not sure if I will be a central part of it, but I will do what I can and what I must. I know that Sara will be a part of whatever is good in my life. I make you this promise. Nothing will harm her as long as I draw breath. I've built a home where I believe she'll be comfortable. If, that is, you would give your consent to our marriage. There is room for you and your family to visit whenever you would like. I look forward to having you come to our village."

"You have my consent, Bren Redhorse. Not that it would matter, if she set her mind and heart on you."

Sara walked from the tent and saw Bren had been cornered. She greeted her father with a kiss on his bearded cheek and gently pulled Bren to his feet. "We have things to do today." She smiled down at her father as she took Bren's arm. Arden Bjornson watched as his daughter walked away toward the gather tents. Her young man had spoken well.

Bren and Sara took their time getting to the traders' park. They made their way to a prearranged spot where they met Ben and Thora. Ben brought the wagon containing the family's trade goods. Bren's horses, carrying a few of his packed hides, were tied to the wagon so they could trail behind. He took a pack containing a few representative hides and headed for the booths. He was surprised at how easy it was to make the deal for his packs of furs. Within the hour, he brought the wagon to the merchant and had more marks than he expected he would get. It had never been so easy.

"Now," Bren said, "the real trading begins." Bren first went to the booth where he'd seen those fine forged steel knives the day before. The quality was excellent, and after some good-natured haggling with the proprietor, he bought three. Two were for himself and one for his father. He found the knife maker had some very small and very dangerous-looking boot knives as well. He bought two of these, one for himself and one as a gift for Airik. He bought his mother and sister each a mirrored box to hold their combs and hair ties. He admired some thin, almost weightless steal arrow points and bought two dozen. He collected all the items that would be necessary to get himself through the long winter months, when there would be little to do but work on equipment and prepare for the spring hunts.

He bought a pound of tea from the herbalist. He and Sara thought it smelled very similar to what they tasted at Joseph's camp. They would take the tea to him as thanks for his help, although, Bren said he was not so sure how much the old one was helping him.

While they were walking through the section of booths selling clothing, Sara's eye was caught by a rack of wool coats. They were very thick and a deep red, with leather fringed sleeves and thick black horizontal bands. They were knee length, with a full hood that completely hid her head. Sara fell in love with the coats almost immediately. She reached into her waist pouch to bring out the coins for a purchase, and Bren lightly touched her hand.

"It would make me happy if you would let me buy this for you, Sara, please. I'll buy one for myself as well. When it's cold this winter, we can wear them together."

"I like the way you think, Bren. Everyone will know you're spoken for." Sara smiled as she helped him try a coat for size.

Bren went back to the clothier who had bought his sister's goods. He bought two pair of heavy winter gloves made from otter skins. One pair was for himself and one pair for Sara. "These will keep our hands warm while we ride your snow sled," he told her. He found a skillfully made pair of oak and rawhide snowshoes, shiny with their waterproof sealer. They would be handy in helping him check his winter traps.

The couple stood looking at the various clothing styles made of cloth and hide both. As they stopped, a young blonde-haired girl ducked under her mother's tables two stalls down and headed straight for Thunder, who was standing at Sara's right side. The toddler cooed as she reached the wolf. "Puppy," she said in a clear, warbling tone as she reached up to throw her arms around the wolf's neck. She buried her face in the thick fur around Thunder's neck then changed her grip and, reaching as high as she could, grabbed him by each side of his mouth and again said "Puppy" as she looked him in the eyes. The crowd froze all around them as they watched in terror. What would this wolf do, confronted by such an unruly young girl?

Bren heard a great intake of air from the surrounding crowd. Every person within eyesight watched in anticipation of the reaction this small girl's innocent enthusiasm might cause. Bren glanced at Sara and relaxed. He saw her looking down at the little one with a loving grin on her face. Thunder opened his mouth just a bit and swept the girl's face from chin to forehead with a wide, wet tongue. The small one gasped at the wolf kiss and promptly let go, falling back onto her rump.

Thunder gingerly reached out with his muzzle and, grasping the front of her overalls, pulled her to her feet. She giggled in glee and once again sunk her tiny arms into his neck ruff. Thunder stood tall, his tail wagging the smallest bit.

A woman, obviously the girl's mother, rushed up from her clothing booth, scolding the girl. "Lizzie, what are you about now, child? You don't know that wolf. You could have been badly bitten, you little imp!"

The woman picked up the child, who was struggling and reaching out for the wolf. Sara laughed and spoke gently to the woman. "Lizzie was as safe with Thunder as she is in your arms, Mother. My Thunder and Winter love the young ones. I can promise you no harm would come to her no matter how impetuous she might be."

The crowd began to breathe again and moved about their business once more.

"I am sorry." The girl's mother smiled at Sara, clearly flustered. "She just sneaks away so quickly. Sometimes I think she's the one who needs a leash."

Sara laughed as she answered, "We were all of us three years old once. She learns something new about the world each time she escapes, I would guess. I'm happy to have the chance to show everyone my wolves aren't the beasts they might think." To the young girl she said, "Lizzie, you may visit my wolves anytime you want, but next time, ask your mother, or better yet bring her along. No more sneaking off, okay?" Lizzie gave Sara a conspiratorial grin as her mother turned to carry her back to their clothing shop.

"I am forever amazed by your skill, Sara," Bren said as they continued through the booths and shop tents. "What you've done with these wolves is fantastic to see."

Sara smiled and looked at her wolves with obvious love. "It's really a very simple thing. I give them the love and respect they deserve. We understand each other. I teach them my world, and they teach me theirs. We are family."

Sara found her sled and harness. As she paid, she arranged for it to be delivered to her parents' camp. The young couple wandered around the traders' booths for the better part of the day, looking at wares from different parts of the country. Several times they were greeted by name from the wandering crowd. They were well entertained watching people trade, argue, and do business.

The two young people sat at the same table they chose the day before and shared a lunch of roasted pork, bread, and cheeses. They drank wine from the vineyards on the west side of the great river.

After the meal, they walked to the music park. The young couple sat on the grass and listened to the music. There were flutes, violins, and other string and woodwind instruments. They came together from across the nation for this time of sharing with new people. They enjoyed learning new music and talking with like-minded folk.

So the two young people passed their days together at fall gather. They were, for the most part, left alone by family and friends, to learn as much of each other as they could. They swam and lay in the sun. They rode along the river and explored the country. They walked and talked together and shared this rare leisure time.

The last night of the gather found Bren and Sara sitting on a grassy hillside under the stars. This night was set aside by long-held custom for saying goodbye to friends who might not be seen again until the next year. Everyone enjoyed the last night of gather. They ate and drank their fill, before starting their journey home to prepare for the cold, more sedentary winter months.

Early the next morning, Bren and Sara said goodbye under the same tree where they first had come to know one another. They held each other tightly, as he breathed in the smell of her hair and felt the softness of her sun-gold skin. He promised her this separation would be their last and much shorter.

"Remember, we'll be in your camp before the winter snows can stop us from coming. I'll hurry my mother as much as I can with her visits. She's beginning to come to terms with the fact I'll not be coming back to the farm. Strange words, those. I've spent my entire life, to this point, being at home there. I will carry part of it with me always. Bren, keep you safe until I arrive. Be nice to the bears, and do nothing foolish! Think of me with every breath, and know I love you more with each of mine!"

Bren spoke softly to her in return, "I've been thinking of nothing else for as long as I can remember. The time will go by like mid-winter days, until you are with me again. Ride with the wind on your way to me." Bren spoke to Thunder, "Keep her safe, wolf, or I'll be wearing your coat as my own." The wolf sneezed loudly with a shake of his head. He got up from the grass to watch their goodbye. Thunder took an almost dismissive, sideways glance at Bren as he had the first day they met and barked once, loudly.

Sara smiled ruefully at her wolf, then softly at Bren as she warned him. "He's begun to listen to the meaning in your words. He understands much more than you think, Bren. If not the words, then your intent is clear. Be careful you don't make him angry!"

She pulled him close to her and kissed him one long, last time. Bren felt the heat rise in his core. He turned to leave her under the tree before he overstayed the moment. "I love you, Sara," he spoke as he turned.

"I love you as well, bear killer," she answered.

Reluctantly he mounted Stone Foot and rode to where he would intercept the train already on the trail home.

Winter pranced alongside the horse for a while, staring up at Bren as if she thought he would give permission for her to follow. Or perhaps, Bren wondered, was the winter wolf committing his face and his smell to her memory? Whatever her reason, after a moment more, she spun and trotted back to Sara. Bren dared not turn to watch them go. The wolves and the girl walked slowly to her parents' wagon, all three turning several times to watch Bren disappear over the rolling swells of the prairie.

The Sweat Lodge

Bren awoke under a still-dark, star-filled sky on the third day traveling home from gather. As he lay quietly in his bison blanket, he realized this was the day he would begin his vision quest. He dreamed vaguely during a restless night of sitting on Bear Butte and speaking to spirits. He had no idea what the dream meant, but he thought now was the time to start learning what was to be. He dressed in his most comfortable clothes and went to find Don. His uncle would know how to find Joseph.

Bren arrived at Don's lodge, surprised to see an old mare already staked outside the lodge cropping what little grass she could find. The rider must have just arrived in the traveling camp, or the horse would have been cared for. He called for a young man he recognized to come and take both his horse and the mare for water and a little grain. He approached the door of the lodge, but before he had a chance to announce himself, Don called to him by name, telling him to enter. Bren entered and stood a moment to adjust his eyes to the dim light. When he could see, he wasn't surprised that Joseph was sitting at the fire. Bren's father was seated next to him.

"It's good to see you again, Grandfather. Your horse has been taken for food and water. He will be well cared for."

"Thank you, Bren," the old man said. "Did you dream of the butte last night?"

Now he was shocked that the old man could know of his dreams. He stood for just a moment before Kennon, also sitting near the small fire, addressed him. "I see you're ready to begin. Sit, while we tell you what will happen."

"Joseph, how did you know to come here this morning? How did you know I would be ready on this day? How did you know of my dreams?"

"He knew," Ben told his son. "That's enough for now. Sit, and let's talk about this." Bren sat close to the fire and listened as Joseph talked. "Joseph was just telling us he will be making his lodge in our new village for the foreseeable future. He wants to come live where all the excitement is." Ben smiled over at the old man as he said this. "Have you eaten this morning?" Bren told his father he hadn't taken time to eat before he came to look for Don.

"Good," Joseph said. "For the rest of this day, don't eat or drink. You can drink this, and we'll smoke the pipe." The old man handed Bren a small clay mug filled with hot liquid. The tea smelled strongly of the anise plant along with other herbs he couldn't identify. He thought he smelled cinnamon as well. The tea steamed as he held it. He allowed it to cool a bit, as he watched Joseph cut tobacco on his wooden board. The old man was always careful to cut just enough of the leaf to fill the pipe, no more. He took a pinch of the chopped leaf and sprinkled it into the fire. He filled the pipe with everything that was left and lighted it from a small stick held in the fire. Joseph held the pipe in front of him at chest level for a moment and said a silent prayer.

He passed the pipe to Bren, who was seated to his left. Bren smoked and passed it clockwise to his father, and they continued in this manner until the pipe was empty. Joseph tapped the ash into his palm then sprinkled it over the small fire.

"So," said Joseph. "Let's begin." Bren finished the tea and placed the cup on the ground in front of him. "We've built a sweat lodge in the old way. Tomorrow morning, we will complete the Innipi, the cleansing ceremony. After this, you will go to the butte, where you will sit at the top and pray for a vision. During this time, you won't eat or drink. For how long do you think this quest should continue?"

Without hesitation, Bren said, "Four days. I would like to follow the ancient way."

Don, Ben, and Kennon exchanged glances, and Joseph said to Bren, "The four-day ceremony is the most sacred of the ancient way. It is also hardest on the seeker. The ceremonial days started this morning as you awoke. The four days of vision quest will start once you reach the top of the butte."

"You should be aware, Bren. Not everyone who seeks a vision is rewarded with what they seek. Some visions are not easy to understand, and some don't come at all. If this is to be, it will come upon you. You will have nothing to be ashamed of, whichever way it goes. You will be assisted in this quest by one male from this village. You will of course have the choice of horses to ride to the butte. Every other choice has been made for you. Who will be of assistance to you, and which horse do you choose?"

"I would like Airik to ride with me, and I will ride my hunter. Airik has been my friend since we were children, and the horse has carried me through many long hunts."

"You will sleep tonight separated from the people," Kennon said. "Your father will speak to your village to explain what's happening. They've expected this for some time but will think good thoughts for you and pray while you're on this journey. From this moment, until the quest is completed, you must concentrate on the ceremony and nothing else. If your mind strays in the slightest, bring it back to the proper place. I can tell you without doubt this will be the most important event in your life, to this point."

"Now you'll go to the shelter that's been prepared. Stay there until the cleansing ceremony tomorrow. In a while someone will bring you clothing, and you'll set aside what you have on now. Go, your people are with you, don't be afraid."

Bren left the lodge in a haze. How did Joseph know to come to his camp this morning? Could the old one see into Bren's dreams? What was going to happen tomorrow after the cleansing ceremony? Why did this ceremony have to be carried out in such a particular manner? He was about to give up, find Airik, and go fishing when he saw his father's small hunting lodge had been prepared not far from the family lodge. It sat waiting for him under a group of light-green willow trees. He thought of Sara and the words he had spoken at the gather meeting. He entered the lodge and sat heavily on his own sleeping furs.

After a few moments, a shadow approached the door. A tiny delicate hand reached into the opening of the shelter, dropping leggings and breechcloth on the floor. Bren thought the hand must belong to White Calf, but he stayed silent. The leggings were of buckskin in a simple, ancient style. The breechcloth was red wool and reached almost to the ground when he stood. The leggings and the moccasins were decorated with a simple and equally ancient quilled design called the broken nose. There was no shirt.

Bren sat into the afternoon, thinking on what was occurring. He was relaxed now. He went over his conversations with Joseph, Kennon, Don, Airik, and with his father over the past few months. He saw the white buffalo calves in his mind as they were on the prairie. He questioned why he'd been picked for this journey, but no answer came.

That night, as a result of the tea Kennon gave him, Bren purged himself and then slept well, without dreaming. He awoke and barely sat up when there was a shadow once again on the door. Bren's father poked his head into the lodge and smiled at him. "Let's go to the sweat lodge," he said.

Bren's horse was ready outside, and they rode through the camp in silence. After a few minutes, Bren saw the sweat lodge sitting on the open prairie. The structure was man high and domed. It was framed with fourteen small willow trunks, which were covered with buffalo hides. The opening faced the east, to catch the sun as it rose. Ten paces from the opening was a fire, where stones were being heated for the lodge. Near the fire, and in line with the opening of the lodge, was a mound of dirt. Joseph stood, small and regal, at the door of the lodge. Kennon seemed to tower over him, at his side.

Father and son dismounted and walked to the lodge entrance, where they stood with Kennon and Joseph. Bren looked around and saw the morning sun shining off the prairie grasses, still damp from the night. He saw the low red hills, dark in the distance, and the fat white clouds over the hills. They floated in the bright, shining blue of the sky. Within himself he felt this day would begin his new life.

He felt cleaner and newer than he had ever felt, as if he were a new-born person just come to the world. He was centered, relaxed, and at peace with himself and this mystery about to occur. He was filled with confidence that whatever this day held for him would end well for his people.

He was startled out of his thoughts by a low, deep droning song of the ancient tongue of his people. Joseph had entered the lodge and was offering a prayer to the six directions. He purified the pipe altar in the center of the lodge with a pinch of tobacco. He purified the pipe first with the smoke of sage and then with sweetgrass and filled the bowl with a pinch of tobacco for each of the four directions, as well as the earth and the sky. Bren recognized the pipe with mild shock. This was the pipe he had seen and smoked in the old man's lodge at gather. Why this was significant, he didn't know, but he felt it was.

Joseph stood with the pipe and left the lodge. He walked along the path to the earth mound and placed the pipe so the bowl faced the west. The stem pointed to the eastern sky and so the rising sun. Joseph returned to the lodge door and entered. He walked clockwise around the central firepit, followed by Kennon, and then Bren, and last Ben. The four occupants of the lodge sat on a deep bed of sage around the central altar. They sat so that Bren was facing to the west and Joseph was facing east and nearest to the door of the lodge.

After they were comfortable, Joseph said a quiet prayer in the old language. Then Joseph's granddaughter, whom he had called by the name White Calf in the Lakota dialect, passed the pipe into the lodge. Joseph handed it carefully to Ben who placed it on his lap, with the stem pointing west. White Calf began passing in stones, with the help of a hoop stick, one at a time from the fire outside to the altar inside. They were placed to the center, east, west, north, and south before being filled in to complete the circle.

Ben lit the pipe and offered it to the directions. He rubbed the smoke over his body and passed it to his left, where Bren took it, thanked Ben in the ritual manner, and applied the smoke to his skin. He in turn passed it to Kennon, who completed the same ritual, before passing the pipe last to Joseph. Joseph cleansed himself with the smoke. He smoked the pipe empty as he quietly prayed and tapped the ash to his palm before placing it on the westerly stone of the altar.

Joseph held the pipe over the altar and again purified the pipe in the smoke of sage and sweetgrass. He handed the pipe to White Calf, standing outside the door. She closed the door to the lodge, and darkness enveloped them. She returned the pipe to the mound of earth, this time with the stem pointing to the west.

Now Joseph began the prayer ceremony. "From the beginning of our time, we have heard the story of the circle of life. We hear how the people lived together in harmony with all living things of the world, how we were once closely related to the other spirits of our world. In the times when people began to populate the land, they also began to drift apart from each other. The spirits around them became less important to them, and the circle of life began to grow weak from the people's lack of spirit and power. The buffalo were all but killed, and the land was laid waste by the people. The time came that the earth mother rebelled. The cities of the people were destroyed, and disease wiped out many people.

"A little at a time, the earth began to heal herself. The people remembered and used the old ways to help them survive in the darkest times. We pray to the earth mother to help us have the strength to complete the circle. Show us the way to continue to heal our world and grow upon her as one people."

As Joseph spoke, Ben dipped a bundle of sage in a bowl of water and shook the water four times on the hot stones of the altar. Bren felt each wave of wet heat as it rolled against his face. His lungs filled slowly with the hot thickness of the air, and it felt good. His body relaxed into the sage bed, and his mind began to be filled with the words he heard.

The pipe appeared at the door again. They smoked as they prayed, rubbing themselves with the smoke and sending the pipe around the circle from Ben to Joseph, left to right. As the pipe was emptied, the door opened. White Calf took the pipe and handed in a bowl of water. The water was passed around the circle and rubbed onto their bodies. Bren felt the shock of the cool water, and his scalp tingled with the feeling. He was soaked through from the sweat and the water. He felt as if he had just awakened from a winter of sleep. His muscles took a moment longer than usual to comply with his commands for movement.

Bren's eyes began to adjust to the very dim light, and he saw the people around him as dark shadow figures. He saw Joseph as he spoke, and he appeared to be moving in one slow and continuous motion to get the words out.

Kennon looked much smaller and more frail than he appeared in the light of day. Joseph, who sat with his back to the door, appeared as a dark, vaguely manlike shape. There was a slight radiation of light surrounding his body. Bren wondered whether it came through the thinner hide of the door or emanated from the ancient man himself. However small, Joseph appeared by far the most powerful and imposing person in Bren's experience. Bren wondered what this impression stemmed from. His mind told him the man was as small and old as he had been when they entered the lodge.

The door was opened after a moment, and the pipe was passed in, as the water bowl was taken out. The pipe was passed to Joseph, who filled and lit the bowl, and passed it to Ben, around the circle to Bren. He held the pipe in the darkness of the lodge and felt the coolness of the stone in his hands. He ran his hands over the decoration on the stem and knew he was expected to speak.

A picture flashed before his eyes of a bull elk standing in a green pasture of knee-high grass and, beside the elk, a bear. Bren recognized the cinnamon-brown hair as the grizzly that he killed that night in camp. The elk had the rack of the bull that Bren had taken in the meadow by the winter camp. Sitting on the elk's rack was a golden eagle, the biggest bird he had ever seen. Bren's head began to swim, as the bird opened his wings to their full span. He was looking directly at Bren, and he felt as if the eyes were piercing his soul. He centered his consciousness on himself and stared back. The bird sat silently peering into and through him. It was clear to Bren that he was being measured.

Bren began slowly in a wet, whispering voice to describe the picture before him and his interpretation of what he saw. The men in the lodge sat quietly listening as they passed the pipe. When Bren described the eagle sitting on the elk, he heard one of the elders say in the old tongue and in a barely audible voice, "Waste Wakan," good magic. Bren heard this and opened his eyes. He looked around the circle, seeing the faces of his elders looking back through the watery haze. Each face registered stunned silence.

Joseph cradled the pipe limp in both hands. The old man came back to himself, gently prodded by the silence. He tapped the ash from the pipe. On that signal the door opened, and a hand took the pipe. A moment later it was replaced with the bowl of water. Joseph passed the bowl, and in another moment, it was taken, to be replaced with the pipe. This time, Kennon took the pipe. He puffed at it for a moment and held it to the sky, looking ancient and fragile.

When he spoke, the alarm Bren felt was eased by the tenor of a voice resonating assurance and power. His heart began to beat in cadence with the words, as the old one told of the vision quest.

"This seeking of a vision is one of the most sacred of the ancient ceremonies remembered by our people. The practice has been carried out since the people came to this world from inside the earth mother. When we are troubled as a people, or as a person, we clean our spirits. We seek the help of the ones who have gone before us and of the ones that are around us as we walk through this world. A very powerful time has come upon us. A time when we are told we may bring the circle to a close and heal the earth our people have disgraced and torn apart.

"We feel the world changing around us and have faith this change will be for the good of the people. All the races of the old world have come together on the plains, the center of our world. We believe the mingling of these peoples has been brought about by the creator for the good of all. We have been given another chance on this island of the turtle. We must continue to be worthy of that task. We are the keepers of the earth and the future of the people who walk here. We pray for the strength to help this young man on the path of a true human being. We share in the power he has brought to us. We are humbled by the chance to be a part of this changing time. We hope to help him continue to walk the red road."

The door was pushed open, and the young girl took the pipe. The ritual was repeated with the water bowl with the pipe being passed on to Joseph again. This time Joseph lit the pipe and kept it in his hands. He said a long, quiet prayer in the ancient tongue and smoked the pipe as he did. He soon passed the pipe to Don and continued to speak in the rasping, rhythmic tones of an ancient time. Joseph lifted the bowl, pouring the remaining water on the stones. Bren watched as a great cloud of steam billowed into a palpable mass around their heads. He felt the wave of heat roll over his body and permeate his flesh, rushing into his blood.

Joseph began the prayer to end the ceremony. "We come here to give our prayers to the spirits for the healing of the circle. We use the sweat lodge ceremony to cleanse the spirit before a great journey and to strengthen the soul of the traveler. Here before us is a man who has been through a great deal in this season. His is the generation that will see the circle complete again, and we are privileged to pray for him. Now is his time to journey to a place of ancient power. We give him our prayer and our strength to carry with him. It is a good day for the people. Let us help him begin the journey." Joseph stood and opened the door to the sweat lodge. The men exited in the opposite order of their entrance. Once outside, they rubbed themselves in sweetgrass smoke and made ready for the journey to the butte.

Bren was accompanied to a creek, yards from the smoke lodge, by all four elders. They dropped their clothing to the ground and entered the water to their necks. Bren felt the shock of the icy water and lost his breath for a moment. Joseph looked at him and grinned.

"You awake, young man?" he said, and their companions laughed.

"I am now, Grandfather. I am now," he answered.

Bren's horse was staked to the grass outside the lodge. On its back were a buffalo robe and an elk robe and a small skin of water. These were all Bren would need for the next few days. He was feeling hungry now as he dressed himself. His belly was empty, but he felt renewed by the sweat lodge and ready to ride. Airik was his usual smiling self, sitting lazily on the back of his horse, as if this were nothing more than a weekend fishing trip. He reached over to Bren and handed him a simple long-sleeved elk hide shirt, which he slipped over his head. He also gave him hide pants and new moccasins. Bren knew by the feel of the soft, comforting hides it was the work of his sister, and he sent her silent thanks.

Joseph said goodbye and handed Bren a small bundle. He felt the now familiar shape of the pipe under the hide. Joseph told him to guard it well as it had come through many generations of his family. Next, he handed him a small skin of water and told Bren to drink it all. He watched as Bren did as instructed. Bren swayed as he mounted the hunter. The horse stood solid for a moment as if he knew his rider needed stability, and they started for the butte.

As he rode, he thought of what he would be doing. The path he would take to the butte was clear in his mind, although the end of the road was not. He thought of his father and mother, of his sister and Sara. He knew that the old ones expected something to come of this vision quest, but he had no idea how he might be able to help the people. Again, just for a moment, he was afraid he would fail his people. He looked back to see his father. He saw Don and Joseph and all the people in the far depths of his mind watching him and drew from them the strength to complete the ride.

Their trip to the base of the butte took five days. They stopped each night to sleep, as the sun sank below the horizon. Bren spent the riding time looking at the country as if for the first time. He recognized many of the landmarks as they passed but saw them now in a new light. Bren realized his vision of the world would be different after this trip. Looking back, Bren savored the memory of his days on the plains. Remembering the many trips he and his companion had taken over the course of their lives, he was once again reminded of how lucky he was to have been born in this time and to these people he loved so deeply.

He slept each night with no realization of time passing and awoke each morning with a growing sense of peace with what was ahead of him. On the third morning of their journey, he spoke to Airik of these thoughts.

"Brother," he said. "I'm grateful for the friendship we've shared through our lives. I know you and I have learned many things through this journey with the people. I feel this time together is a culmination of that part of our lives. I also know we have many years of learning before us. These next few days are not a test, nor are they an ending, but a time for learning the ways that will take us into the future.

"I have no doubt those gone before us ride this path with us today. They follow us, and they ride before us. This journey is just as much theirs as it is ours. We ride also for the people of the village. For all the people of the plains, the woodlands, and everywhere the people live today. No matter what comes, I couldn't have chosen a better friend to ride beside me on this journey."

"I've known since we were children, Bren," Airik answered him, "that you would do great things with your life. You have a way of looking at this world that sees and understands in a way others can't. You walk through the world with a humility that draws people to you, and often you don't realize how or why. You taught me as much as any teacher we have had in our lives. I'm also grateful I live in this time. That we can take this ride together, for our people. I look around us and know we need to do whatever we can to keep ourselves on the proper path through this life."

Bren looked into the distance. He saw the mountains as they approached and answered his friend, "We, Airik, we all will do great things together. And yes, whatever we need to do to follow this red road must be done."

A Vision from the Sky

Early on the fifth day, they dismounted in a bowl between two fingers of land sloping down from the butte. They stood at the foot of the place called Bear Butte. Here there was a winding path to the top. Airik would leave Bren to climb the butte by himself. Airik would take the horses and make camp several miles from the butte, where he would wait until Bren sent him a signal to return.

Bren took the pipe and his robes from the back of the horse. Making a bundle with the tie chords, he slid it onto his back. "Make sure you travel a few miles before you stop."

Airik answered him. "We passed a stream back about that far, that's where I'll camp. Be well, brother, and have courage. All will go well."

Bren left Airik standing with the horses and started up the path toward the top. The sun was strong on his back. The sky was clear, and there was just the whisper of a breeze. On every green bush and tree limb on many of the rocks, he saw small bundles of hide or brightly colored cloth tied with string or sinew. Some of these were recent, some were very old, faded by time and weather. Some were tied singly, and others were tied in bunches of many small bundles. These were tobacco offerings left by travelers from past times. Travelers who came to the butte either to search for a vision or just to seek help from the spirits who were said to dwell here.

Bren came upon a snake in the path as he climbed. It sat in the strong sun warming itself. His shadow fell across its body, and it coiled, looking in his direction. The tail began to vibrate and rattle as it looked toward him, warning him against attempting to attack. "I mean you no more harm than you do me, brother. If you would be kind enough to give me the path so I can pass, I'll be gone, and you can lay in the sun. The hillside is too steep for me to go around without the chance of a fall, or I would do so. I'm too tired to want to crawl up this hill again today." The snake had stopped its rattle as Bren spoke. After a moment of stillness, it moved off the path on the downhill side. Bren continued to climb. Looking back a moment later, he saw the snake had resumed its place on the path.

The higher he climbed, the more enthralled he became. Although he had seen the butte before from the prairie, he'd never climbed to its crest. The trail took a turn to the left and the pitch of the slope increased. Bren felt the hair on the back of his neck stand as a thrill rippled through his midsection. His legs were weak from lack of food over the past days, so they began to shake a bit. He was moved by the serenity, the holiness of his surroundings.

The slope increased again, and it was now even more difficult to climb. He passed a shale spill on his right as it fell from a narrow outcropping in the trees. He felt the breath of the almost indiscernible breeze in his face, soft and billowing, as if forgotten voices spoke to him. After a few minutes, the trail climbed sharply again, finally leveling out onto a small grassy knob. Bren walked to the edge and looked over the valley to the north of the butte.

The valley stretched in front of him until it disappeared over the horizon. He saw rivers, lakes, streams, and the waving undulation of the many different grasses on the plains. There were washes, plateaus, draws, and the prairie ocean that went on forever. There was the forest and the lines of trees that bordered each side of the waterways as they ambled through the country. He could see small dark specks of what he was sure were thousands of buffalo among the grasses into the distance.

He spread the buffalo robe on the ground a man's length from the edge and sat amid the rocks there. His legs still burned slightly from the climb. He felt the warm, loose feeling in his body that he always enjoyed after running a distance. Bren leaned back and looked up into the sky. He felt the fur of the robe brush against his legs and relaxed more with the familiar texture. Bren saw the familiar crystal blue of the sky as it merged to the west with the purist of white clouds. These clouds seemed to flow like the foam on an ocean in the sky, slowly making their way toward the butte. Their slightly darker shadows followed along the ground as disciples of the winged white messengers of change.

A thought came to him, and he gathered four small round stones from the ground around his robe. He placed one stone on the robe in front of him and the others to the side. He would use the stones to count the days on the butte.

He felt himself surrounded by the crowns of the trees he had passed on his walk up the hill as they peeked over the crest at him. He had no doubt he was in the midst of countless souls and spirits from an age long past but still very near. It seemed he could hear them on the edge of his conscious mind, and he was glad for the company. He wasn't frightened but encouraged by the spiritual power of this place around him. Bren closed his eyes and focused on his breathing. He silently solicited the help of the ones around him for answers to his presence on the butte.

He opened his eyes and saw the silky white clouds floating closer toward the butte. He said a silent prayer there was no rain to come. The air now was comfortable, almost still, with only enough movement to send it rolling from the prairie, up the slopes of the butte, and gently across the surface of his skin. The sun shined down on him and felt soothing on his arms and face.

He found a shallow, dusty depression in a group of rocks close to where he placed the buffalo robe. Gathering small branches, he started a very small fire with the flint and steel he always carried. He carefully unwrapped the pipe Joseph handed him. Inside the bag he found a small pouch of tobacco laying with the stem and bowl. Offering a pinch of tobacco to each of the four directions, he filled the red clay. He lighted it with a stick retrieved from the fire and, walking to the edge of the butte, lifted the pipe to the heavens. The wind gusted as he did this, blowing the pungent smoke over his face and through his hair.

Bren's hair flowed out behind him, and the flaps of his breech-cloth blew through his legs in the wind. He lifted his voice in a prayer to the spirits of both worlds, shouting above the sudden gusts, for help in the quest he was on. He smoked the pipe empty, tapped the ash onto his hand and into the wind. Bren once again sat on the robe, with his legs crossed and his back as straight as he could manage. He held the pipe in his hands, closing his eyes. He was feeling the weakness of hunger strong in him now. Concentrating on breathing helped a lot. He felt as if he gathered sustenance from the air drawn into his lungs. He was curiously empowered by the feeling radiating through his belly and into his limbs. He gained strength from the emptiness within him.

He sat through most of that day with his eyes closed, concentrating on the simplicity of each breath. His mind was opened to what might await him on the butte. He could feel the grassy prairie at the bottom of the butte. He felt the life that lived there, cycling through its generations for countless ages. He felt the warmth the rocks gathered from the sun each day, casting it back to the world in the night. He saw the small four-legged ones and the crawling ones as part of the earth, as all things were. As the sun fell and the night began to cool, he pulled the elk robe over his shoulders for a blanket. He thought of the day he had taken the elk and thanked him again for the sacrifice.

When the waxing moon rose and traveled over the Big Horn range, it splashed a diffused tinted glow over the floor of the valley. Bren looked out over the ethereal scene presented to him and thought again of the luck he had in being born into this world, at this time, and in this place. He thought, whatever small travels he'd reveled in, this country was the most beautiful to his eyes and heart.

He watched the stars dance in the night above him and remembered the story told around a fire long ago. The story explained the many stars of the milky way. The lights in the sky were the campfires of the people who had passed on from this life, as they made their journey to the next. Bren thought back on the people he'd known in his life. He wondered if they were with him now. He saw the occasional trail of shooting light as a star streaked through the air to the earth or burned itself out before falling all the way. Bren followed the path of the constellations through the night sky. He felt a certain affinity to the one his father pointed out, to Bren the child, as the great bear.

As night turned to dawn, his head began to swim, his eyes watered with the brightness. He saw tiny flickers of yellow flame through closed lids, almost as if the stars fought the return of the sun. He once again concentrated on his breathing, and the flickers subsided. He noticed a decrease in the light through closed lids and opened them to see the clouds advancing much closer to the butte. He pulled the elk robe around his shoulders, anticipating rain. The winds died again to an almost imperceptible softness, but the clouds continued their march toward the butte, all but blocking out the sun.

Bren sat for what felt like days. He felt a sudden decrease in the air pressure, and the robe was sucked to his body for a moment. Slowly, he opened his eyes. What he saw made him sure he'd slipped into a dream state caused by the lack of food in his belly.

Flying in great double-wedge formation toward the edge of the butte was a huge convocation of both bald and golden eagles. Bren guessed their numbers to be in the hundreds. The largest of the eagles was an immense golden flying at the front of the group. This was the biggest bird Bren had ever seen. He remembered the eagle from his dream. This one looked much like the rest of the formation in color and shape, but Bren had no doubt. This was the bird he had seen perched on the elk's head.

The entire group circled the butte four times. Bren could hear the sound of the wind through their wings and feel it against his face. On the fourth pass, they turned as one toward the crest of the butte then floated in the last few yards with hardly a twitch of wing. The leader touched down a few feet in front of the buffalo robe, on a crested point of rock, forming a crown at the edge of the butte. The great bird settled itself with awkward steps and unfolded wings as it found purchase with its needle-sharp claws. The raptor turned its head and looked into Bren's eyes. He felt the creature was once again peering deep into him, past the flesh and into the soul.

Bren sat amazed as the scene unfolded around him. He pulled his eyes away from the bird for a moment to look down at the robe. What he saw startled him again. There were four counting stones laid out in a row in front of him. Was this the fourth day? His confusion made him dizzy. How could the time have passed as the stones suggested? He didn't remember placing but one stone. He remembered only the passage of a single night! He remembered to breathe as the dizziness threatened to overtake him.

A sound startled him as a low, warbling hum began deep in the furthest reaches of his subconscious. The sound gradually grew in intensity, until he heard the hum of a single note from many voices. It reached a pinnacle of sound that vibrated in his very bones then subsided to an audible whisper.

Bren heard a voice speak to him, "We are not in your dream, Bren Redhorse. We are the embodiment of your awakening, and we mean you no harm." The voice was soft, comforting, and full of self-assurance. The sound warbled warmly, like the deepest notes of a flute.

"The wheels of time have circled round to a day when we will once again speak with the people, from time to time. This is a new beginning for us as well, so have patience with my speech. Do you hear me well? Do you understand the words I speak?"

Bren hesitated, thinking on the portent of speaking to an eagle. He realized he was the only human on the butte and said aloud, "I understand. I hear you well." At the sound of his voice, several of the eagles abruptly opened their wings as if to take flight then settled once more, their chest and head feathers puffed and airy.

"When this continent, this turtle island, was first visited by the two-legged people, our race was an old one. All of the animals that lived on this world were close to one another. The four legs and the winged ones, all beings lived in natural harmony. Everything flowed with the rhythm of the world. The circle was whole, and the earth mother sustained every soul.

"This changed as time passed. The two-legged people were first to begin to spoil what the earth mother gave them. They began to compete, one with the other, for dominion over the earth. They attempted to own the land as they drifted farther away from the truth of the circle. This caused the circle to weaken, tearing away at it until it was broken. The earth mother survived in this manner for as long as she could, until a cleansing began. The fire and water storms ended much of what humans had built and become.

"Generations have passed since the change, and the circle has begun to heal. The four legged you call the buffalo have returned in great numbers. They are bigger and stronger once again. Our people, the winged ones, have returned to the sky, the mountains, and the lakes in greater numbers. We are regaining the stature that we had long, long ago. The two legs are learning to walk within the circle, once again beginning to travel down the pathway you call the red road."

The bird shifted his footing a bit as he finished speaking. He raised his wings to refold and smooth the feathers, as if contemplating what he would say next.

"How is it that I hear you?" Bren asked. "How is it that you come to this place, at this time? What has happened that you've met me here?"

"Your first question may be the most difficult to understand fully, so we will take that first. Bren, our thoughts have substance and so, also, do they have power. That substance and power exist on a plain which isn't easy for us to feel or see, so it is easily disregarded by our minds. Our ancestors in the far dimness of the past knew these things, and we are beginning to remember. The substance of our thoughts can travel, through the power of the mind, across pathways we really don't understand. In this manner, we hear what one another has to say. The spoken word also has great power, and since it is much easier to convey, your people have forgotten to use the mind to its potential. We will learn this again, together. Maybe with time we will learn together more about the ways of it."

Bren sat still on the buffalo robe and listened, as the eagle continued. "You and I were chosen by the life force that is the essence of the earth and sky. We were chosen by that which is a part of every living thing there is or, truly, ever was. We were chosen by every rock, stream, tree, and mountain. We were chosen by the ancestors that were and the ones to come after we are gone.

"The eagles and many of the beings of this world have been changing for some time. Or better to say we have been learning again to be as we once were. We have been returning to the place we were before men began to change the world. We found, not long ago, that we were able to direct our thoughts at men. We've been studying on this and the languages of your peoples for ages of our kind.

"I am called Wanbli in the ancient tongue, the golden eagle. My kind believe that your people are at a place where we can work toward living in harmony once again. We can help each other as we did in the time of the ancient stories. There are people in the world today in need of our help. Some, indeed, most don't understand what's happening or how to live in harmony with the earth mother. Many men and women don't have the foresight or the spirit that is needed to see the circle is healing. We have the opportunity to take advantage of the healing to start anew in this world.

"The stories that are told of the spirit guides in the ancient world are more than stories. Once your people were closer to the bear and the other four legs and to my people. We can come together again, to make the world much as it was in the days when the people were young upon it.

"You have finished this part of your journey. You have seen your spirit helper. There is, however, a difference in your journey. Sometimes, one who seeks help from the spirit of an animal is chosen by more than one. This may be the truth of your vision. I am Wanbli the warrior eagle, and it is my path to help you through yours. I'll return to your people with you. Through what follows, we will be spoken of in the stories of this world for the remainder of the generations of our peoples. So I am told."

The birds turned as one and unfolded their wings to the wind. They sang into the sky the most amazing song Bren had ever heard. The sound pierced into his soul and held him rooted to the earth with its spell. He sat as he was and watched the birds take wing, flying into the northern sky.

Wanbli stayed behind and moved to Bren's side. They watched together as the convocation of great birds disappeared into the line of the horizon. "Wanbli," Bren vocalized the name. "This will take some getting used to. I'm not accustomed to having a conversation with animals." The bird looked straight into the eyes of the seated man.

"But you do, Bren. You make prayer after you take the life of your meat. You talk to the wolves, who are friends to the young woman. If you watch and listen closely, you will see they also speak to you and one another. I think, most importantly, you believe in the old ways of your people. I have seen the soul of you, or I wouldn't be here.

"You'll soon learn you don't have to vocalize what you say to me. In fact, you may find it easier. Think to me what you want me to hear. This will be useful from time to time, I'm sure. It's worked well among us as we fly. You should also be aware some of your people will not be able to communicate with us. They may be frightened or not interested in our help. We'll work with this and overcome what difficulty might result."

Bren and Wanbli spent the rest of the afternoon talking. The young man mostly listened, as Wanbli explained to him the recent evolution of the eagles and their means of communication. He became more comfortable with the mind-to-mind transfer of thought into speech as the day wore on. Late in the afternoon, Bren told Wanbli he needed to start down the butte, to meet up with Airik. He wanted to spend one night at the bottom of the butte before leaving for home. Bren carefully wrapped the pipe and gathered his robes. Wanbli watched as Bren started down the mountain, then took flight. He flew east around the Butte and disappeared over the trees.

Awakening the People

Bren made a small smoky fire as a signal to Airik the time had come to meet. On the way down, Bren saw Airik coming with the horses and realized his friend hadn't waited for the smoke to signal his time on the butte was over. He met his friend at the spot where they had separated. Was it really four days ago? Airik looked pale and bewildered. He sat on his horse and stared at the small birds that seemed to be clouding the air around them.

He handed Bren a dripping skin of water and told him to take small sips. Bren hadn't realized just how thirsty he was until he felt the wet coolness of the container in his hands. He uncorked the skin and held it to his mouth. He felt the life in the water spread through every part of his body as he swallowed just a little each time.

Airik swung a leg over his horse and dropped to the ground. He took a small cooking pot and mug from a bag on his horse and sat near the path. He gathered a handful of twigs and began to make a small fire. Airik circled the fire with stones and sat the cook pot on them. He took a second waterskin from the horse and filled the pot, adding several chunks of jerky and a handful of rose hips.

While the broth was simmering, he sliced small bits of an apple from a pouch on the horse. Airik handed the slices to his friend and told him, "Chew it well, more for the juice than the apple." Bren thanked Airik for the kindness, as his stomach roared for more. "I was given strict instruction on what to do when you came from the butte, by both Lanis and Kennon. I don't want to be on the bad side of either."

Bren grinned at his friend as he chewed the apple slices. His stomach seemed to knot around each swallow as he sat next to the cooking broth to wait. He took in more of the water and began to feel better. A headache he didn't realize he had began to fade to nothing as he felt the water move through his body.

Suddenly the air was filled with music. All around the two men, the smaller birds of the prairie sat in the trees and sang out in a chorus of chirps and trills. From the direction of the butte, a shadow glided softly over the prairie to light on a scrub tree close to where Bren stood. The birds became silent as Wanbli met the gaze of the amazed Airik. The bird said quietly in Bren's head, "Your friend is frightened. Tell him, please, I'm also a friend to him. I would speak to him directly, but I don't think it would bring comfort at the moment."

Bren grinned as his friend continued to stare at the eagle. "Airik, this is our friend Wanbli. He came to me on the butte during the vision quest. He has spoken to me and wishes to speak to you. He and his clan, the eagles, are going to help us with our plans in the days to come, and we will help them as well."

"He...he spoke to you, Bren? Are you sure you know what you're saying? The hunger and the lack of water have made you weak. You are hearing things that aren't there." As Airik finished the sentence, his head twitched, and his body jumped. He looked at the bird, still calmly perched on the tree branch. His knees wobbled, and his legs gave way. He sat hard on the path.

"What trick is this? How is this possible?" he asked and looked up at Bren, clearly terrified.

"I didn't hear him speak that time, what did he say?"

"He...that bird!" Airik looked up from the ground at his friend's feet. "A voice was in my head! I heard it clearly! It spoke to me not to be afraid of him, that our people were partners in the old time of the earth, and now that the circle is healing, he says it's time for us to be partners again."

"Thoughts have substance, Airik..." Bren began to explain but stopped. "Never mind. You'll understand in time."

Now Wanbli spoke to them both. "We'll be friends, the three of us. Bren has been chosen to begin this fellowship. In time we will learn together, and my people will be great friends with all of your people. As it was in the days when we were new on the earth, so will it be again. Each of my kind will make the choice whether to speak to a man or woman, but it may be that Airik will have a friend who flies. He is easy to speak to. He accepts the voice well enough where others will not. He'll learn not to let the voice make him thump upon the ground.

"I hear the many questions in his voice, but they will have to wait for another time. This meeting has been taxing for me as well. I will hunt, then rest. You will go to your people, and I will go to mine. My mate and many others will soon build their nests. I will be there to meet you at your winter village when you arrive. Travel well, Bren. Remember, we are brothers. If you have a need, send your thoughts to me, and I will help or send my brothers who will."

The huge raptor left the perch with a leap and a downward sweep of wings. He screeched a short, sharp note as he lifted himself toward the top of the butte and disappeared.

Once again, the smaller birds began to sing around the travelers. Bren saw them dancing in and out of the trees and fill the sky with their movement. Airik sat in the trail at Bren's feet and again stared at nothing. "He spoke to us!" He looked up at Bren. "Didn't he? People will never believe this. What a strange time is coming."

"Oh, brother," Bren said to his friend, "I believe you have no idea how strange!"

Bren reached out to his friend and took his arm, helping him to his feet. "Get up. He'll meet us at home, and the people will believe. This is the beginning of a new time. I'm hungry, and I need water." Airik came back to himself and poured some broth into a mug for Bren.

"Go easy with that and the water. It's been a few days for you, and you need to take care."

The horses stood silently, as if unaware of the presence of the bird, taking the opportunity to grab a few mouthfuls of grass. Airik handed Bren another handful of elk jerky as they mounted and started on their way toward home. The trip would take a few days, and they were anxious to get to the village.

They traveled quickly through the high grass, stopping seldom but enough to keep the horses from becoming fatigued. The trip home was fairly uneventful, excepting for the birds. The whole distance home, the travelers were surrounded by a profusion of winged creatures dancing in the air about them. They seemed to celebrate the adventure that had started on the butte.

Airik asked his friend many questions as they rode. Most of them Bren was able to answer easily. He told Airik of the strangeness with the counting rocks and how the time had passed so quickly; he thought he had been there only the one night. Airik asked Bren to tell the story of speaking to the eagle over again, several times. He was having a difficulty coming to terms with it.

Home

For three days and nights they traveled through the tall grass prairie. They slept but little at night. More for the horses to rest than their own need. They found themselves too overcome from the experience on the butte to rest much. On the fourth day, the prairie gave way slowly to the trees of the mountains. Bren could see the area where the village was but was heartened to see there was no sign of it from where they sat on the prairie. Visitors would have to know where to look to find the people.

The two men relaxed as they entered the familiar paths that would take them home. All the distance to the village, they were serenaded by a chorus of small birds, finches, starlings, hawks, and falcons. They swooped through the trees in a display of aerial acrobatics that had Bren feeling sure they would collide in the air. The chorus ended in a crescendo of song that left the people of the village staring at the travelers as they entered a clearing at the heart of the village.

Airik was smiling and looking about him with his hands raised, waving as if the commotion were a greeting for him alone. Bren's father approached with the elder council. As they came within speaking distance, the chorus was abruptly quieted by a loud, trilling song that echoed through the clearing from above. Bren looked over his shoulder in the direction of the sound and saw Wanbli back wing to land on a large crescent-shaped oak limb behind him.

The council stared at the eagle, saying nothing until prompted by Bren. "I've come from the butte with a friend. This eagle is called

Wanbli. He is a messenger to our people. He's told me a bit about what will be in the coming days. Times are changing, and we will need the help of the winged ones and any others we can find to help. The circle is healing, and we will be a part of it.

"Wanbli's mate is ready to build her nest, as are many of her kind, and they will need our help. We will become friends with the eagles through this help."

Joseph stood in the forefront of the group, and now he came forward to meet Bren. The young man dismounted his horse to greet the old man. Joseph clasped Bren's hand in both of his. Bren felt the power of the old man and the emotion as Joseph said, "I believed you would be a power for your people. The ancient prophecies are coming true, and I'm proud to be alive to see this thing. We must talk, but first you need to eat and rest. Your lodge is prepared for you. My granddaughter is waiting to assist you both."

Bren and Airik walked their horses slowly through the heart of the village, surrounded by the elders. Logan took the horses from the men to be cared for. Bren thanked him as he left through the trees. The people of the village grouped a little distance from them and watched their passage. The bird flew past the group and settled in a tree above Bren's cabin, as if he had been there before.

Bren stepped into his cabin and found a meal of meats, bread, and fruit laying on a low wooden table near the fire. He remembered the young girl who met them, from Joseph's lodge at gather and from the cleansing ceremony. He sat on furs, opposite the fireplace, and removed his foot gear, as Airik sat next to him. White Calf took their moccasins and quickly disappeared. She was back in a moment and served them the meal. The last few days were a jumble of many emotions, melting into a string of thoughts and feelings that left him drained and in need of sleep.

The two friends ate in silence as they sat on the floor before the fire. The fatigue from the last few days hit them now. Bren hadn't realized how tired he was until this moment. The stress of the days on the butte caught up to him. He felt as if he would not make it through the meal before giving in to the sleep his body needed. Airik ate in silence, also feeling the effects of the days waiting for his friend.

White Calf was very attentive to them both. The girl's attitude seemed to have changed since last they met. She was no longer withdrawn, although still she spoke in hushed, almost reverent tones, using his name for the first time he could remember. She placed some of the tea he remembered from gather on the food tray.

"Bren, if there is anything you need of me, I'm here for you. Grandfather has told me to stay near to you until I'm no longer needed. I can make your meals and make sure the young hunters care for the horses. You rest after you eat. Bedrooms are ready for you both. I'll make sure meat is available for our new friend. He's given me the honor of speaking to me, so I'm familiar with what he will require. He's told me he will be staying close by for a time so will appreciate assistance with his food. I'll see to it."

For some reason he couldn't put to words, Bren was in awe of the young girl. He felt this small, unassuming young woman was in every way his equal. She far surpassed his skill levels and importance in the scheme of the world, in many ways. He was not comfortable with her servile attentiveness to him. Bren thanked her and started to tell her of his thoughts. She interrupted him with a smile, saying, "We all have our place in the mystery, my friend. Mine is here for now."

Her simple hide dress made only a whisper of sound as she moved fluidly through the cabin. He noticed Airik kept a very close and wondering eye on her. He watched her with a familiar gleam. Bren made a mental note to speak to him about it, soon.

The companions finished their meal and went to their beds. Bren drifted off toward sleep, his thoughts moving toward the eagle that he felt on the periphery of his conscious mind. Wanbli was perched above his head. A quiet voice spoke to him in his head. "Sleep now, brother. I'll stay here with you and we can speak tomorrow." The bird's voice was soothing and reassuring to him.

Bren awoke to the quiet, bustling sounds of White Calf as she moved from one task to another in the great room of the cabin. He watched the girl for a moment from the door, still a little asleep. She looked at him and said bluntly but with a slight smile, "If you want to watch, sit and do it. Very little that you do escapes me, and be assured, you will not embarrass me. Are you ready for coffee?"

Bren was shocked into silence and only nodded, as the girl stepped to the fire. He looked over to see Airik standing on the threshold between rooms. He was also barely awake but grinning at him hugely. He said quietly, "I like her a lot! I could get used to this treatment as well! I've noticed she is very pleasant to look at, brother. There is something about her that holds my attention. Though she is such a small girl, she seems very wise, even powerful, doesn't she? I believe the wolf girl would not be pleased with this young woman taking such good care of you."

Airik was still grinning at his friend, and Bren didn't like it. "Us, Airik, she is taking care of us. Because she is kind and considerate. I noticed the way you looked at her last night, and it will stop! She and Joseph have been very kind to us, and that's not an appropriate way to repay them."

"I think it will not stop!" was Airik's response. "She is lovely. She is kind to us. But I will respect her, brother. You should know the truth of that!"

Airik only smiled wider as White Calf approached the table. She was carrying a pot of coffee, two heavy mugs, and a basket of hot breads. The friends came to the table, taking the coffee and bread.

"You are very kind, White Calf, to tend to us," Bren told her.

"You're kind to allow me, Bren. You and your friend Airik are people of honor and magic. I've come into this world for this time. The healing of the circle is a sacred thing that has been spoken of and awaited since the people first walked on this land. You both walk the red road, and I'm honored to serve in whatever small way I may." White Calf continued as she sat. "Do you know that your fame has spread across the continent? You are spoken of throughout our village and across the plains. It won't be long before your name is on the lips of every person who is alive and some who have passed beyond."

Bren felt the eyes of his friend on him and felt a slight shiver as the girl spoke of the people who were gone.

She has come into this world for this time? What could she mean by that? Where had she been before? He was uncertain what happened beyond this life but hadn't thought of speaking with those who had gone to the next, if there was a next world. White Calf looked directly into his eyes as she said, "There is indeed a next life, Bren Redhorse. As sure as I am standing before you. This life and the ones before this are but a preparation for those that come ahead. This is why it is most important what path we walk." While speaking these last words, White Calf looked pointedly at Airik and raised an eyebrow. He stopped chewing a bite of bread to stare back at her. His mouth turned suddenly very dry, and he tried to move it several times, as if he wanted to speak. He could only look at the girl.

Now it was Bren's turn to grin. He watched as Airik sat dumbfounded, looking from Bren to White Calf and back again. The conversation pointedly directed to him. "What?" was all he could manage.

"Very little that you do escapes her, you know. For a waif of a girl, she is indeed wise and powerful, isn't she?" Bren could only laugh and thought he detected a hint of a blush on the girl's cheeks. He asked White Calf to sit with them for a bit. She laughed with him as she sat. Airik sat looking from one to the other until he also began to laugh. The tension was eased, and the young people sat for some time, talking quietly and eating.

Bren and Airik finished their meal and decided they would take a bath in the heated pools of the cavern. He left the lodge and looked up to see Wanbli seated on his perch above.

"Good morning, Wanbli," he said aloud. The bird shifted slightly as he looked down at Bren.

"Good morning." He returned the greeting silently. "It is good to hear you laugh. The young woman you are with is full of magic and a very powerful human being. Her light shines brighter than any I've seen before. She will be helpful to us all in the future. Do you know if she is interested in the eagles?"

"We haven't spoken of it, friend," Bren returned. "But I can ask her. Why do you ask?"

"Time is near when the eggs will hatch."

"You see a light in her?"

"Some people's light we can easily see. The aura is a manifestation of the life force. It's helpful to see what a person has inside them, and that usually shows in the aura. Some people have none, or at least none that is visible to me."

White Calf stepped out of the lodge and looked directly at the eagle. "I am now and always have been interested in your kind, Wanbli," she said aloud. "I'll be honored to help you in any way I can." Bren and Wanbli looked at one another in surprise.

"She hears my voice," Wanbli said.

"Yes, Wanbli, I hear your voice and the voices of all the great birds."

Bren and Airik walked toward the opening to the cavern, with all eyes of the village on them. They were greeted by young and old as they made their way. Bren's parents and sister met them outside their lodge and fell in with them. Aria took her brother's hand and looked at him closely. "You've changed, brother. You look more…grown up than you did before," she said as she giggled at him.

"I am the same brother you had at gather, Aria. Have you met my friend?"

"I've gone to look at him, but I didn't stay too long. I didn't want to stare, and he frightened me a bit. I've never seen such a large eagle."

"There is no need to be frightened of Wanbli, Aria. He's not going to hurt you."

"I know that, but it doesn't keep me from being afraid. I've never been close to such a one. The way he looks at a person! I think he can tell what you are thinking!"

"If he wants to, he usually can. I've talked to him for hours, and he listens better than many people I know. He will love you like I do, Aria. Speak to him with your thoughts, with your mind, and listen for his answer. It's fun!"

The people working outside stopped to watch the small party walk across the village. Bren and Airik were surprised to see so many changes had been made to the cavern. The entry walls had been made more or less square with mortar and stone, and a great pair of oak doors were set in place. The interior was lighted by oil lamps and candles. Several large tables were set around the room.

The hallway leading to the bath chambers was also lighted, and the floor had been leveled with sand from the creeks around the village outside. They came to the bathing chambers and found low wooden platforms had been built as flooring at the edges of the pools with benches set in place. The men made their way to the pool next to the waterfall and, dropping their clothing on the benches along the wall, slipped into the warm water.

"It's very warm," Bren said, slowly submerging his body. "This will come in handy in winter." Airik lay languidly on the pebbled bottom, supporting his upper body with his arms wrapped over the rim of the pool, his back to the rocky edge.

"It's too bad the elders saw fit to separate the men's and women's pools. This could be very interesting, in any season."

Bren could think of no proper reply, so he just lay in the warmth of the water, feeling the tension ease from his body.

The room was lighted by the sun coming through the veil of the waterfall and accompanied by the hushed music of the water. Bren opened his eyes in time to see a shadow approach the watery curtain from the other side of the falls. He watched as a shape appeared and broke the water barrier. Wanbli flew through the mist at the edge of the waterfall and landed on the ledge of the pool. Airik sat up startled and looked at the bird face-to-face. He shook the water from his feathers and greeted the men so both could hear.

"Hello, this is a very good place to bathe, is it not?"

"Good day, Wanbli, it is a good place to bathe. Have you come here before?"

The bird answered. "My people have known of this place for many lifetimes. When we stay in the mountains through the winter, it is a warming place for us. There are many such places in the mountains. Many more in this mountain alone. Some are connected to this place by tunnels, and some are not."

"Will you show them to us when we have the time?"

"Some of them we will show you, and some of them we will keep to ourselves."

Bren laughed and said, "That sounds fair to me, friend. We will be able to use any of them that you care to show. I'm sure the people will be pleased to give you privacy in the others." He smiled as he said, "We have much to learn about your kind."

Wanbli told Bren he had used the time it took he and Airik to travel from the butte to find a nest site in one of the caves high on the mountain. He and his friends had begun the task of building their nests. The eagles were a few days from laying.

Bren and Airik soaked in the warmth of the water, listening carefully as the bird told them what was expected of the people. Bren felt again the excitement of what was happening for his people and for the eagles. They were entering a new time for the earth, when the people of the plains and the winged ones would again work together to heal and live upon the earth mother. He heard the bird say, "This is right, brother. We're surely seeing a new beginning for the world. Soon we can once again fly the path as it was meant by the earth mother. We will be together in this. We will help one another to do the right things for this earth that gives us home and hope."

They sat a long while then in silence. The great bird and the two men, allowing the bond between them to strengthen and grow. The only sound was from the water as it cascaded from the tops of the mountain or bubbled up from the depths beneath, into the heart of the village. After a time, Wanbli said softly so both men could hear, "Rest for a time. We both will have much work to do in the next few days. You with your new village and I with mine. I will see you each day, and if I am needed in between, you have but to call me with your mind. I will come as quickly as I'm able."

"Tend to your family, Wanbli," Bren answered. "Let me know if there is any way my people can help." With that, the great bird lifted himself and again flew through the water, this time shooting up along the face of the waterfall and away.

Airik lifted his head to watch him go and said, "I'm still getting used to his coming and going. It is something to see, isn't it?" Bren just lay back on the rock of the pool and smiled. He was pleased with the turns his life was taking in the past few weeks and eager to see what the weeks to come held in store for himself and his people.

Bren spent the next few days sleeping and attending meetings with the elders. They discussed the finishing touches on the village and plans for the coming spring. He advised them of the preparations Wanbli told them must be completed. The egg laying would come within the next several days.

He had moved into his new cabin before gather and so stayed there again after his first night back from the butte. Airik stayed with him from time to time, as did Aria, when she wanted a night away from her parents' lodge. The young people enjoyed the evenings sitting on the front porch or by the fire after the night got too cool.

Bren's mother and father came to dinner once or twice during the week. His mother would cook for them or bring food when they came. Bren was looking forward to the delivery of the glass windows he had ordered at gather, before the winter came. It would be good to be able to look out on the winter world from the warm cabin, when the snow started the long winter season.

Bren had made an eagle-sized nest platform he thought would work nicely for Wanbli and his mate when they visited. He placed it on four long lodge poles near the cabin. Wanbli told him they would use it when visiting, but right now, he and his mate had completed their nest in the ancient stone eyries high on the mountain. He thought they were appropriate for this new beginning of the old ways. Bren agreed and told his friend the nest would be available whenever they needed it.

He and Wanbli talked at length with Lanis until she had a complete understanding of what was required of the people of the village when the current nests of eggs began to hatch. Because the eagles were getting larger now and there were more hatchlings in each clutch, the people would help the mother eagle by making sure there was enough fresh meat cut and available any time it was required.

A select few young villagers would be able to get close enough to the eagle chicks to help feed them as they grew. In this way, the young people of the village would learn to become accustomed to the eagles and their needs.

Since Lanis had taken over the coordination of this task, Bren used the time to walk through the village, speaking with the people he would meet. He saw more meat-drying racks and smokers than he could remember for many years. Everywhere he looked, he saw people working on the drying and preparation of meats and other foods that would feed the village through the winter. He saw racks of drying fish and berries. There were baskets of turnips, onions, potatoes, and beans. Women and young people were everywhere working on hides in various stages of the tanning process. He inhaled deeply the smell of the soft, pulpy wood that was used to smoke the hides in the final stages of the process. The smoke would give them the warm brown tones and water resistance. Bren preferred these colors over the whiter hides the young women used for their dress making.

His sister took him hunting for porcupines during one afternoon, and they caught enough of the prickly creatures to keep her busy with needles and hide all winter long. Aria explained to Bren how she felt her role was to be a teacher of her craft. Her quillwork and tanning of hides was important to her. She felt the need to keep her art alive within the village and through the plains communities.

Bren hugged his sister to him when she told him of her plans. He told her how happy he was she had made this decision. Everyone had a place, and he was sure she was choosing the right path for herself. He'd seen her sitting for hours in the shade by their parents' lodge, cleaning and dyeing the quills and sorting the long, thin guard hairs into piles of different lengths. Bren felt a warmth run through him as he saw his sister and his people coming of age.

In the evenings, Wanbli would invariably come to him around the time White Calf was preparing meat for the birds' meal. She always had a large bowl of uncooked elk, deer, or sometimes whole fish. He would take a portion to his mate then return and allow her to feed him. He sat on a low perch in full view of the village. The sight of the eagle feeding had quickly become a regular treat for the young people and those that weren't busy elsewhere.

On this day around noon, Bren walked down to his cabin to finish some of the furniture he was building to make the cabin more comfortable for winter. White Calf was placing three large buffalo steaks to cook on the low fire outside the door of the cabin. The cast-iron grill Bren had picked up at gather was working perfectly over the open fire. White Calf would always make sure Joseph had his meal and was comfortable before she walked to Bren's home.

As he approached the cabin, he saw Airik grinning at him from a buffalo robe under the shade of the huge old oak in the front yard. He had taken to spending more time at Bren's cabin since they returned from the butte, even when Bren was away. Bren grinned back at his friend and sat beside him. Bren knew the two young people were using this noon time ritual as an opportunity to meet and talk to each other. They talked while they waited for the meat to cook. He saw several ears of corn on the stones of the fire, and the aroma awakened the hunger in him.

Bren heard a commotion ripple through the village from the south, moving toward them at the western edge of the village. Several young boys were running ahead of two eagles that were gliding slowly toward Wanbli's usual perch in the oak. The golden eagle that was accompanying Bren's friend was even larger than Wanbli and a most beautiful creature.

The birds came to rest and slowly looked over the small gathering. Wanbli turned to Bren and spoke slowly and with deep emotion. "This is my mate. She is known to me by a name you couldn't speak in your language, or the ancient tongue of your people. It would please her if you were to call her Tayla." She sat regally next to Wanbli. She carried herself upright, and her feathers shown in the sun as if highly polished. Her beak and feet were as shining clean as the flat stones in the creek running through the meadow. "It is close enough to the name we use."

"Your friends have done a very good job attending us, and we are grateful."

Bren looked into the approaching crowd and saw Lanis leading the group. She was staring intently at the pair as Wanbli spoke. "I've heard the words he spoke, Bren, and I'm honored I've lived up to the trust you've all placed in me. Everything is ready. Tonight, we'll have a feast and tomorrow we will be ready for what comes."

White Calf asked Lanis to help her feed the two birds, while Bren watched the steaks. They had a great time chatting and feeding the big birds, as the villagers looked on. The two eagles made short work of the offered meat and soon were ready to rest.

There came a low warbling trill from the eagles as they sat craning their necks to the sky. Tayla took wing, and after her, Wanbli, so they flew almost wing tip to wing tip toward the mountain. Soon they were out of sight, and the people slowly returned to their tasks.

Lanis asked Bren and the elders to meet at the central village lodge after their meal. They needed to discuss the events that were to take place when the birds called them to care for the chicks. Bren's mother had organized several women of the village to prepare the meal for the evening's feast.

After the meal, Bren and White Calf made their way to the center of the village. Lanis told all in attendance which of the children had been chosen to help and what would be expected of them. The meeting went on until late in the afternoon, when the women informed them the feast meal would be served shortly. They needed to get the central lodge cleared out for the setup. If the council wanted to dress in fresh clothes, they would have to be quick.

Bren had chosen the quilled buckskin pants and shirt his sister made him to wear at gather. He wore a wide red wool belt over the shirt and his newest pair of moose-hide moccasins. The shirt hung long over his waist, and the fringe on the sleeves hung well below the hem of the shirt. The red quills shined brightly in the firelight against the white quilled background. The white glowed as if the moon was reflected in its surface. He chose to wear an old-style roach that his sister made him from the guard hair of the porcupine. He was not accustomed to wearing head gear but thought this a fitting time to dress as completely in the old way as he was able. His father had finished carving the lower jaw of the great bear and fashioned two beautiful belt knives for him. These he placed in sheaths with quill-work matching his shirt. The bear jaw knives turned out so beautiful he promised his father he would use them for decorative purposes only. Last, he placed the bear claw amulet over the shirt, so it hung on his chest.

He opened the door of his cabin and stepped into the light of the full moon. He was greeted by White Calf and Airik coming for him from the village. She was dressed in a beautiful cloud-white dress of the softest antelope skins. The yoke of the dress was covered with off-white and caramel elk teeth. The fringe on the sleeves hung almost to the ground. Next to White Calf walked Bren's sister, in a sand-colored moose-hide dress. The yoke of her dress was filled with row on row of sky-blue bead work trimmed in tiny white beads. She turned for him, and he saw the design on the back was a bald eagle with outstretched wings spreading across the back of the shoulders. Both girls wore their hair braided down to their waists. They each took an arm, escorting Bren toward the main lodge.

"Well," he said, "I'll be the most envied man at the feast tonight. Look at how beautiful you both are." Both girls beamed at him as they walked. "Airik will be jealous when I show up in your company, White Calf." She looked up at him to speak, as a voice caught their attention from a short distance away.

"Not so fast, bear killer!" It was, of course, Airik come to join them from an adjoining path. He looked very fine, in deep-brown elk-hide pants and shirt decorated with Aria's quillwork in blue and yellow. "I am very jealous," he said. "I asked White Calf to accompany me, but she crushed my heart. She told me she had previous plans. I was tempted to send a runner with a message to Sara."

White Calf quietly took Airik's hand in hers as he caught up to the group of friends. Under her breath but loud enough to hear, she said, "Please shut up now." Airik grinned down at her. Bren was surprised and pleased as he saw how comfortable they were, walking closely together.

As they entered the hall, Bren heard soft flute music playing from a group near the east end. He saw a raised platform there. On it were four peeled willow backrests trimmed in soft red cloth. The whiteness of the wood glowed against the red of the edging cloth. The floor was covered with buffalo hides. The girls escorted Bren to this place, where he could see his mother and father waiting off to one side. His parents stepped up to the platform and showed Bren to a seat at one of the center backrests.

The two young girls sat on the steps of the dais. Lanis took one of the backrests at the end, and Joseph seated himself at the other end.

Bren thought, *How appropriate that Lanis should be honored tonight. She's worked so much harder than anyone else to accomplish these tasks.*

Bren sat against one backrest, and Airik took the remaining seat. Bren looked over at him and saw him grinning hugely. He was conscious of all the eyes in the hall on him, but the smiles of his friends and family eased his concern, and in a moment, he was smiling also. Shortly after they sat, the flutes stopped, and he saw two forms, one after the other, drop from the smoke hole at the top of the building. First Wanbli, then his mate dropped with wings folded. As they cleared the center smoke hole, the crowd gasped in astonishment. The birds spread their wings and glided smoothly to perches on either side of the group seated on the platform. Wanbli was just to the left and behind Bren, and his mate was at Bren's right shoulder.

"Quite an entrance," Bren said in his mind to the birds, and a soft, warbling voice whispered in his head.

"We thought it fit the occasion," Tayla said.

Bren was surprised at her words. This was the first time she'd spoken directly to him. He caught Lanis's eye and her amusement was obvious. She was keeping several things from him, he thought. "An honoring is much better if it's unexpected," said Wanbli's strong tenor voice. Bren took note of the amusement he heard there as the bird continued. "This is a wonderful time. You have done well and deserve to be honored a little. Tayla thinks the hatchings will start tomorrow, and then the work will come. The weeks ahead will be a challenge for many of our peoples. This night is to relax, celebrate, and honor."

As his winged friends' words were fading in his head, Bren heard a soft rumbling drumbeat from behind the dais he was seated on. The sound grew louder and suddenly stopped. Joseph raised a hand in a silent greeting to the group on the dais, and then he turned slowly to the assembled village. He greeted them and then said a short prayer in the ancient language of the plains.

Joseph let the words of the prayer waft through the room then began to speak in the modern language of the people. He spoke softly, barely above a whisper, but his words filled every corner of the great room. "Now before us is the beginning of a new age for the earth. We who sit here tonight are blessed to be living in the time of a great healing, when old things will become new again. We have watched two young sons of this village embark on a journey that has been passed down through the people of the plains. This journey was foretold since the sun first warmed our lodges on the prairie. We've watched the progression of events spoken of in the chronicles of our nation, passed down from father to son, from mother to daughter. We've seen the legends become reality and new legends being born. Tomorrow, all of us here will become part of the legends told by future generations. The healing has begun, but there is more work ahead for us all. Tonight, we'll share the company of one another. I ask that we all reflect on what was, what will be, and what we will do to make sure we see the sacred circle healed and whole for all the generations to follow. For all the future generations of our people to be allowed to walk the red road upon this earth, our mother, our home." Joseph's warm smile spread across his wrinkled face. "Now table the meat and pass the skins. Let's eat, drink, and dance."

Joseph seated himself at the front table. A group of young men dressed in dance regalia made their way into the cleared circle at the center of the room. They were dressed in traditional buckskins, quills, and head gear of the plains peoples. The village people ate and talked and watched as dancers and musicians took turns at the center of the floor. After Bren ate, he wandered from table to table, talking with the people. He stayed for a few more dances then sneaked away to his cabin. He felt the real celebration would take place in the morning with the hatchings.

Hatching

Bren awoke to the gentle shaking of his foot and saw White Calf standing at the foot of his bed. She was dressed this time in a muted tan work dress. Her hair was plaited and tied in a bun behind her head. The sun was up but just barely. He dressed quickly in his clothes from the night before and met White Calf at the stove. She gave him coffee and warm bread, and they talked about last night's feast.

"Why are you dressed so plainly?"

She answered, "The hatchings started early this morning. Things are going well." She added at his startled look. "I will be working for the whole of this day and probably into the night. It makes no sense to me to wear my best while working."

"Good point," he told her, amused by the common-sense approach to the event that had most of the young people in a panic for the past few weeks. "Whatever you are wearing, you had better be off, or you will miss something good. I'll be along in a few minutes. Thank you for my breakfast, White Calf."

She walked away toward the caves with enough of an urgency in her step to make Bren chuckle under his breath. She gave him a backhand wave as she left. He set his coffee on the big dining table and collected the pipe, in the bag that Joseph had given him. He didn't know if it would come to any use, but it felt reassuring in his hand just now.

He joined his family on the path to the caverns, and they talked quietly as they went. There were young people in small groups and singly scurrying here and there, clutching their bowls of meat, baskets of straw, or other such things Bren couldn't identify.

When he got to the caves, Lanis explained to Bren she already had young people high up in the caves. Wanbli had called to Lanis early in the morning to tell her the hatching had begun. He showed her where the nesting caverns were high up on the wall of the mountain. He told her where she would find a passageway inside and up that would take her to the nests. Lanis had awakened several of the young people of the village, and they in turn awoke the rest.

The workers had climbed up steps high inside the mountain and found many small nesting caverns. Some were already being used as nest sites. The young people were quietly busy bringing soft hay and grass into the caverns to make additional nests in the empty caverns.

Many of the nests had at least two, and some had three eggs. The caretakers from the village separated the newborn eagle chicks as they hatched after the mothers completed their inspection. They would leave one chick with the mother, and one child would stay with that chick and mother to help with feeding or anything else necessary. They took the newborn chicks to the empty nest sites so each one could have the undivided attention of a young person. The young people who were not lucky enough to take charge of a newborn chick were hauling meat or nesting material up the lamplit passages.

Bren asked her, "The mothers don't mind that their chicks are being taken?"

"Believe me, Bren, if they didn't want those chicks separated, there is no safe way we would lay hands on them. They are being taken to nests right next to their birth mothers at any rate. The mothers have found the chicks are so big when they are hatched it's difficult to keep more than one of them fed. They are dangerous to one another because of their hunger. This is one of the reasons we were asked to help.

"The mothers are more likely to have successful hatchlings, and the children of the village can bond with a chick. The mothers and their mates will visit each several times through the day, so the chicks imprint on them as well. The children will be helpers, and the mothers and fathers will be teachers, both to the chicks and to their human friends. The mothers will, of course, at some point, need to teach the fledglings to fly and to hunt. This is the first time, at least in memory, we have tried this, so we are all learning. Hopefully the grown birds will be lifelong friends to the village. We just don't know for sure at this point, but things are going as well as can be expected."

"How are the children accepting this new challenge?" Bren asked her.

"So far they're doing wonderfully well. They are all tired, of course, but there has been hardly a complaint from them. Even when the newborn chicks are more than a little, well, aggressive about taking food from their hands. Both chicks and children seem to be learning the tasks of eating and feeding.

"The children figured out quickly once the little bellies are full, the chicks will sleep. They've fetched sleeping furs up to their eyries and curled up in them to sleep when their young charges do. Let's go up and see them. We can watch the feeding, and you can see how well it goes."

Lanis took Bren and Airik up the cavern tunnel through the mountain. The rest of their group waited in the first cavern to allow for ease of movement up the mountain. The tunnels were passable but little more than shoulder wide. They had to turn sideways often as they made their way up, to pass someone going in the opposite direction with an empty bowl or to be passed from the rear by a full bowl or basket of straw, many times at a run. Several times they passed a wide place in the tunnel they used for ease of passing. Bren, Airik, and Lanis stepped into these over and over again in order to let someone hurry past with their burden. Despite the candle lanterns every few yards, the tunnels were still just barely lit enough to see the floor. Bren looked up and realized he could see nothing but darkness overhead. He reached as high as he could with only empty air above him.

The tunnels turned right and left so many times Bren soon couldn't tell whether they were traveling north or south. He knew only they were moving up. After what seemed like a very long time, the small group came to a shelf opening into a large cavern. There were children seated here on furs laid out on the floor. There were candle lanterns everywhere, hanging from the rock walls of the chamber. They cast a golden light across the floor of the room but here again didn't penetrate to the ceiling.

There was a table off to one side covered with bowls of meat. Baskets of straw were stacked next to the table. Two young people were standing at the table, ready to be of service. Bren saw passages all along the left side of the cavern. Every few moments someone would pop out of one of these and ask for a bowl or join the group of young people on the floor or head down the corridor toward the outside. Some children were asleep and waiting to be called. Others were sitting wide-eyed and talking animatedly but quietly in the dimness of the cavern.

Lanis crooked her finger at them both, and they followed her through the first corridor to the left of the long shaft they had climbed. They went several paces before Bren noticed the slight movement of air in his face and natural light on the walls.

They soon came to a smaller chamber, and there they found White Calf. She was speaking to a small group of attentive children in a subdued tone. She took one girl by the hand and told her, "Come with me, please." The girl looked back at Bren and Airik through tousled black hair and with widened eyes shot both of them a huge open-mouthed grin. White Calf was explaining as they disappeared through a low opening what would be expected of her as she met her eagle chick.

Lanis touched Bren on the sleeve to get his attention and ducked through an opening on her left, obviously expecting him to follow. Bren tucked his head through after her, and Airik followed. They crouched in a small tunnel and moved onto a flat stone shelf. More than half of the shelf was taken up by a huge nest of twigs and grasses. There was a young boy of about eleven years lying asleep on a buffalo robe next to the nest. His dark brown hair was mussed and covered his face. The shelf a few feet from where Bren stood was opened to the air, and a view of the whole valley below spread out before them.

Tayla was perched on the side of the nest at the open edge of the small nesting cavern. Bren looked out the opening and could see the whole meadow and his cabin, sitting at the far edge of the woods. He was taken aback by how high on the mountain they were. Tayla greeted both the men quietly with words whispered in their heads.

"Good morning Bren, Airik."

Bren silently answered the mother eagle and, as he spoke, saw a single hatchling asleep in the nest. Right away Bren noticed the size of the chick. This was a big bird, as big as a full-grown raven, even larger! He was amazed they could fit into the small space the eggs contained.

As he stood, he wondered what their grown size would be and asked Tayla the question.

"We don't know yet, really. Each clutch has produced larger young and bigger numbers. This one has been most successful so far. One eagle mother has laid five eggs. The chicks all seem to be quite healthy and bigger than before. We are very grateful for the help to feed them, and with all the food they are getting, I'm confident they will continue to grow large and healthy."

Lanis motioned to Bren. It was time to go. "Thank you for allowing us to visit your nest, Tayla," he said. "You're most welcome anytime you have a moment, Bren Redhorse. And you as well, Airik. This thing we're doing together is helping to make the old world new again. My relatives are all very excited to see what's next."

The three companions ducked out to the main hall and back into the cavern, where young people continued to come and go quietly. Airik met White Calf there and spoke quietly to her for a moment. Bren began moving down the corridor toward the bottom of the mountain. After a few minutes, Airik caught up with Bren, and they started toward the entrance cavern.

They passed a steady stream of young people purposefully coming up or going down. The young men were forced to stop at several of the wide spots to speed a worker's movement through the mountain.

Finally reaching the main cavern, Bren and Airik both stopped and grinned at each other, as well as the group waiting.

"What a wondrous thing to see!" Airik's enthusiasm was plain to see. "The cave is honey combed with corridors, tunnels, and nesting caverns open to the sky. Look at these children! They're working inside this mountain as if they've done it all their lives!"

Bren stayed at the entrance for a time. Lanis appeared and was speaking to the villagers gathered there. The parents were curious about what their children were up to. Bren listened as she advised them what to expect in the days to come. The children chosen would be busy almost constantly for several days. They would be required to provide much of the care the mother eagles would give in a more normal nesting situation.

They would be cutting meat and feeding the chicks. They would be spending many hours bonding with their young charges, as well as with the adult eagles. They would also hopefully be becoming familiar with the mind-to-mind communication that Bren knew so well could be frightening to the uninitiated.

Bren took the afternoon to spend time with his mother and father, whom he hadn't seen a great deal of since returning from the butte. He found them sitting outside their lodge, leaning one against the other and talking quietly.

"Hello, Bren," said his mother. "We were just saying how proud we are of you. The things you've done in this summer make my mind swim. You've accomplished more in this short time than many will in a lifetime, and it's being talked of around our village. We're happy with this new winter place as well. Although your father spends much too much time away from the lodge, seeing to one thing or another."

"Yes, well," Ben said. "If I didn't take charge of the things that need to be done, it would be left for one of the other elders to do, and they'd talk of what a lazy husband your mother has. I would soon find that I had no lodge to come back to at all. I'd find myself begging at my son's door for a place to lay my head."

"I'm sure you have little to fear, Father," said Bren. "Mother knows well there are many who would take in such a man as you."

Bren's mother returned her son's comment with a disgusted sound, as Bren sat at her feet.

They spent the afternoon talking of what they would do for the rest of the season, before the snows began. Bren and his father made plans to go on another hunt. Ben heard word from the village men of a sizeable herd of buffalo seen not a day's ride from the village. The grass was still in good condition on the plains nearby, and the animals were busy adding to their layer of fat to see them through the winter. There were still many elk and deer both to be found in the surrounding hills. They also talked about scouting out areas where they could lay traps for the beaver, mink, and fox that always had prime winter pelts.

Thora told him of the lodge she and Aria had been working on for his sister. This shocked Bren a bit, until his mother told him the lodge would be set not ten steps from her own, at least for the winter. She had every intention of keeping a close eye on her daughter through the cold and sometimes lonely winter.

"Mother, you don't need to worry about Aria being lonely this winter," Bren said. He got a shocked look from both his parents. "I mean only that she has made plans to teach quillwork to many of the girls in the village. They'll be coming and going all winter long, I'm sure."

They began to speak of Sara and what would happen when she and her parents came to visit with them. "The lodge will be done by that time, and we can offer it to them for their stay," Ben said. "I think they'll be ready to spend some time on a soft fur floor after so many days in the saddle or a hard wagon seat. I'm hoping you'll be ready to make a commitment to the girl when they arrive and possibly have a wife to winter with."

Bren flushed slightly at his father's comment. "I've already made a commitment to Sara and to her father as well. We both know we were meant to be together, and we've told her family so. Remember, my cabin is finished. I was planning on offering them the cabin while they're here, and I'll stay in my lodge just behind. She'll be my wife before the snow falls, and they'll leave her here for the winter when they return home."

Thora and Ben laughed at their son's obvious discomfort. "You've made a fine choice in her, son, just as she has made a fine choice in you," Ben said. "We're proud of the way you have both conducted yourselves through this courtship."

Bren asked his father indignantly, "What other way could we have conducted ourselves?"

He laughed as he answered. "You've continued the old ways, and it's a good path to walk."

Aria returned from visiting friends in time to help her mother with the evening meal. Ben left for a time to conduct an inspection of a cold food storage cavern with some of the elder men. When he returned, the family sat and ate their meal as they had before the events of the summer changed their routine. As they were sitting to eat, Wanbli arrived and perched on a log bench at Bren's side. Aria offered him pieces of an elk roast she was just about to put into a cast-iron pot, which he gratefully accepted.

"You're quiet this evening, Wanbli," Bren said.

"I'm tired from the work of hatching. It's not all mother's work, no matter what they might tell you. Also, something is coming. There is a task before us that needs to be done. We will have the telling of it in the morning, I think. It might be good for us both to sleep early tonight."

Try as he might, Bren could not get the bird to tell him anything more. He would only repeat they would have the telling of it come morning, and it was nothing he should worry about for the present.

They finished their meal with coffee and more conversation. As the moon rose, Bren left for his cabin with Wanbli shadowing him through the trees. He was no more on his bed when he fell into a deep, fitful sleep. He dreamed for the first time in many nights of the bear that had come from the dark to meet him and of the elk with the great bird on its rack. He heard the unmistakable voice of the war eagle in his mind.

"I'm here with you, friend. We are one and will always be together. Send the dream away now and rest, for we have a road to follow soon."

With this, the dream left him, and he slept the night through.

Spirits Guiding

Bren sat bolt upright in his bed, instantly awakened in the predawn darkness by the scree of an eagle in war song. He pulled open the door to see the stars still in the sky and Wanbli coming in to his perch in a claw-first, full-flight landing. Bren was sure the bird would hurt himself. At the last moment, he spread his wings to break his speed, lighting on his accustomed perch just outside the cabin. "Thunder comes," he said. Bren looked around but could see only a cloudless sky filled with stars.

"There is no thunder, Wanbli, only stars. Are you all right?" he asked.

"I am always all right, Bren. Thunder comes in the shape of a wolf. The story is about to be told. You should get dressed for travel, I think. He is just now making his way through the village to us."

As Wanbli finished this thought, Bren heard a commotion in the village behind the cabin. He saw a shape running the wide path between lodges. It was Thunder, the wolf that was Sara's constant companion. His heart leaped as he thought this could only mean she had arrived in camp, but why would her family not camp for the night and come into the village in the daylight? His hope turned to concern and then terror. The wolf grew nearer, and he could see the animal was in poor shape. The wolf's coat was matted and dirty. His body was thin, as if he had not eaten in days. Bren's heart crashed as he saw a gash down the left side of his body. It was old but oozing thick red blood.

"He has lost her, he says." This came from Wanbli in short, choppy, matter-of-fact sentences. "He has traveled far and fast to find you. To bring you to her. She's been taken by the murderers in the north country, and they ride as we speak. Away to the north and farther each moment. We need to hurry, or she will be lost. He says he tried to fight, and she sent him away to come find you."

Now Thunder barked twice, loudly. The last bark turning to a howl so pitiful that Bren had to reach down and hold the wolf close to him. He felt the pain and the terror that the dog had been holding back. "Send for Lanis, Wanbli. Tell her to come quickly, and I'll get ready to travel."

Wanbli answered, "She comes. I've sent word to her already. She comes with her medicines for the wolf."

As he spoke these words, Airik skidded into the camp on his heels, carrying his bow in one hand and his war club in the other. "I thought you were being eaten by wolves, Bren. What happens here? That's Thunder, Sara's wolf. Did he attack you? Is she here in the village? What happened to him?"

"I'll explain as I dress, Airik. Come inside and build the fire. Light some lamps. Sara's wolf has been injured, and Lanis will need light to dress his wounds." Bren dressed in heavy buckskin as he told Airik what the wolf said, stopping to explain that the eagle had translated for him. Ben arrived in the firelight and was asked to saddle Bren's fastest horse, Stone Foot, the hunter.

Lanis ran into the camp and almost over the wolf in her haste to find out why she had been called. "I was awakened by Wanbli's voice in my head. He told me only that an animal was in need and I must come to heal. That's Sara's wolf. What's happened?"

The whole village was awake now, and a good many of them were standing near Bren's cabin. Airik quickly told Lanis what was told to him, and Lanis took charge of the wolf. She picked him up gently and carried him into the cabin. Thunder made no protest but groaned as his feet left the ground. Airik followed her inside and was in the process of lighting candle lamps.

Lanis had Airik put water on the fire to heat and placed the wolf on the dinner table. She was soon cleaning the wound on the wolf's side. She applied a salve, and Bren watched the animal relax under the gentle hands of the healer. She sent for food and water for the wolf, and her apprentice was soon back with bowls full of both. Lanis stirred a powder into the water bowl and urged the dog to drink sparingly of it. Thunder drank slowly from the bowl.

Lanis worked on the injury as Thunder lay very still. The moaning of the wolf as it lay under the lights was heart-wrenching to hear. Lanis closed the wound with several small stitches. She insisted the animal needed to rest several days before it could walk, let alone travel, but Bren quickly stopped her.

"This wolf knows his mistress like no other could. He'll be able to help me find her. He will leave this village when I do. I don't believe there are enough people to prevent him from going. If there is something more you can do for him, then do it. If not, give me medicines that I can take with us when we leave."

Lanis looked at Bren with heat in her eyes. "If this wolf worsens, it's on your head, Bren Redhorse."

"Yes, Lanis," Bren answered. "It will surely be."

White Calf stepped from the darkness to kneel at the side of the wolf. She reached for him and gently, carefully inspected the injury. "You're a most skillful healer, Lanis. This wolf will live for the care you've shown. I have something that will help him regain strength and heal the wound quickly. He must be with Bren when they find Sara. Better for the wolf as well as the man." White Calf quickly stepped into the darkness and away.

Ben walked through the cabin door with food and extra clothing in a travel pack across his back. He sat the bundles down on the porch of the cabin and spoke to his son. "I've gathered what I could for us to take. We'll have to travel light and quickly. Your mother has packed enough jerked meat and dried fruit to last a month."

"Father, there's no need for you to go. There are things here that need to be done. Mother couldn't live if something was to happen to the both of us."

Bren's father held up his hand. "Enough, you're my son. Sara is soon to be my daughter. You go to meet the people that have your woman, and I'm going with you. There can be only one people who would do this thing. I know their language and can be of help. Your mother knows this is a battle for us both to fight. She also knows I won't send you to meet them alone. We're wasting time arguing about it."

Ben said this with such force of will Bren knew there was no arguing. Wanbli said, "You forget, Bren, I am with you always, and you will not be lost. This is the beginning of the time we were chosen for. We will do battle together, if we must, and they will sing songs of us for all the seasons of this world. We go, and we will bring back this young woman. This is what I say. Let's make ready. The night awaits."

Bren quickly packed moccasins and a change of clothing into his traveling bag. He was stepping from the cabin when White Calf returned carrying a small pouch and a bowl of thick yellowish paste. She handed Bren the pouch and knelt beside the resting wolf. Thunder's eyes were rolling from side to side as people spoke. White Calf touched the paste to the wound, and the wolf relaxed at the touch. She applied the paste with tiny fingers, rubbing it gently into the stitched flesh. The animal seemed to relax more as she worked, his eyes half lidded in obvious relief.

White Calf stood and addressed Bren. "Use the salve twice a day. A horse will carry the wolf for the first day and further if there is need, but I think a day and night should be enough. He has lost blood and will be weak, so watch him carefully. Give him water and give him food when he wants it. Don't forget this. Now go and bring back this woman. I wish to speak to her again before she chooses to make her life with you."

Bren stared at White Calf as she said this, and a warm smile broke across her face. Bren could not help but return the smile. He hugged her tightly to him. How odd, he thought, that this tiny young girl could carry such power and infuse him with calm and confidence. He hugged her close to him once again and thanked her quietly.

"I have another sister," he said.

"You have another sister," she answered. He mounted the horse Don was holding for him, as Ben mounted his.

Airik lifted the wolf carefully, looking into his eyes as he did. The wolf didn't protest but lay easily upon a platform of woven reeds laced to the saddle of Bren's packhorse and padded with soft hides. Ben took the leads that were attached to two other horses, and they made their way down the path leading toward the northern plains. Bren looked back and saw the people of the village watching them go. There was his mother standing with Aria.

Airik raised the war club above his head and gave a loud, shrill war cry. They rounded a curve in the path and entered the trees. The dark village disappeared from sight.

The sun was just coming up over the curve of the plains as the riders came from the forest. They picked up speed, and Bren saw the eagle soaring smoothly above their heads. Soon he was a small spot near the horizon, and soon after he was gone from sight entirely. They cantered easily for a long time. Bren could not tell how long. His thoughts raced through the possibilities of what was to occur. He swore to himself he would wreak vengeance on those responsible if any harm was to come to Sara. He heard the warbling, familiar voice of Wanbli answer to him that Sara was, for the present, well and unharmed. They would return her to her people safe and whole. Fire burned in Bren as he looked down at the wolf, sleeping as they rode.

The miles flowed quickly by, as if the prairie were a landscape built in his dreams. Bren looked over at the wolf many times, to see him sleeping easily as they rode. He felt the spirits were moving the world under their feet. The country changed from the tall green grass of the prairie to the shorter scrub of the more northern flat lands. There were patches of bunch grass and wild rose.

They crossed stream after stream and larger water courses one after the other. Bren had little time to wonder how they could pass the miles so quickly. Whatever magic was working, he was grateful to the ones that were guiding them and sent his silent thanks to the sky and into the earth. He looked over at his father. Ben was looking often at the ground and at the line of the horizon to their front. Bren recognized that cold, determined look on his father's face. He'd seen it only a time or two since he was old enough to ride with the adults. It always struck a cord of fear and awe in him. He seemed to have changed from the peacemaker Bren had always known into a fierce and terrible warrior. He was proud to ride with him.

"Father, you ride with the elk dreamer in you!" These words he shouted into the wind but came from Bren's mouth in strangely muted tones, as though he were hearing them underwater. His father looked over at him and nodded once.

"He is in me tonight. He guides us on this journey!" Ben answered. And his father's voice sounded muted as well. They continued to ride across the night-covered prairie in silence.

Bren made a quick inspection of his weapons as they rode. He had the bow he'd hunted with for several seasons and a quiver of twenty arrows. He had his stone war club and two of the good steel knives he bought at gather, one on each hip. These would have to be sufficient. His father carried his bow, slid into its beaded case next to a quiver of arrows. His hunting knife was tied in a matching sheath at his belt. Airik appeared to have changed from his usual carefree self. He was quiet, his face stern, but composed. He carried his war club always ready in his hand.

The sun was setting to their left as they came upon a rise. There perched Wanbli, the war eagle, on a gnarled and dwarfed pine of the high north country. They stopped for the first time beside the great bird to let the horses rest for a few minutes. "The sun is flying through the day, and the world is turning under the feet of the horses. There is something magic working here," said the bird. He seemed larger and full of life to Bren. He appeared to be surrounded with a bright and shining light. Bren wondered if this was the light that Wanbli could see in White Elk. The eagle's voice was almost jovial in Bren's mind. "Yes, Bren, that is the light I spoke of. The same light surrounds you as well. The circle is healing, and the world knows this thing that has happened will not help. The spirits of the world help us set things right again. They don't want to rip the fabric as it heals. There are spirits traveling a path toward our goal that will be terrible to see, but they will go to war beside us if need arises. When you see them, you must not show fear. Remember this."

Bren repeated the words Wanbli spoke, and Ben said to the eagle, "I trust the words of my brother, and I'm thankful you're here with us. I've seen this magic work and I'll remember."

The stars appeared as muted, vague smears against the sky, as if he were looking at them through a high, thick fog. They rode into the darkness of night, stopping only to rest the horses and see to the wolf's injuries. The moon was full when it rose, casting a shrouded, watery light onto the path they took. Hours of riding fell away behind the group. The horses moved as if they were fresh from the pasture, seemingly tireless. The earth churned and flew under their hooves. Bren noticed the constellations were still recognizable. Most prominent was the great bear. He felt a presence streaming down from it, filling his heart.

Deep into the night Ben stopped the riders at the bottom of a small dark draw. He told Bren and Airik they needed to sleep for a few hours. They wouldn't do Sara any good if they arrived exhausted from the ride.

Bren made to argue with his father but saw the look on his face and the futility in the argument. The rest would do them all good, horses and men alike. Wanbli said Sara was all right, but that didn't stop the worry from seizing him in its grip. They dismounted and walked the horses into a group of willows, their branches closing around the small band, hiding them in a curtain of gray green. Bren thought there was little chance they would meet an enemy on this plain, but he felt more relaxed within the protection of the trees.

Bren carefully took Thunder from his nest on the packhorse's back and set him on the ground. The wolf walked around a bit, as if testing his muscle against the injury. He lay near the base of a tree and was soon asleep. Bren took the opportunity to see to his wound. He was amazed as he applied White Calf's salve at the healing progress. Airik picketed the horses inside the circle of trees, and the three men lay down near the sleeping wolf.

What seemed like a moment later, Bren felt a hand on his shoulder. He came fully awake without moving, right hand still gripping his club. His father was bent over him, telling him it was time to ride. Ben quickly got the horses ready to move. Bren helped Thunder onto the packhorse and got him settled as best he could. The wolf struggled for a moment to be on the ground then resigned himself as Bren spoke quietly to him.

The horses ran smoothly through the darkness into the morning. Before the sun was at zenith, Ben slowed the group to a trot and then to a walk. They seemed to be unaffected by the rigors of the journey and so began to run again.

The miles passed beneath them, and they ran into the night. Bren watched the moon rise in the sky as if the world was turning at twice its normal speed. He felt unaffected by the hours in the saddle, as if they had just left the village. He realized he wasn't hearing the normal nighttime sounds of the prairie. No night birds were singing, nor had he seen any fly. He had not seen an animal moving around them or a movement of any kind since they started their ride.

Neither did he care. If the earth mother, or whatever spirits were helping them, chose to ease their journey, he wouldn't argue. Whatever got him closer to where Sara was in trouble, he could only be grateful.

In the night sky, the barely waning moon was flowing across the sky as rapidly as the sun had in daylight. Bren's mind wandered back to Sara, as Stone Foot ran beneath him. He was terrified things would go badly for her and tried to pick up the pace. His father, riding beside him, reached over and grabbed his son's arm. "Let the horses choose the pace, Bren. Feel their movement. See how the moon runs across the sky. There is power here that runs with us. Let it work. Trust these helpers."

Hearing his father's words, Bren began to relax into the rhythm of the run. He scanned the country to their front, not really knowing what landmark to look for or even where they were. They passed giant sage and stunted pine growing amongst boulders strewn about by an ancient mountain of moving ice. The miles faded away behind them. Time could not be measured in the movement of the moon or stars. On and on the horses ran.

The sun would not be held, and in its inevitable dawning light, the wolf stirred. Seeing his friend awake once more, Bren called a halt to check on him. He dismounted and took dried meat from his pouch. To this he added a small palm full of the powder White Calf had given to him. Thunder held his head high as he ate and stood on firm legs while he drank. Bren was moved to see the wolf regain some of the vigor he had seen in him at gather. Ben advised they should rest the horses and sleep again for a few hours. Wanbli, who had dropped from the sky as they halted, concurred over Bren's objections. Finally, he gave in and sat dejectedly, looking around at the small group.

Dark thoughts pulsed through his mind until he heard the now familiar voice. "I'm here with you, Bren, and I watch. Your young woman is safe for the moment, and we will need to be rested for what is to come. We have far to go, and a few hours' rest will make a difference to the horses, no matter what magic is protecting them." Wanbli said this as he sat on a rock next to Bren. He felt the closeness of the bird as warmth on his shoulder, and the wolf's warmth at his feet. Ben allowed the horses to roam without hobbles over a nearby patch of grass. The men settled into a deep, dry buffalo wallow at the bottom of a hill. Thunder lay at Bren's feet and slept. Wanbli moved his perch to a shrub oak on a small rise, within sight of the camp and the horses.

Sometime later, Bren was nudged awake by the muzzle of the wolf. He rolled to his feet as Airik came to him with the horses saddled and ready. The sun was coming up, and the sky was a piercing blue. A thick ground fog sat in the low places surrounding the small group. Bren was amazed at the progress they had made. He had never been this far north. He was unfamiliar with the country but knew it to be far from home.

The wolf made it known he would not be placed in the saddle again and loped along with the horses. Bren found himself constantly watching his movement lest he should falter. He appeared not to have been injured at all, though Bren could still see the wound on his side. The day rolled by without a rest stop. Wanbli flew ahead, circling back often to reassure the riders. The weather was clear, and the day stayed as cool as the dawn had been, so they continued.

Night found the group surrounded by Beaver Marsh, and Ben called a halt as the moon rose full once again. The light of the moon cast a glow on the surface of the marsh, creating an eerie picture of the countryside. "We are in the country of the enemy now. We may come upon them at any time if they have guards out," Ben said, as they ate a meal of smoked buffalo meat and cold bread. Bren shared his food once again with the wolf and added another small palm full of the powder from White Calf's pouch. "I've never seen an animal recover so quickly from an injury such as that," Ben remarked. "The girl has some remarkable power in her touch."

Bren answered his father, "I don't believe the girl's touch is the only one the wolf is feeling, Father. There is something else at play on this journey."

Wanbli returned from scouting the country. He advised Bren that they were indeed in the country of the enemy people. He was sure they would not come upon them soon. There was no one around for miles, he said. They remounted after a short rest and rode quickly through the night and into noon of the next day without incident or halt.

A bit after noon, Thunder stuck his nose to the ground and stopped still in his tracks. He growled low over his shoulder at Bren and took off at a full run directly into the north. The men galloped the horses after him for several miles until Thunder stopped again and turned, growling deep in his throat. He had recognized the scent of his Sara.

They continued quickly, and Wanbli again disappeared over the horizon. He was back once more at dark with news that excited and chilled Bren. "The camp is but a half-hour walk ahead. We will go cautiously now. We must get close enough to the camp to surprise them at dawn."

"What is happening in the camp?" Bren asked. "Could you see what they've done with Sara?"

"She was in a lodge guarded by a single warrior when I flew over the camp. The white wolf is hidden nearby, unseen by the camp. There are many warriors there, women and children also. They'll move the camp soon, I think, but for tonight, all is quiet."

Wanbli continued, "We have help coming from the west. The one I told you about is very near to us. He will be among us before the morning. He is the beast you call Griz, but he's here to help. Try not to kill this one, Bren." Ben gave a chuckle as he smacked his son on the back, and Thunder chuffed.

"Your bird is talking to me now. I think he wanted me to hear his joke."

"My kind are not without humor," Wanbli said with a grin in his voice.

Bren said out loud, "What would they hope to gain by this theft of a woman from her family? Does someone want her for a wife, or is there some other plan in what they do? Do they know who they have in that lodge?" These were questions that had been bothering Bren since they left home, and now he voiced them aloud.

"These are people who have reverted farther than most into the old ways, son. Since the destruction, they've kept mostly to themselves. They have been relatively alone for a very long time, by choice. In the buffalo days, the people of different bands would sometimes take captives during their raids. They would take children, women, even men. After time, they would adopt them into their families and give them every freedom one raised with them would have.

"This was a way to add diversity to the people. The new blood would be added to the pool of their village. In many ways, these people are carrying on a custom that is as old as the original people of this continent. They cannot be blamed for seeking the old ways, excepting that this particular band has gone too far into the past, as they have in this instance. They will probably be expecting to make the girl a member of the band and a wife of a warrior."

"They may be expecting that, but it won't happen. They will probably be waiting for someone to come after her. I think that's why they'll try to move the camp. We'll surprise them at dawn. We must plan to arrive in a way that will give them no pause for thought or preparation. Wanbli, I need to know of the surrounding lands of the camp. We need to know which way will give us the best approach."

Wanbli told them what he'd seen as he flew over the camp. He detailed the village with attention to the smallest hill and the number of men, women, and children he saw. He told of the number of lodges and where they lay, as well as where the lookouts were positioned in the nearby woods and on the ridges. When the bird was done, Bren had a map in his head of where they were going.

The men talked and planned their approach as they waited for the dawn light to break. While the hour grew near, they made their weapons ready and finally mounted the horses for the ride close to the camp.

They came to within a quarter mile of the camp, and the horses became suddenly uneasy. Fearing they would make too much noise, the men dismounted. They sent the horses toward the south, where they might graze and wait.

Wanbli, who was soaring nearby, suddenly folded his wings and dove toward the men. "He comes from the west. You should wait here for him. This beast will be of great help to us in what we are about to do. Remember, Bren, that he knows what we are here to accomplish. He's been prepared for this meeting. Many wolves come also. They are friends to us but will be fierce and deadly warriors if the need should arise."

Bren felt apprehension mount in him. He could allow nothing to go wrong in this confrontation. Everything of value in his life was at stake. His blood rose as they waited. His father closed the distance between them until they were shoulder to shoulder, and they knelt together in the damp and dark. A moment later, a shape came into view over a near hillock. The form grew to an enormous size as they watched it lumber over the prairie. The bear walked on all fours as it approached to within a few feet of the pair and then sat, regarding them with tiny eyes glowing with the remaining light of the stars. The wolf at Bren's side trembled with the need to protect the small band from this creature. Their kind were ancient enemies.

Bren reached out and touched Thunder's back. He turned his head and licked the cheek of the young man. "We will accept the help and the friendship of this one, Thunder, as well as the friends he brings to the fight. They are all one of us in this battle. We need to trust the word of the eagle. He won't let us down."

Bear Killer Comes

The bear made a huffing sound and turned to Wanbli. After a moment, the bird spoke. "This one says he knows of you, Bren. He's heard you are the bear killer. He knows the one you did battle with in the camp and says that one had a bad spirit. He needed killing, as this was the only way the spirit would be released from him. It was a service you provided him. He says he never liked him anyway."

Bren grinned at the bear. "I'm glad that's settled."

The group was suddenly aware of others watching them. Bren looked into the darkness and counted twenty pairs of eyes peering in. A large white wolf trotted calmly up to Thunder and sat close beside him. It was Winter, Sara's wolf and Thunder's litter mate. They looked at each other, and she rubbed her head on his wounded shoulder as he huffed a greeting. Airik cursed quietly under his breath. "We're surrounded by wolves, you know."

Bren stared at the group in amazement for a long moment, until the bear turned and ambled off a few steps. He looked back pointedly, and Bren began to follow him. Thunder and Winter disappeared into the growing dawn.

"They go to free the woman of the wolves," Wanbli said. "Death will come to those who come between."

He took the lead as they approached the camp. They came upon a meadow of giant sage brush they could use as cover for the final approach. Knowing there would be a lookout waiting on the hill at the head of the meadow, Bren halted the group and crept ahead on his own. The air was cool with the coming morning and damp as the stars dimmed in their last moments. Clouds rolled in and were covering the last light of night. He made his way slowly up the hill, searching for the man he knew was there. Halfway up the hill, he heard a small noise at his side. He turned to see Thunder crouching in the darkness. The wolf was looking pointedly at a grouping of rock on the crest of the hill to their front.

"Thank you, friend, this would have taken much longer without your nose." Thunder broke his gaze from the rocks long enough to glance at Bren, then back to the rocks. "I'll go alone from here. Wait, and come only if you're called."

Bren went the last forty yards on his hands and knees, feeling the bite of the prairie grit on his palms. He crawled slowly, weaving his way around the rocks and sage. He kept his eyes on the rock outcropping where he knew the lookout was waiting.

He moved to his left around loose shale at the bottom of the outcropping in order to come into the rocks from behind the watcher. As he approached a large boulder, he felt the breeze change, wafting cool air over his back and into the rocks. He saw the head and shoulders of a man raise from the rocks six feet from where he crouched and knew the watcher had caught his scent. He came to his feet, heart thumping loudly as the shadowy figure knocked an arrow into his bow. He heard a muffled growl, and the dark figure spun his body, raising the bow. Bren covered the distance in a leap and brought his club smashing into the back of the lookout, between the shoulder blades. The thud of impact was the only sound as the shadowy figure dropped in a pile at his feet. Thunder hopped from the darkness between the boulders at Bren's side, his tongue hanging slack from an openmouthed grin. The wolf looked sternly at the unconscious man, a blank look in his eyes. Bren whispered, "So I owe you my life yet again, wolf. This time I'm grateful that you didn't listen to me."

He quickly tied the unconscious man's hands and feet and stuffed the toe of a spare moccasin into his mouth. *You're lucky it's a new one,* Bren thought to himself. Thunder again disappeared into the brush. Bren searched the top of the hill for any sign of a second lookout and, finding none, made his way slowly back to his father. "I found only one man and left him gagged and secured. We will have no others, I think, between us and the camp if we make a straight line."

The group made their way down the shallow draw toward the camp. They moved west in order to come into the camp over the south side of the bowl. The breeze continued to rise as they went. Clouds moved quicker over their heads with every step.

The great bear kept pace without effort or sound. The group of wolves fanned out to the left and right of the men. Wanbli moved ahead and waited in a huge cottonwood tree at the top of the bowl. He was keeping Bren appraised of the movement inside the camp. The village was making preparations for the morning that was coming, dousing fires around the edge of the camp, leaving one main fire for last. Wanbli guessed forty warriors were still afoot inside the camp. Bren grimaced as he passed this news to his father. The muffled clap of thunder boomed loud as they closed the last few yards of cover between themselves and the camp.

The group crested the top of the bowl as thunder and lightning clashed and lit the skies in the same instant. The storm was upon them, directly overhead, but no rain fell. The three men stood abreast with the bear as sheets of lightning backlighted them. The wolves fanned out to their left and right, standing stiff legged and clearly ready to fight. Suddenly a man cried out from camp, and all heads turned toward them. Shouts came from around the village in a language Bren didn't understand. Lightning turned the night to daylight as Bren's father said, "They are saying the bear has come. They're scared out of their wits." The great bear spread his arms as he stood and issued a roar that rattled Bren's teeth.

Bren lifted his war club above his head and shouted into the bowl. "My name is Bren Redhorse, I am the brother of the eagle and friend to the bear!" Bren's father repeated his words in the language of the captors. "You have taken the woman of the wolves, and we come to return her to her friends. You can stand aside, or we can take her while your women grieve over your bodies. The choice is yours, but make that choice now. I won't ask again."

Hearing these words, a warrior jumped upon a horse staked near a lodge. The man shouted, "I am Long Runner. I am a warrior of my people, and I took this woman. She is mine."

Bren looked at the man and said, "Make no mistake, warrior. This woman belongs to no man. She is her own person, but she does belong with me. She decides who she keeps company with. You would find she will never be your woman, after the way she came to be with your people. If you were truly a warrior, you would know what I say is the true way of it."

Long Runner's horse cried out in rage as the man whipped him up the bowl toward the group. Wanbli left his perch and glided silently toward the horse. At a few yards distance, he spread his wings, stopping in midair. There came a scream from the war bird that shook the ground in the village. The horse was frozen in step, and the rider was thrown to the ground like a leaf in the wind. The bird circled lazily, as if nothing had occurred. He came to perch on the head of the bear, who was standing at his full height next to Bren.

The warrior got to his feet, breathing heavily and gathering his wits. He gave Bren a look of pure hatred and began running at him. Bren stepped forward and away from his companions. He took several steps and stopped, waiting as the warrior closed the distance between them. At the last moment, Bren sidestepped the warrior, coming forward swiftly on his right. He crouched and stepped forward as his right arm flashed out quicker than thought. He slapped the man heavily in the chest with his open palm, moving into the strike. The man's feet flew to the sky as the smack of the contact reverberated. Long Runner landed on his back with a loud thump, and his air left him in a rush of noise. Bren stood and looked calmly down on the warrior who was straining soundlessly for breath that wouldn't come.

Two of the largest wolves Bren had ever seen trotted forward from the ranks behind him. They flanked Bren on either side and looked up at him for direction. "Brothers, stand and watch this man for me. Do him no harm, unless he tries to rise." The wolves took their places on each side of the downed man. One stood at his feet and one at his head. There was such menace in their stare it was apparent they waited greedily for him to move.

Everything seemed to stop, even the wind subsided. The people in the camp stood rooted in place. The clouds seemed to stand still in the sky. Bren spoke without raising his voice above a normal tone, though it carried to every ear. "We have come for the woman who you took from her family. We mean you no harm, but we will take your lives if we must. Look about you. My friends are terrible warriors to oppose. The world is changing. The circle heals. Yours is a true and ancient people, and your knowledge has a place in the healing. We need your skills. There's enough of this world for all of us to share when we live on it wisely. We can be one people."

Bren began to walk as he spoke. His father came to his side, and Airik followed. The bear towered over them all, looking down on the village people. Ben disarmed the man who called himself Long Runner, as he lay on his back. He took his bow and club and a knife from his belt. The man looked at Ben and his companions in terror, seemingly unable to speak. The bear walked with them into the camp, and the people shrank from the small group of warriors, as if to be near them was to die. They walked to the fire, turning to face the people of the village.

Bren said, "See now, the Winter wolf comes to the world and brings Thunder with her." As he pointed, the people turned as one and watched Sara emerge from a lodge across the clearing. She walked accompanied by the two wolves, Thunder at her left and Winter at her right hand. Sara went straight to Bren. She embraced him and, taking his hand, stood tall at his side.

The sun rose below the clouds and shined into the bowl of the camp as Sara spoke. "Know this, people of the northern plains. This man is the bear killer and the healer of the circle. He walks the red road into a new world. I am Sara, woman of the wolves. I belong with this man, and he belongs with me. I can forgive you your transgression because you have lived separate from the world for too long. We can live together in peace upon the earth mother, but hear my words! If you bring wrongness and war to my people again, I will rain down upon you a storm of destruction such as your people have never seen, and your warriors will be no more."

There was such fire in her eyes and her words that many of the villagers could not bear to look directly at her but were forced to look away in shame and fear. As Sara spoke, the wild wolves trotted from the rim overlooking the village, pushing aside the warriors who dare not move, with snarls and snapping jaws. Reaching Sara and Bren, they fanned out behind them. Their eyes shined in the light of the rising sun. They looked over the villagers with predatory purpose, huge bodies poised to attack at the slightest provocation.

Sara turned to Bren and showed the weariness of days with little sleep. Her cotton dress was wrinkled and worn, but she stood erect and proudly at his side. The wind blew through her blond and tangled hair. As she clung to him, she whispered, "My father and mother. My family, I didn't see them when they took me."

"Alive and well," he reassured her. "And waiting for you." He heard a sob escape her as they stood. He felt the trembling in her shoulders and was overcome with a seething and terrible anger.

Thunder broke his mood as the wolf stood in front of Sara, a pup once more. He was wagging his entire body, and his head swayed with the effort. He calmed himself and stood on hind legs, his paws lightly placed on Sara's shoulders. He placed a long, wet tongue on her cheek then dropped to her side, tilting his head up to meet her eyes. Sara knelt to the wolf and encircled his neck with trembling arms. "I thought I'd lost you forever, my friend. I knew if you lived you would bring Bren to me."

Sara reached to share the same embrace with Winter. She told Bren as she hugged them both, "She followed us the whole way to this camp. She showed herself to me in secret, after they took the hood from my head. She was telling me I wasn't alone." Sara hugged the wolf tightly as she said, "You are my beautiful sister, dear Winter wolf."

A small man with deeply wrinkled skin came forward and motioned Bren and Sara toward a lodge on the eastern edge of the village circle. Wanbli was perched on the lodge poles that flew the banner of the elk dreamer.

The bear sat on his rump in front of the open lodge door with all eyes of the village on him. He opened and closed his mouth several times, making chuffing sounds as if chewing the air. The noise echoed menacingly across the village. The wolf pack opened their mouths and seemed to be laughing at some secret joke the bear told.

The group of friends entered a warm and comfortable lodge, one very much like that of Joseph's, where Bren and Sara had sat at gather. Ben, Airik, Bren, and Sara sat on the furs at the fires edge, as did the old man. Sara's wolves refused to leave her side.

"I am Black Moccasin," he said. "I've been told, in dreams, that someone such as you would come. I was told of the bear and a man that would walk among the wild ones as family to them. I was not told of the eagle. I've spoken to the young ones of this village until my voice left me, but they're young and proud.

"The young man you bested in the field a moment ago is lost in the fear of responsibility. He leads some of the young warriors but doesn't know the road to take. It was he who led the party that stole your woman. The young men followed him out of boredom and for the glory. They've lived without many things for too long.

"I heard you speak of the healing of the circle. Most of the old ones of this village have passed, and the ancient stories are forgotten. I am the last, and few listen. I thought the dreams were speaking to me of the healing, but as I said, I am old. Seeing you walk with the bear, the wolves, and the eagle as your family, I believe my people are thinking now they should have listened more carefully to an old man."

Bren acknowledged the man's humor with a smile. "The stories are true, Grandfather, although they're being…exaggerated, as they're passed from fire to fire. I've seen strange and wonderful things. I've fought the great bear, and I've walked with his brother and the eagle as my friends. I've traveled the prairie while, it seemed to me, the spirits of the old world slowed the race of time itself and worked magic in the night sky. The circle is healing, and the earth mother is awakened as if from a long winter sleep. The people have a renewed chance to honor our mother the earth. We'll need all the power and skills that remain in the world and your people have remembered many of the old ways. They have an important place in this thing that is happening, if they choose to accept it. I'm taking this woman from your village. It's up to your warriors how that happens. Regardless of the outcome, I would like you and whatever of your people remain to come to my village when you can, and we will talk."

They stood together, and the old man led them outside. As they left the lodge, the bear stood on all fours and regarded the crowd with a clear challenge. The old man stood next to the great bear, with his hand on the giant shoulder. He addressed his people, "We come to a good time again. These warriors have come to us as messengers and friends. The circle is healing, and we will be a part of the world again. This woman was not yours to take, and they will leave with her. Those of you who wish to prevent this may try, and we will bury you without honor. I will fight beside the bear."

The village stood quietly looking at the old man. No one spoke, though several of the villagers, men and women, walked to stand beside their elder and the newcomers. Bren, Sara, Airik, and Ben followed the bear and Black Moccasin to the edge of camp.

"Thank you for your help, Grandfather. We hope to see you in our village when the snow melts," Bren said as they parted. He walked to the bear and placed his hand on the giants' shoulder. "I'm thankful for your help, brother. You'll be welcome in our village whenever you can visit."

Wanbli glided by on silent wings and spoke to Bren. "The snows are not long away, and our homes are distant. We should leave soon." The group turned back from the rim of the bowl and saw the whole village looking after them. Long Runner stood staring, sullen, at the center of the band. Bren embraced Black Moccasin before the old man started down the slope toward his lodge. Black Moccasin took Long Runner by the arm as he walked past the warrior. He turned and followed the elder into his lodge. The bear looked at Bren and walked off to lay at the lodge door of the old man.

"He will stay with the old one for a day or two. He says he hopes someone will need to be eaten." Bren glanced up at Wanbli. "He's still a bear," the eagle said, and the humor in Wanbli's warbling chuckle was clear. "I don't think the people will come to violence.

The village will gain status from this, and the old one will be venerated, as he should be. They'll begin to listen to him again. We need to hurry back now. There are travelers for us to meet on the prairie. The wolves will watch the camp for a day, to see that we are not followed." The wolves were disappearing into the prairie as they heard the words Wanbli spoke.

Ben walked at his son's side. His voice was tight in his throat as he spoke. "I've been proud of you always, but I have never seen the like of this. My son has been honored as the healer of the circle. You walk the road of a true human being, and it leads us now toward a new home and a new age of this world."

Bren answered, "I haven't healed the circle, Father. Whatever has happened on this journey has been accomplished by the work of greater spirits than mine. I wished only to return the woman I love to her parents. If anything, I've just helped to show these people the way a little. I think much more will need doing before we're done with our tasks."

Wanbli led the group to where the horses were grazing on the damp grass, in a meadow some two miles from Black Moccasin's village. Thunder's bed was taken from the horse he had ridden to make room for Sara. They started for home with the morning sun still low in the sky.

A few minutes later, Airik rode up to where Bren and Sara were riding and spoke. "There are wolves following us on every side."

Sara laughed as Bren explained, "Brother, they aren't following us, they are our company. Or more precisely, they are making sure Sara gets to where we are going safely. They'll probably stay with us for several days, maybe more. They have become quite fond of Winter and Thunder and consider Sara a mother to them all."

Airik looked from Bren to Sara as they smiled at his wondering expression

The trio saw Wanbli fly ahead of their party, and he was soon out of sight. The day went quietly and quickly as they rode. They stopped around noontime at a spring to allow Sara to bathe and clean her clothing as best she could. Afterword, as they made a lunch of the last of the dried meat, fruit, and bread, Bren listened as Sara told her story in starts and stops. He saw the fear and helplessness bubble and then drain from her as she spoke.

Sara and her family had been a day's ride from the village of her grandparents when the group of warriors met them. Sara saw her father go down under blows from several warriors, while she was grabbed from behind. The world went dark as she was blindfolded. She could still here the screams of her mother as Sara was thrown over a horse and led away. She had seen Thunder go down as he fought by her side. Her grief was overwhelming. She thought the wolf she had raised from a pup, the one she had stayed awake with through so many nights, laying alongside and coaxing to live, had been killed. She was almost sure she had seen Winter alive and well, just before her eyes were covered, and that was something to cling to.

Her captors had been very careful with her, almost kind. They kept her tied the whole distance to their camp, traveling night and day without rest for the horses or themselves. They were in camp several days and nights before Bren found them.

On the morning of their second day toward home, the travelers looked over the landscape and saw a small pack of wolves galloping toward them. Sara jumped from her horse and hit the ground running, followed by Thunder and the white wolf. They met on the prairie grass and danced and rolled. They hugged one another for many minutes, before Sara turned and walked back to her horse. Now she was surrounded by all seven of her wolves.

In the distance, they saw a small train of people on the prairie. When they got close enough to see, Bren could make out two canvas-covered wagons, with a large man driving the lead wagon. There were several armed, mounted men riding with them. They were headed north and traveling with a purpose. A hundred yards from the train, Sara could wait no longer. She urged her horse into a gallop toward the group. Bren held out his hand to stop the rest of the group, to let her ride alone. They sat their horses and watched as she shot from her horse once again and into the arms of her father and mother. The wolves danced once more around the wagon. Bren's group sat for a few moments to watch this reunion before continuing. This moment belonged to the family.

When they reached the train, Bren dismounted and joined Sara at her father's side. His head was bandaged, but he looked well otherwise. Sara's mother stood to greet him. "I brought your daughter back to you, sir. I would ask a great favor. I have loved this girl from the moment we met. I would be honored if your family would follow me to our village and allow me to make her my wife before the winter snows fall. I'm tired of waiting." He smiled as he waited for Arden's response.

Sara looked into the face of her father.

"If this is what she wishes, we will follow, of course. Try as I might, I could never keep her from something she wanted."

Sara laughed as she said, "I wish it, Father. We'll be happy, he and I. This man walks the red road, and I intend to walk that path with him."

The group set out for Bren's village, talking together and sharing the news of the last few days. Sara rode alongside Bren. They stopped at nightfall as they traveled, and Bren spoke of their mystifying ride over the prairie to Sara and her family around a campfire. All sat in rapt attention as he told the story. In the telling, Bren came to understand more clearly what Joseph and Kennon had been telling him. They traveled leisurely and arrived at the new winter village six days after their meeting on the plains.

Their impending arrival having been announced by Wanbli, the village was out in mass as they came out of the trees into Bren's meadow. Ben wasted no time spreading the word of the wedding of his son to Sara of the wolves. The ceremony was set for two days from the evening of their arrival.

Bren saw eagles everywhere. Young ones and adults were perched everywhere he looked. Wanbli informed him the young chicks were already starting to fledge, taking their first tentative flights. It wouldn't be many days before they were flying longer distances and then hunting on their own. Several eagle pairs and many of the young had already made their intentions clear. They would stay in the village and in the mountain through the winter.

As Bren approached his cabin, he stopped short, realizing something looked amiss. Something was different. Walking closer, he discovered what it was. His windows had glass in them. Real glass windows. Apparently, the glass panes he ordered at gather had come early. Looking into the faces of the assembled crowd, he saw grins and sheepish looks on several faces. Don spoke up and confessed.

"Your windows came while you were away, and not wanting them to sit idle to be damaged, several of us took the liberty to put them in. I hope the work will be satisfactory. They sealed and trimmed in quite well!"

Bren could only say, "Thank you, Uncle. Thank you, everyone. I'm grateful, and I'm sure the work is very well done!"

Bren saw to it that Sara and her parents were settled into the cabin after he took care of Stone Foot and the other horses. Bren and Sara would, of course, sleep separate while the village prepared for the wedding. He settled into the lodge behind his cabin. Sara with her parents in the cabin that would soon belong to the both of them.

After they were settled, he showed them around the cabin. He pointed out the details he was most proud of as they looked. Sara and her mother both marveled at the skill with which the cabin had been finished. Arden made sure to tell Bren what a fine job he had done.

"The logs are tight, nary a draft of air will get between them, I judge. You would have a future in building if you chose!" he told a beaming Bren.

After Sara and her parents were comfortable in the cabin, he and Sara walked together through the village.

Everywhere they went, they were greeted by smiles and pleasant words from Bren's village. Seela called out to them as they passed her lodge. "Bren, have you heard, the people are calling this the village of the eagles now. Many of the great birds will stay for the winter. The children and all the people are pleased, nephew. You've done well."

"Auntie Seela, the children have done most all the work themselves, along with the parents that have taken up their chores while they fed their charges. I can take no credit nor any blame either, mind you," Bren told her as they passed. He turned and grinned at her as they walked toward the mountain.

They toured the caves and the baths, and Sara was taken aback by the chance to have a hot bath anytime she wanted. Even in the deepest months of winter. "Wait 'til my mother sees this! She'll want to live in these caves!"

Bren showed Sara the place where he had killed the bear. Sara held close to Bren's arm as they came upon the spot. As they walked, they talked quietly about how they would pass time in the winter. Sara told him Aria had promised to teach her the skills of tanning and quillwork. Bren showed her the spot where he would build a barn in the spring, where the horses would stay.

Sara was very pleased with the kennel he had built the wolves. It looked exactly like the one at her parents' home, she told him. She showed him the sled and harness she brought from gather and helped him unload it from his father's wagon. She spoke with joyful anticipation of how they would teach the dogs to pull, through the woods and over the plains, once the winter snow was deep enough.

In the morning, Sara's father pulled a wagon up to the front door of Bren's cabin. He uncovered a huge black cast-iron stove in the back of the wagon. Sara said it looked very much like her mother's. Airik, Ben, and several others walked from the village and helped them unload the stove and carry it into the cabin. Bren spent the morning cutting a hole in the roof and stacking the vent pipes through the hole. He made it weather tight with pine pitch and tin flashing.

Sara and her mother made the first dinner on the stove for her family and for Bren's parents and sister. Bren, his father, and his soon-to-be father-in-law sat on the porch and watched the horses in the meadow.

Sara's father spoke of how well he thought the meadow would do planted in alfalfa, for the horses to eat in winter. He told Bren he could expect two or three cuttings a year, if it was watered right. Arden questioned whether there were streams or rivers close to the village. He asked of their depth and width and if they ran strong through the summer.

"There are several streams, almost small rivers really, that answer those needs within a day's ride of this village. After the wedding and when you are ready to leave for home, we can ride through the area, and I'll show them to you," Ben told him. "Why do you ask of these streams?" Ben asked, with a knowing look in his eye.

"Ellie and I will miss having our daughter in our home. We've thought we would like to be closer to her as she makes her new life in this place. There will probably be grandchildren, you know, sooner or later. We can't miss that. I've always wanted to build a sawmill, and I think this might be a good place for such a thing. It would be a small mill, built for local use only. I don't want to cut down your forests or ruin these lands. Only, of course, if we would be accepted here."

Ben reached out and took the man's hand as he told him, "You will always be accepted here, Arden."

Sara called from inside the cabin that dinner was ready, and they should come to the table. The two families that would soon be one sat at the long log plank table that Bren had made. They shared buffalo steaks, wild turkey, corn, potatoes, and bread that Sara had made fresh from her new oven. She beamed as she sat between Bren and her mother, to share the first meal in her new home.

They shared wine and coffee after the meal and spoke about what Sara's father had spoken of with Ben. Thora came to stand behind Ellie and put one arm around her in acceptance. They would have to spend the winter at home, of course, Arden said. He needed to sell the farm and make arrangements for the delivery of the saw-mill pieces.

Sara was delighted beyond words for her parents' plans. She pulled Bren aside and whispered to him, "Is this all right with you?" concern showing in her expression. "Did you know you would be marrying my whole family when you chose me?"

"Sara, I didn't dream that you would come with all of this," he told her honestly and watched her attempt to hide her crestfallen eyes. Bren took her in his arms and felt the warmth of her against his chest. "I would do anything to make you happy. Your mother and father are good people, and I will be forever grateful to them for their gift of you to the world. I would welcome your whole village if that's what it took to have you as my wife!" Sara turned in to his embrace, and their mouths met gently.

The two mingled families and their friends continued into the night in conversation and laughter. They spoke of the gather just a few weeks past and gathers of years gone. They told stories of their families and, in the telling, came to know each other as an extended family. They drifted off to their beds in singles and pairs, and finally Bren had to take himself away to his lodge. He said good night to his parents as they left for home and said a quiet good night to Sara at the door of their future home.

"One more night alone and the rest of our nights will be together," she promised him after a gentle kiss.

Bren hardly found sleep that night. His mind was full with the happenings of this past year. It seemed to him everything had happened so quickly. Time had rushed by him like a swollen spring stream since the night he and Sara sat with old Joseph in his lodge, smoking the ancient pipe. He felt as if the hands of the spirits had pulled him through the events of the past weeks.

He talked for a moment with Wanbli outside the lodge, watching the stars in the sky. The great bear constellation was out tonight, glowing brightly over the people of the village. He thought of how the bear had affected his life, one way and another. The spirit of the bear had almost taken his life and then stood beside him on the hill, outside the village of the people who had taken his woman. Wanbli had shown him the way to her and shown him the way of so many other things as well. He wondered as he lay in the furs of his lodge, for the last time as a single man, would he be able to lead the people effectively in the days ahead? Could he be brave enough? Could he be smart enough to help guide the people into the days ahead? As this thought crossed his mind, he heard a reassuring warble. "We are together, friend. We can do what has to be done."

As he drifted into his dreams, he felt the presence of the old ones who had gone before him. It seemed they whispered the ancient songs into his mind from the past. Words that brought him strength drifted in the crisp night air. The rustle of the eagle's wings as he and his mate settled on the oak branch above his lodge brought him peace, and at long last, he slept.

Bren awoke as the first rays of the sun brought steam from the walls of the lodge. The golden light filtered between the lodge poles, bringing with it a sense of quiet peace. The sky was leaden in the north with low clouds fighting the sun for possession of the sky. There would be snow soon.

As he lay in his robes, he could clearly hear a song of peace floating through the pines on the cold morning breeze. Bren saw a shadow approach and heard a scratching on the lodge door. He pulled the door to the side, and there stood his sister with breakfast on a wooden plank. Aria served her brother a breakfast of freshly roasted elk, eggs, and coffee, with bread still warm from the baking ovens. She sat and spoke with him for a few minutes, asking if he was nervous about the coming day. She giggled as he told her he was, a little.

Halfway through the meal, she left him alone to eat but returned shortly with the moose-hide clothing she made him for the gather. The pants and shirt were cleaned and smoothed. The quillwork glowed in the early morning light. She had made him a pair of high-top moccasins decorated to match the clothing. He knew he should be nervous but felt more relaxed as he thought about the coming ceremony. He was ready to be the husband of the woman of the wolves.

A Wedding in Elk Meadow

As Bren dressed himself, Joseph scratched quietly on the door of the lodge and entered. The old man carried the now familiar ancient pipe bag in his left hand and a buffalo robe over his right shoulder, dragging the tail on the ground. The bag contained the pipe of his people. Joseph laid out the robe hair side down and pointed out to Bren the pictographs of the history of the plains people painted there. Years almost beyond counting were remembered on the soft surface. Joseph handed the pipe to Bren, telling him he was passing the honor, as keeper of the pipe, to one who had earned the right.

He sat by the fire and motioned the young man to his side. Joseph lit the pipe and smoked quietly for a moment before passing it back to Bren. He gave Bren his blessing in quiet ancient words. Bren took the offered pipe reverently from the wizened hands of his true friend. He held it, sitting quietly for a moment, then smoked. The strong mixture sent the message it carried deep into his soul and up to the heavens as Bren exhaled.

Bren and Joseph sat and smoked for a short time, until there came still another shadow to the lodge door. Aria was there, waiting to escort her brother to his wedding ceremony. Bren stepped into the cold, clean light of the morning and was greeted by the shining eyes of most of the village. His people lined the path from his lodge toward the center of their new village. The great birds were there also, filling the trees around the path.

Thora took her son's arm, with her husband, Ben, next to her. Airik was there, accompanied by the hunters of the village. Aria fell into step between her father and brother and took both their arms. The drums and flutes of the village played in a quiet, gentle rhythm that touched Bren's heart.

They made their way to the meadow where Bren had taken the elk. It seemed like a long time ago, though only weeks had passed. The meadow grass had been kept clipped short by the horses. Crimson flax and blue lupine, tall spires of snow-white bear grass, and purple elk thistle poked their heads from the lawn, as if waiting to take their part in the ceremony.

In the middle of the meadow, an arbor had been built of willow and covered with sweetgrass and the small white flowers growing at the creek's edge. He could smell the perfume of the burning sage and sweetgrass. Bren caught sight of Sara as he turned to take his place in front of the arbor. She was standing behind him at the meadow's edge. She wore a snow-white antelope hide dress that hung perfectly to just above her ankles and white moccasins beaded in white, pale blue, and dusty pink. Her hair hung almost to her waist in otter-wrapped braids. The flowers in her hair were the same small white ones that the arbor held. She glowed, even more beautiful than Bren had seen before. He was stunned, again, at how easily this young woman could steal his breath away.

Joseph stepped to the altar and began to speak in the ancient tongue of the plains people. He told the story of the circle of life in the world and the red road. He told how the old ones spoke of a day when the buffalo would return, the circle would heal, and the people of all the nations would unite again to live in peace. He told of how the journey began for Bren and for Sara long before they were born.

Bren felt a peace come over him as Joseph's words rang true in his heart and filled him with voices of the ancient ones. He felt the blood in his heart warm as Joseph began the wedding prayer. He heard himself answer the promising questions as if from a distance.

He turned toward Sara and saw her shining eyes as she quietly answered the promising questions in her musical, lilting voice.

Finally, Joseph asked the two young people to turn toward their families, and he introduced them for the first time as a married couple.

The sun broke through to a patch of blue in the clouds and shined on the meadow. A light powder snow began to fall, and the snowflakes reflected the light like tiny torches. The eagles lifted to the sky in unison. They circled the meadow four times, singing to the people below.

As Wanbli led them toward the south, Bren heard his friend's familiar voice in his head.

"The snow is here. You will have company for the cold months, but I will see you from time to time. Remember that we walk the red road together, my friend. The circle is healed, and we have done it together, your people and mine."

Sara looked at Bren, wonder clear in her expression. She was hearing Wanbli's words. She looked toward the birds as they ascended into the clouds and said aloud, "Our home is open to you always, Wanbli, you are our family now."

After the ceremony, Bren and Sara held to each other as they were escorted by the whole village, laughing and talking into the heart of their new home. The people had been busy most of the night, setting a huge feast in the meeting hall. There were roasted turkeys, buffalo steaks, and buffalo hump roasts. There was a firepit built outside the building, and a whole elk had been roasting over the low fire for most of the night.

The tables were filled with breads and cakes. Every kind of dish that Bren could remember from his childhood and many that he couldn't were stacked everywhere. Sara's family had helped as well, and her favorite foods were there. There were wines, coffee, and teas in abundance.

The eagles were represented by Wanbli and Tayla, who were perched on either side of and behind the head table. Bren and Sara were assisted to their seats by White Calf at the head of the table. Sara's wolves, Thunder and Winter, Smoke and her young ones, paraded into the hall and lay behind the head table. The immediate families were on either side, and the village filled in down the huge table. So many were in attendance that the party spilled to the outside, where tables were set under arbors of lodge pole pine covered with pine branches. Everyone sat to eat, except the young people, who would serve before they sat.

Joseph stood to speak, and as he walked to the front of the table, the whole village became silent. The old man stood between the eagles. Thunder and Winter stood and walked on either side of Joseph and sat close to him looking out at the crowd. He spoke of the beginning of a new time on the earth. He talked about the healing of the circle and the coming together of the people. He spoke about the joining together of the two fine young people who sat at the head of the table and what they meant to the village and all the people scattered across the nation of this place the ancient ones called turtle island.

Bren took Sara's hand as Joseph asked the people to remember they were at the dawning of a new beginning for the earth. To listen to the old ones and learn from them so the earth was not spoiled again like it had been in the past. He ended his speech with a prayer in the old language of the plains, to place a blessing on the union of Bren and Sara and all the people of the nation.

White Calf followed Joseph to his seat and made sure he was served before she sat next to Airik. The party drank, ate, and talked through the afternoon into evening. There was music and dancing, and many gifts were placed on a table placed for that purpose next to the entrance of the hall.

The eagles and their extended families were fed raw meat by the children, who had learned during the summer to take care of their young ones. Many of which sat on the shoulders of the children as they went about their tasks.

Sara's wolves were fed in a like manner. They were approached reverently by the young villagers, thrilled at being chosen for the task of taking care of the pack during this wedding feast. They took this duty so seriously, in fact, that Sara had to quietly ask them to stop feeding the wolves after the second huge helping. The younger pups looked at her wistfully as the third serving was taken away.

Bren and Sara rose to dance, and the wolves moved to the wall to watch. The flutes and violins played a soft, slow tune as they came together and moved slowly around the dance floor, beaming at one another.

The music stopped, and Airik rose to ask White Calf to dance. She placed her hand on his shoulder and pointed to the wolves who had joined Bren and Sara. White Calf spoke to the musicians in the old language, and a drumming began slow and quiet. The flutes joined in an ancient melody that intensified and brought to mind the wind in the trees and the sun on the plains.

The wolves began to dance around Sara and Bren. They moved with a sensuous, predatory grace that held their audience spellbound. The wolves wove their way in and out, around one another, and around Bren and Sara.

Sara looked at Bren with tears in her eyes and said to him, "They are accepting you into the pack! They are making you a member of their family, a binding not even death can break. We need to dance with them to secure the knot they weave." As she spoke, Sara came closer to Bren and began a slow, liquid movement in the center of the wolves. Bren had no choice. He was swept up, not against his will, but involuntarily into the mystic counterpoint of the movements.

He had no idea how long they danced, but the music stopped after a time. He felt the heat radiating from his body and saw the flush on Sara's cheeks. Her hair had fallen to cover a bit of her face, and her eyes were smoking with a fire Bren had not seen before. He held her head gently between his hands and brought her mouth to his in a kiss he was afraid he could not stop.

"Are you all right?" he asked her, his voice husky with pent emotion.

"I need you. I've never needed you so badly," she said. Every muscle in her body was tense. The need in her eyes a beautiful thing to see.

A moment later he realized they were not alone and remembered the crowd. He felt the presence of the wolves and looked down to see the whole pack surrounded them, their muzzles side by side and their noses pressed against his thighs and Sara's. The whole room was silent and staring at them in confusion and wonder. Bren dropped to the floor and was encircled by the great hairy heads of his new family.

Sara came to a knee as well, to join her husband in the enveloping love of her pack. Bren thanked them aloud for their acceptance. He was almost overcome yet again with a wave of love and affection emanating from each of the wolves.

They stayed in the embrace for a moment, and then Sara stood, sending them back to the wall with a smile and a gesture of her hand. They bounced and pranced as they went. The younger pups affectionately mouthing each other's muzzles. Thunder and Winter looked regal and proud. Bren looked out at the company still seated around the table and saw on their faces looks of amazement and pride. The music started again, violins this time, drums and flutes and guitars joined in. Bren's voice rose above the music for a moment as he said, "Let's dance!"

This time when Airik rose and took White Calf's hand, she stood with him, and they walked to the dance floor. Bren's parents and Sara's, Aria and Cade took to the floor as well. Bren and Sara sat and looked at each other while the dancers spun elegantly across the room.

Sara smiled at her husband and told him, "I hoped they would accept you in this manner but had no idea they would choose that moment for it. It was a perfect thing, don't you think?"

"I have no words to tell you the feelings flowing through me as they started the dance. It is as if they were projecting themselves into my heart. It was even more intimate than when the eagles first spoke to me. I felt overwhelmed with acceptance and a love that went beyond a kinship."

"That's the way of the wolf, husband." Sara grinned at him, and her glacier-deep eyes flashed darkly sensual once more. "From this day forward, you belong to me...to us, and we belong to you. Heart, body, and soul, we are one pack. Not time, nor distance, nor any circumstance in this world or another can separate us."

Bren held her close to him and told her in a whisper of emotion, "Sara, I'm humbled and grateful for this gift you give to me. Not just the friendship of the wolves, but this love I feel for you. It charges me with life and blesses me with a spirit I can't explain."

"Bren Redhorse, you've made me your wife. You are my husband and the leader of my pack. That's all the explanation I need. I feel a love for you that knows no bounds and no end. I feel love from you that will take us through this life together."

"I know what you say is true, Sara, but you need to know this also. This pack must be led by the both of us, together. I meant what I said in the village of the eastern tribe, you belong with me, not to me. I'll cherish your life forever, but never claim to hold sway over it. We are one, to walk the path of true human beings together, and we will make the choices this life holds for us together."

"Yes, husband, that's the way of the wolf and the way of our family from this day forward. Let's dance with our village. I have energy to burn, before I do something to embarrass us both."

They danced, laughed, and feasted the afternoon away into early evening. It seemed that every person in the village stopped to congratulate them as they rested between dances.

White Calf and Aria sat them down near the end of the evening and showed them their gifts one at a time. Their families and the whole village had given them many fine wedding gifts. From time to time, someone in the crowd would speak out loud, "My daughter made those mugs for you, Sara," or "I found that pot at gather and thought of your new cabin, Bren."

Aria made for Sara a pair of thick elk-hide pants and shirt, beaded sparingly in light blue and white. She explained the beading would hold through the hard work of winter much better than quill-work would. There was a matching coat with no beading but lined with fur. The set was completed with a hood trimmed in otter fur and a pair of lined winter moccasins as well as a heavy pair of leather mittens.

For her brother, she had made a similar set of winter clothing of soft, thick moose hide, also with warm winter moccasins and mittens. "For pulling that new sled through the trails all winter," she told him.

Sara hugged Aria with tears on her cheeks. "I feel so blessed, Aria, to have been accepted by you and your family."

"We love you, Sara of the wolves. I always wanted a sister," Aria answered as her eyes welled.

From Bren's parents, they were given a set of cast-iron pots and pans they recognized from one of the shops at gather. Sara's parents gave them a small wagon that could be pulled on wheels in the summer months and a pair of sled rails that could replace the wheels in winter.

It seemed every villager gifted them with something. There were blankets of warm buffalo, thick cotton quilts and bedding. There were utensils of every sort for making a home. Sara was even given a beautifully made bow of Osage wood and a dozen arrows. Sara picked up the bow, in awe of its construction, and felt its perfect balance. Don said to her from the back of the room, "When you're ready to shoot, Sara, come find me. I'll have you shooting better than Bren within a fortnight!" The crowd laughed as Sara accepted her new uncle's challenge. Each person called out to them as their gift was shown so that Bren and Sara could give their thanks without worry of leaving someone out.

The afternoon wore into twilight and came the time that Sara spoke quietly to Bren. It was time for them to go home. Bren's eyes widened as Sara looked at him with a smoky innocence and raised eyebrows. His grin back at her spoke volumes, and she laughed out loud.

Her parents had moved their things into the lodge set for that purpose, next to Bren's parents. They would leave for home the next day. Bren's cabin was theirs alone.

They forced themselves to make their way around the hall and speak to everyone in groups or singly, to thank them for the gifts and for the gift of spending their wedding day with them. The whole of the village knew it was time for them to leave, as they had started lining the pathway toward the cabin as soon as the wedding couple started circling the hall giving their thanks.

Bren and Sara stepped outside and into a light snowfall. They smiled as they saw the procession lining the path. They took their first steps and were joined from behind by their immediate families. The wolves formed a wedge to the front and were wagging and prancing as they went. An eagle arose from seemingly each tree they passed and joined the convocation in the sky over the couple.

Belonging

A distance from the cabin, the wedding party dropped back and gave them their privacy for the night. Except, of course, for the wolves who followed the couple to the door and stood expectantly, looking up at them both. Bren said to them, "I would appreciate if you would all sleep outside tonight and guard the cabin from mischief makers." Thunder huffed a few times, and the pack dispersed into the twilight shadows.

They walked into the warm and inviting great room of the cabin. Someone had taken the time during the party to make sure there were fires in each of the fireplaces. The table was set for two, and there were platters of meat, bread, and other dishes as well. There were bottles of wine and mugs also at the ready. A dozen candle lamps glowed through the great room and into the main bedroom.

On a cupboard next to the stove sat a basket of eggs and one of breads for the morning. Bren and Sara marveled at the thoughtfulness of their friends and family as they made their way through their new home and toward the bedroom. The fire there made the room comfortable, and the bed was turned down. The bedclothes were of cotton, and they recognized them as the gifts they had seen just a while ago in the hall. A beautiful star quilt in browns and reds topped off the bed. There were real feather pillows tucked at the headboard. The first Bren had ever seen.

Bren left to blow out the candles in the great room. He climbed the ladder to the loft above the front of the great room, to make certain they were alone. Satisfied, he made his way around the cabin, snuffing the light from the room. All that was left was the fire in the front, which he left to die in its own course. When he returned to the back bedroom, Sara was standing next to the bed and looking at him with wonderful intent in her glacier-green eyes. She was holding up her dress with one hand. The other she held out to Bren. As he crossed the floor to her, she dropped the dress. Once more, and not for the last time on this night, she took his breath away. Her hair hung loose around her face and down her back. Her eyes glowed in the lamplight with a dusky innocence that almost stopped his heart.

He took a moment to shed his shirt and pants before he joined her next to the bed. She gently put her palms on his chest and whispered to him, "I have a confession to make to you, Bren. Two actually." That stopped him in his tracks. He could feel her warm breath against his cheek, and Bren could feel her body tremble slightly as she continued. "First, I have never been with a man before. I know you've been with other girls, and it makes no matter to me. You are mine now and forever. I know how everything works, believe me, but I don't have the experience you have. Secondly, I have spoken to Lanis, and she gave me herbs to drink so that we might not have a child until we're ready. She assured me there will be no permanent change, and I sought the advice of other women I trust as well."

Bren put his arms on hers and looked into her eyes as he spoke. "You're right in everything you said. You've thought about this I think more than I have. I should have been thinking more about how you might feel, and for that, I'm sorry, Sara. I've been with other girls before but never a woman and never someone I have loved. Sara, I'm yours now and forever, and nothing can ever change the love I feel for you. How this love could grow stronger I can't imagine, but I know it will. What I said at gather is as true for me now as it was then. Your body is your decision, and I'm happy you spoke to Lanis. If you choose to have children, I'm here for you. If you choose not to have children, I'll support your decision as well. We have plenty of years together to decide about children and much hard work to do. Now is a time to get to know each other even better than we do. We'll learn to think and act as one." He felt her relax against him as he spoke. As he finished his thoughts, her mouth came to his, and she pulled him into the kiss.

He lifted her gently onto the bed and lay down beside her slim, smooth body. She reached out to him, and they melted together, kissing and touching for a long while. Sara became more and more insistent, until she pulled him on top of her body. He looked into her eyes, and he told her, "This is going to hurt at first, you know."

"I'm aware of what will happen," she told him, but he could see apprehension in her eyes. "I've felt pain before. I'm more afraid of disappointing you than the pain."

Bren pulled her closer to him still and said, "Oh no, Sara girl. I'm quite sure you could never disappoint me in whatever you do."

"I've waited long enough to have you join with me, Bren. We have all night to ease the pain and the rest of our lives to practice." Her insistence grew as she grabbed the hair on his head with one hand and guided him into herself with her other, and Bren was through thinking for a while.

They lay together after this first time, speaking softly about what had just happened and then both fell asleep. Bren was startled awake sometime later with a tap on his chest. Sara leaned over him on one arm with her hair tented over his face. She whispered a single word into his mouth, "Again." And so they did and yet again.

In the small hours of the night, Bren awoke to the soft rhythm of her breathing close beside him. He lay in the darkness of their home, lighted only by the embers of the fire across the room. He was completely relaxed in the bed, thinking of how lucky he was to have this life. Softly she rolled toward him and laid her leg on top of his. She gently squirmed closer to him and began kissing his chest. "Are you awake?" she whispered to him.

They awoke wrapped together, as the sun's light began to peek over the edge of the earth, into the windows of their bedroom. *Our bedroom,* he thought. It astonished him that he should be lying next to this beautiful young woman. His thoughts again went to how lucky he was to be alive in this time, to have this woman to share it with. Her breathing changed, and she popped up on an elbow again. Her hair was everywhere, and he reached for it, running it through his fingers. She looked at him in such a childlike manner that he was shocked for a moment, and then her countenance changed.

Her eyes became cauldrons of fire, and her mouth opened. "This will be the first full day of our marriage," she said to him. "Let's start it right, shall we, Bear Killer?" He laughed out loud as she rolled on top him.

Hours later, Bren got up to start the fires in the house. A light snow was falling again, making the world a soft and quiet sanctuary. Sara sat up in bed and told him she would start the fire across the room, while he tended the one in the great room. He watched her slip from the bed and walk to the fire on cat feet. Laying there watching her, he felt he could stay in this one spot forever.

He threw back the covers and slipped on his pants as he went to the fire. By the time the flames were dancing in the front fireplace, she was out and building a fire in the stove. She had pulled on a simple red-and-white cotton dress, and he could see her shape outlined through the material as she closed the stove.

He was staring as she finished, stood up, and turned toward him. She smiled at him through her rumpled hair as she realized what he was doing. She pointedly raised her eyebrows and told him "I like this marriage thing a lot!" as she giggled impishly. "Shall we eat first, though?" Bren laughed as he sat at the table and watched her make ready the coffeepot and set it on the stove. He marveled at her graceful movement. She could make even the most mundane task an enticing dance. She moved to drop some of last night's elk steaks in a skillet to heat, and he was awed by the slender length of her legs below the dress.

While the food was cooking, she walked to the bedroom and came back wearing short moccasins and the winter coat he had bought her at gather.

"Watch the eggs, please, I'll be back in a moment."

"You're not going out in the snow in that dress?" he asked her.

"I'm a mountain girl now." She turned and smiled at him as she closed the door. Bren dutifully stood and walked to the stove.

They ate breakfast leisurely, sitting before the fire in the great room of the cabin. Sara brought Thunder and Winter inside with her when she returned, and they lay on the buffalo rug just behind her and Bren, accepting small bits of meat or bread with practiced ease.

Thunder and Winter had become used to sleeping under a roof from time to time, to protect and be close to Sara. All the wolves really preferred not to be indoors, although they had learned to sleep under the cover of the kennel in the coldest months. They made their home in Bren's new kennel quickly enough, choosing spots on the straw-covered floor.

Bren walked to the outhouse, while Sara cleaned up their breakfast. When he returned, she was not in the great room. Both wolves raised their heads and looked at him as he passed. Winter sleepily thumped her tale against the floor twice then snuggled into the buffalo hair.

He entered the bedroom and found Sara sitting on the edge of the bed surrounded by the buffalo blanket. Her golden honey hair was brushed and hanging down over her breasts. Her smile sent a warmth through Bren's core that staggered him as he dropped his clothes in a pile at the foot of their bed.

They spent the rest of the morning in bed, talking and sleeping. It was late afternoon when Bren was awakened by the calling of his name. It took a moment for him to realize what he was hearing. Airik was in the yard of the cabin, calling out to him. Bren put on pants and pulled a shirt over his head as he walked toward the door.

Thunder and Winter were both standing quietly at the door and waited to the side as Bren opened it to look out. Bren saw Airik standing several yards from the front door, with Smoke and the young wolves pointedly blocking his way. Sara stuck her head around the door and smiled at the scene.

"Smoke, let him pass," she said, and the wolves complied. They broke their line to give Airik just enough space to pass between them.

"Next time I'll bring meat," he said as he approached the door, with the wolves close behind. Bren stood in the door with no thought of allowing Airik entry to the cabin.

"What do you want, brother?" he asked, with an agitated expression. Airik came up short of the door and looked sheepishly at the both of them.

"My apologies for bothering you this afternoon. Sara, your parents are leaving within the hour and thought not to bother you. They will camp at the creek five miles east and leave early tomorrow for home. I thought you might like to know since winter will soon close the traveling roads, and we won't see them until spring."

"Airik, thank you. I would hate to have missed them. I'll be out in a moment to say goodbye. Please, would you delay them until I get there?"

"Of course, Sara. Again, I'm sorry to interrupt your...your day," he said with a huge grin as he turned to leave.

"Airik." Sara stopped him with his sweetly spoken name, and he turned to her once again. "It won't help, you know."

He looked at her perplexed as he asked, "What won't help, Sara?"

"Bringing the meat," she told him, returning his grin. "If they don't want you to pass, you will not pass."

Smoke poked Airik in the small of his back with her muzzle as he turned to go. She chuffed loud enough for all three to hear. Sara giggled as Bren closed the door on Airik's retreating back.

"I love those wolves," Bren said as he laughed, and they moved to get dressed.

"He is a good friend to you, you know," Sara told him as he found his moccasins.

"Yes, he is a thoughtful friend and very nosey."

In moments, Bren and Sara were headed to his parents' lodge, with seven wolves traipsing around them. Sara's parents had stayed the night in the extra lodge, not wanting to intrude by staying too close to Bren's cabin.

The wagons were ready to go, as were the mounted escort of Arden's friends who had met them on the prairie after Sara's ordeal. They stayed for the wedding as well and were welcomed by the village. Bren spoke to each one of them, thanking them for their time and trouble. One of the men was the young blacksmith who had taken such good care of Bren's horses at gather.

He told Bren of his wish to return with Arden and Ellie in the spring and set up his forge near Arden's sawmill.

"I'm sure you'll be accepted and do well, Oren," Bren said. "Many people have commented on the work you did on my family's horses. Stone Foot has never run so well as he does with iron shoes. I'd be willing to bet you'll stay busy when you get back."

Sara pulled her mother aside and was speaking to her quietly, as Bren busied himself with the rest of the group. He hugged Arden, who was looking sheepish, and told him to hurry back in the spring. The big man thanked him again for saving his daughter and for the hospitality of his village.

"We're family now, sir. Please be at ease about Sara. I'll take good care of your daughter. That is, if these wolves allow me to," he said, grinning.

"We are family, yes," Arden echoed. "That being the case, I would be pleased to have you call me by my name, at least."

"Thank you, Arden. Travel safely home and return as quickly as you can. We'll all be watching for you come the spring."

He hugged his father-in-law again, and then Sara took his place. With tears in her eyes, she said goodbye to her father. The wolves encircled them both, trying hard to be part of the hugging. Arden went to one knee and spoke a few quiet words to both Thunder and Winter before walking to the wagon.

Bren approached his new mother-in-law and wrapped her in his arms, saying goodbye and safe travels. She pulled back from him just enough to look up into his face and told him, "I'm very proud to call you son. I'm also proud of the choice my daughter has made. I know she'll be well with you and build a fine life. I promise to you we won't be a bother when we return."

"You couldn't be a bother, Ellie. I look forward to the spring and helping you both build that sawmill. You'll be welcome in our cabin until you have a suitable home."

Ben mounted his hunter and made ready to leave. "I'll show them the creek five miles east. We'll see if it might suit his purposes come the spring. They will want to be off early in the morning, and I'll be home shortly after," he told the group.

The wolf pups followed the wagons and horses across the meadow and through the stone wall that hid the village from the prairie. Soon they came sprinting back, looking at Sara and sniffing in the direction of the departed wagons. "We're staying here, sillies." Sara smiled at them. "This is our home now. Our pack is together, and Mother and Father will be back soon after the snow leaves." The pups seemed to accept her words and scampered off to play and explore.

"Sara and I should get back to the cabin," Bren said to the group. "It looks like more snow and cold is to come after noon. I want to start the fires in the cabin before it begins to fall."

"Yes, you'll want to start those fires, won't you," Airik teased.

Bren gave him a withering scowl as everyone, except Bren, broke out in laughter. In a menacing tone he said, "Bring meat next time, Airik. Our wolves will be waiting on your return. But for now, let Sara and I make fires in the cabin, and we will meet in the caves for a dip in the pools. Is that acceptable to everyone?" With affirmations from White Calf, Aria, and Airik, he took Sara's hand and walked away. They both turned, smiling and waving to the crowd as they made their way back home.

The evening did turn cold as the sun went down, and Sara worried aloud after her parents and their small company. "This snow will melt and the sun will return before winter settles in. My father wouldn't have allowed them to leave if this was a trail-closing storm, Sara. We have at least two weeks of sunshine coming and going before winter settles on our village." Sara's fears were calmed, and they each chose a fireplace in which to build a fire.

In moments they were finished with the chore and making their way to the baths in the caves. Sara carried a satchel with soaps and brushes and two cloth towels wrapped inside. She gave Bren a towel when he told her he'd never seen such a thing. He was used to sitting on a rock and drying in the sun or brushing off the water with his hands. "These will be very popular items when the village sees them, Sara. How many of them do you have?"

"I have a half dozen at home and these three. Mother saw them at gather and thought they would be useful. There are many things commonplace in the east that are not available here, Bren."

"We are a simple people, Sara. We live fairly simple lives on the plains. I hope you'll be able to be comfortable here." Bren was starting to worry that his people were a bit too simple for this eastern girl. One more thing he hadn't thought of before now.

She stopped in the path and looked at Bren with smoldering eyes. "I'm a farm girl raised in the way of the country, plainsman." Her golden hair swirled in the breeze around her face, and her eyes flashed with fire. "I've gone without more than a few times. I made do with what I have or can find in the woods for my whole life. I am no town girl, with fancy dresses and tea at noon. If I'd known a simple cloth towel would set you to wondering, I'd have left them on the farm."

Bren grinned at her sheepishly and pulled her close to him with one arm. "I beg pardon, farm girl. You're like no one I've met before, and I want you to be happy with my people. I'm beginning to realize that in many ways, we're learning each other's ways as we go. And... if you please, farm girl, don't take my towel before I have a chance to try it on for size."

Sara grinned back at him as they entered the caves. They were met by Aria and White Calf, who told them Airik had gone ahead to the men's side of the bathing pools.

"The men and women are separate?" Sara sounded crestfallen, and White Calf giggled.

"There are both men's and women's caverns, and there are several smaller rooms that can be used by a family or a couple." She said with a wiggle of her brow. "You will accompany us this afternoon for the purpose of telling us all about married life. Bren can go meet Airik and tell him all he knows about how to be a husband."

Bren looked at White Calf with a shocked expression, trying hard not to blush. The girls giggled louder, and Sara kissed him soundly.

"Go find Airik, Bear Killer. I have stories to tell, and this may take a while. Please, though, don't leave without me?"

The girls continued to giggle as they walked away, following the cave wall toward the baths. Bren continued to blush, wondering what stories his new wife would tell. He found Airik in their usual bathing spot, folded his clothes on the wooden bench, and slowly lowered his body into the hot water. The thick, wet air felt good in his lungs. The steam coming off the pool began to relax his muscles as he sat back against the walled edge.

He could feel the stare he was getting from Airik. He closed his eyes and leaned his head back against the rock wall. A slow, contented smile spread across his face.

"So?" Airik said.

"So, what? The hot water feels very good!" was Bren's answer, eyes still closed.

"So how is married life?"

"I've been married slightly more than a whole day, Airik. She's a wonderful woman."

"We all know she's a wonderful woman. How did the night go?" Airik pushed.

"Really, brother? You want me to tell you how it is in bed with her?"

Airik defended himself, "You know as well as I do that's what the girls are talking about as they bathe, Bren. Sara is telling them every last thing about last night."

"Well, then you should go join the women in their bath. Better yet, ask Sara to tell you the story," Bren said as his smile grew across his face. "Right now, I'm going to soak myself, relax, and regain my strength!" Airik smacked water at him, leaned back against the wall, and was silent.

Almost an hour later, Sara walked into the men's bath wrapped in a towel, her hair almost dry and shining straight down her back. She was humming a tune from their wedding party as she walked through the steam. Airik started to stand and then thought better of it, instead, trying to get as low into the water as he could. The whole time his eyes were locked on Sara.

She bent to Bren, whose eyes were still closed, and whispered in his ear. "Bear Killer, I'm done with my bath. The girls say they want to bring dinner to our home, but it will take an hour or more to prepare. Shall we go home and…wait for our dinner?"

Bren stood and walked to his towel and clothes. All this time, Airik's eyes didn't leave the sight of the small girl wrapped in her towel. "Sara, this is the men's bath! What if I were out of the water?" he stammered at her, shock apparent in his tone.

Bren answered for her as he was pulling on his pants and shirt. "She's a farm girl, brother. She's seen lots of animals' equipment before." Bren was obviously enjoying the moment, as Sara continued.

"Close your mouth, Airik, you will surely drown." She laughed. "Are you coming to dinner?"

"I'll be along," he said as he motioned her toward the door with his hands.

"Give us at least an hour before you knock," Bren told him. "Otherwise the wolves will have you sitting in the tree outside. Bring wine, but don't bring meat!"

As they left the caves, Bren chided his bride, "I'm beginning to believe you're more wolf than woman! You are shocking this whole village! What am I going to do with you, woman?"

She hugged his arm as they walked and answered him in her husky voice, "We only have an hour, let's hurry home and I'll show you!"

Bren smiled as he tried to match her quickened step.

Over an hour later, Bren was drowsing when he heard a knock on the cabin door and the latch moved. Thunder and Winter were both laying in the great room and each chuffed a greeting, so he knew it was White Calf and Aria. Sara lifted her head from his chest and padded, naked, to the bedroom door. Again, the sight of her took his breath away.

"Hi, girls," she said, peering around the opened door. "The stove is warm, and you know where everything is. We'll be out in a moment."

"I should listen to my uncle. I need to learn to bolt that door," Bren told her as they both got dressed.

"No one will pass my wolves if they are not loved by my wolves, husband." She paused and cocked her head to the side. "I like the sound of that word...*husband.*" She giggled as she pulled a soft red cotton dress over her head. "Hurry, husband, our friends have brought food and wine!" she told him, and she laughed like a little girl as she went to greet their company.

Bren joined them just a moment later and found Sara helping White Calf around the stove. Aria was in a pile of wolves in front of the fireplace and looked up at him as he approached. "I love your wolves, brother," she told him, with her head on Thunder and her legs thrown on top of Winter. Both of whom looked completely relaxed and at home, as she rubbed one's back and the other's head.

"I believe they love you as well, sister!" He smiled down at her. "You're welcome here whenever you would like, sister. Especially when you bring me food!" he told her as he stoked the fire.

"*Us!* Bring *us* food!" She whispered under her breath and looked pointedly at Sara as she tilted her head in her direction. Winter raised her head from the rug and tilted it curiously at Bren as well.

There came a knock on the door, and Bren pulled it open. Airik stood with his nose exactly where the door had been, holding a bottle of wine in each hand. There were five wolves standing immediately behind him and staring at him expectantly.

"Are you going to let me in?" he asked as he handed over the bottles of wine.

"Let me check this wine first" was Bren's response. The wolves brushed the ground with their tails in unison, and Smoke's mouth fell open in what Bren could only assume was an amused smile.

Sara opened the door for Airik to walk past her, while Bren could only laugh. "They're playing with you, Airik. They've discovered how uncomfortable you are in their presence, and I'm afraid they're having fun with you now. Relax with them and tormenting you will cease to be fun," she said with a laugh in her voice, and added as sweetly as she could, "Thank you for the wine."

"All right," he said to them both as he handed the wine to Bren. "Come after me if I don't return. Don't eat all the supper." He turned and closed the door behind him as he stepped down into a yard full of wolves.

A few minutes later, the door opened, and there stood Airik, sheepish but safe and whole. They all grinned at him without a word and went about the business of readying the table. White Calf beamed at him as she said, "Such a brave man you are. Any wounds to heal?"

"None you can see, at any rate" was his answer.

White Calf said in turn, "I'll check closely later if you would like."

The room became immediately silent just for a moment, everyone staring pointedly at the young woman. Then everyone began to laugh, and it was White Calf's turn to blush, just a bit.

Airik sat at the table, while Bren opened a bottle of the beautiful red wine. He filled cups and passed them to each empty hand. Sara and White Calf set the food on the table, and the friends sat down to dinner. They ate buffalo steaks, rice cooked with onion and spices, and biscuits with fresh butter and honey. They talked about the winter to come, and the classes that would be held in the village center.

Sara told how much she was looking forward to getting started on training the wolves to pull her sled. They were all certainly big and strong enough now. Bren assured her in no time at all there would be ample snow to get started. They planned out there first training route and who would be in what pulling position.

The night was on them before Aria and Bren finished cleaning up. Sara went to look after the wolves while they cleared away the last of the dinner. She walked in the door just in time for goodbyes. Airik and White Calf rose from in front of the fire. Their friends said good night on the porch, where Bren and Sara stood to watch them disappear toward the village.

"I love this place. I didn't realize how much fun it would be to have good friends close by," she said and leaned against his chest, watching their friends along the path. "I feel a sense of family here already, like I've belonged all of my life."

Bren wrapped his arms around her and said into her hair, "You have belonged here, Sara, all of your life. You just lived elsewhere for a while."

They made their way to bed and slept deeply after a while. The morning sun flowed soft over the windowsills and set the air aglow inside the room. Bren felt the presence of the woman lying close to him and reveled in the warmth of the bed. He heard the rhythm of her breathing change, and she placed her arm on his chest.

They came together and lay entwined, for how long he couldn't judge. Bren was thinking of the coming winter and the wild wolves who helped him bring Sara home. Had he dreamed of those wild wolves last night? He drifted off again and awoke still wrapped in Sara's arms and legs. He rocked back and forth just a bit, and she responded with a sigh. "Let's stay just so for the winter, shall we? We can sleep like the bear. Waking only to make love, then to sleep again, over and over until the spring brings the flowers and the warm golden sun."

"We will do just that, Sara of the wolves, I promise to you. But between the sweetness of those nights, there will be work to do. We must keep those wolves busy through the snow months, with that sled work you promised them. I need to set traps along the streams in the mountains, to collect many winter pelts. I have a family to take care of now."

"*We*, Bren Redhorse. We have a family to take care of," she reminded him.

"Yes, wife, we. Now though, would you come with me to the baths? When we return, we can think about breakfast. Maybe after that, you can tell me who will pull that sled and from what position. We can talk while we ride."

"Where will we ride?" she brightened at the prospect.

Picnic on a Mountain

"I want to go to the mountains for a few days. I would like to map my trap sets in my mind before the snow comes too deep. I need to build a few shelters for the winter trapping. Maybe we can bring home an elk or a moose for fresh meat. We have plenty in the ice rooms of the cave, but more meat at winter's start is always a good thing. We need to feed those wolves all winter, you know."

"Yes!" Sara was excited at the thought of spending a few days in the deep mountains with her new husband. "Although the wolves could fend quite easily for themselves, I will ask Aria to stay here with the wolves and feed them while we are gone. Thunder and Winter can come with us?"

"I wouldn't try to keep them from it" was Bren's answer.

Sara sprang from the bed so quickly that both Winter and Thunder pounded into the room to see what the excitement was about. Bren put on plain hide pants and moccasins, as did Sara. They both grabbed their matching wool coats Bren bought at gather. Bren put his on without a shirt, as did Sara. He raised both eyebrows at her. She cocked her head as she pulled the coat open just enough for him to view.

She said coquettishly, "I'm a farm girl first and now a mountain woman. Get used to it, husband."

He smiled at her knowingly. "It will be my pleasure, farm girl." And he turned to leave the room. Sara followed as she answered, "Yes, I believe it will, Bear Killer."

Their wolves followed them to the bath caves and lay next to the water as the two newlyweds soaked. They chose one of the smaller, private pools for their bath. Sara was about to show Bren how to use her soaps to clean his skin and hair, when he stopped her with a raised hand. He picked up the two roots he had set on the side of the pool and handed one to her. "Soap root," he explained. He pounded his with a fist-sized rock against the edge of the pool. The root crushed into a fibrous mass. He handed the rock to Sara, and she did the same with hers. They submerged them both in the water, and Bren rubbed the root over her shoulders and arms, producing a slight lather. "The root will clean the skin and hair but leave no scent for those who live in the mountains to smell."

"Ohhh, I like this, Bren!" She broke out with that smoky smile as she stood in the thigh-deep water. "After you wash me, I'll wash you." Bren laughed and continued with his welcomed task.

They washed each other slowly, twice. Then sat back in the pool and watched the light of the morning through the waterfall that was their only wall from the outside world. Sara marveled out loud at the pools Bren had found. How the pool they were in drained over the edge nearest the waterfall and into the woods fascinated Sara. She explored the floor of the pool with the wonder of a child, using one foot, until she found the cracks where the hot water flowed from below the mountain and into the room.

She sat in front of Bren and relaxed her wet body against his. "What a wondrous place you found for us to make a life. I feel blessed beyond belief that we are together to share these things."

"Yes, we are rich beyond imagining, I think," Bren answered her from behind closed eyes.

They soaked for a while longer, then dried each other well with Sara's towels. Wrapped in their coats, they made their way back through the village, catching a few glances as they were trailed by seven massive wolves. The village was getting used to seeing the pack roam through the woods. They waved or said hello in passing.

The village dogs kept their distance from the wolves for the most part but didn't appear to be nearly as frightened as they once were. A few of them even ran alongside the pack for a short distance.

The wolves paid them little mind. They knew their status in the hierarchy of the village and accepted the smaller dogs as friends to be acknowledged.

On their way back to the cabin, they came upon Aria on the way to visit friends. Sara told her of their plans and asked her to take care of the five "outdoor" wolves while they were away. She asked, "You want me to be a wolf handler? Of course I will. Much more exciting than eagles, don't you think?" The wolves danced in a circle with her as if they were aware of the arrangement. She agreed to meet them a bit later to go over the feeding details and was off to tell her friends her happy news.

They began packing for a five-day trip as soon as they returned to the cabin. Bren folded two pants and two shirts into his pack, along with six pair of new woolen socks he found at gather. He wasn't much used to wearing them under his moccasins but was told by the merchant they were very warm and would last for years. Besides, Sara wore socks almost all the time.

Sara, he noticed, appeared to be packing for a much longer trip, and he left her to it. They were taking two packhorses as well as their saddle horses and so had room to carry extra. She would learn in her own time to pack much lighter when they carried all they would use on their backs.

"Let's go get the horses," he told her as she finished her packing. They set the packs near the door and made their way toward the meadow where the herd was being kept. Halfway there, they met Logan on the path. He was leading Bren's four horses behind him.

"I heard you were leaving up the mountain for a while and thought your four would be useful," he said. "Good day, Sara. I hope you are settling in well?"

Sara smiled at the young man. "Very well indeed, Logan, and thank you."

Logan dipped his head in response and handed the reins over to Bren. "I left my dogs to stay with the herd. Thought you might have your wolves, Sara."

"You're thoughtful, Logan, but don't again change your habits for my wolves. When we get back off the mountain, I expect you to bring them to the cabin for dinner." The young man beamed in response and turned to walk back to the horses.

"It was kind of him to think of us. Was I out of my place to ask him to dinner?"

Bren took her hand in his empty one as they started back to the cabin. "Of course not, Sara. It's your home too. This is not the first kindness he's shown me, and I've neglected to thank him, up to now. Thank you for reminding me it's past time I paid him at least a small kindness. He thinks an awful lot of Aria, you know."

"Really, he's told you as much?"

"He hasn't had to. I've eyes in my head. I believe she thinks well of him also, from what I've seen, that is."

Sara smiled with excitement and said, "Hmmm, this could be a very fun dinner!"

They tied the horses to the post rails in the yard and made ready to leave. "Saddle, or no?" Bren asked.

"I've seen you ride," she answered him. "I'll ride with just the pad as you do, if you please. I've done both in past and may as well get used to the lack of a saddle."

"We'll be gone at least a seven day, Sarah. You're sure?"

"Yes, thank you," she reassured him.

Aria walked into the yard, excitement brimming from her eyes. Smoke and her pups greeted her, and Sara took her to the kennel, while Bren packed the horses. On their return, Bren asked his sister, "Would you be willing to stay in the cabin while we're gone? I'm sure everything will be fine, but I thought it would be best to have someone close. Smoke's wolves have just come a long way to a new home."

"A wonderful idea, Bren," Sara said. "You can stay in the second bedroom, Aria. The bed is very nice. The wolves will want to sleep outside but will stay close to the house."

Aria hugged them both and ran to pack a bag. "She lives not a quarter mile that way," Bren said as he watched her leave.

"That's not the point, though, is it?" was Sara's answer as she smiled after the girl. "I would bet this will be the farthest she's stayed away from her mother's fire, ever."

"You would be right," Bren said, thinking back. "I spoke too quickly. I should have talked to our mother before making the offer."

"Bren, your sister is very nearly a grown woman. We've both known girls to be married younger than she is today."

"Be that as it may, I believe we should leave as soon as possible," Bren said, casting a glance toward the path Aria took.

Sara laughed, as they both saw the girl running toward them with a bag over her shoulder. She was grinning from ear to ear as she skidded to a stop in the yard. "Mother said it was a fine idea!" she told them both. "Father said he would be here often to check on me. He'll probably have to race Mother to do it, though. Thank you for placing your trust in me, both of you."

Sara called Smoke and the pups to her and told them what was to happen. Smoke listened intently and went to stand close by Aria. Sara released her with a gesture, and they were all off again. The three walked into the cabin to settle her in her room, and as they went, Bren told her, "No one that is not immediate family is to be in this cabin until we return. Do you understand?"

Both the girls stopped in their tracks as he said this. "Bren, I will not break your trust," Aria told him and looked crestfallen that he should say such a thing.

"Aria, you know our mother will ask what I told you. That was said for her and not as much for you. You have my total trust. You always have. But still, no boys."

She raised her chin at him and, turning, carried her bag into the bedroom. She was soon settled, this not being her first visit, and they gathered in the yard.

"If you need anything you can't find here, go to Mother. Will you be afraid?" Bren asked as he and Sara mounted their horses.

Aria gave Sara an exasperated look and told her brother, "Have fun on the mountain, Bren. Stay two weeks if you will. I won't burn your cabin down."

Sara laughed as they turned their horses out of the yard, and Bren stuck his tongue out at his sister.

They rode through the meadow and entered the wood across from the cabin. Bren looked back to see smoke rising from the chimney in the great room of the cabin. "She's making me pay for the comment. She knows I can see that smoke rise."

"Ride, plainsman. Take me into the mountains," Sara told him.

They passed the afternoon riding up and over established game trails that allowed them easy passage. Sara rode first, and Bren followed with the packhorses, watching carefully as she rode. Thunder and the winter wolf followed along behind, occasionally heading off trail following the scent of something that took their notice.

He noticed she sat the horse well with only the pad between her and the back of the animal. She adapted to the movement with ease no matter if the trail was rough or hard, up or down. Truthfully, he thought she would have a difficult time riding the mountains. It pleased him to watch her skill on the horse.

She read the trail well and told him what she saw as they went. She saw the passage of every animal from deer to bear and showed him the direction a mountain lion took after it followed the trail for several yards. She kept her eyeline high, to see what was well ahead as well as at her horse's feet. Bren was impressed.

The trail opened into a high meadow after several hours, and Sara stopped. Bren came along side, and she told him they should let the horses breathe for a bit.

"You've done this before, wolf girl," he teased her.

"I've been horseback since a child, Bren, and lived away from town or village. This is the first time I've been high on the mountain, though, and I'm glad you're with me." She smiled at him, as her two wolves bounced across the meadow, searching scent only they could read.

They stepped down from the horses and allowed them to graze the still-green fall grasses. They found a large flat rock in the middle of the meadow to use as a table. Sara spread a lunch of bread, cheese, and cold meat. From their vantage point, they could look out across the mountain and see their back trail.

"That direction," Bren said, pointing down and across the mountain, "is home."

"These are beautiful mountains," she told him, "and I'm having the time of my life. This place is full of beauty and spirit that casts a spell over you." She leaned back on the rock and looked around her. Bren grinned with pleasure as he watched her happiness and chewed on an apple.

"So look at the map in your mind and tell me, where are we?" he asked her as he ate his apple. She thought about it for only a moment before answering.

"We traveled probably ten, twelve miles from the cabin, straight line distance. I'd say west and a bit north of the village, and we're about nine thousand feet up the mountain." She smiled at him as she ate cheese and bread.

"I would say the same." He smiled at her as she raised both fists to the sky. "You're very good in the mountains, wolf woman. For a farmer."

"Nothing wrong with a farm girl, mountain man," she told him and took another bite of bread.

"Surely not," Bren said.

They finished their picnic in the mountain meadow, and as they picked up the remains, Sara asked him, "What now? Which way to our camp for tonight?"

"I think we have gone as high as we need to for this trip. The trail we followed here looks to go across the mountain, and I say we follow that. In four miles or so, we can start down. Hopefully, we can find a passable trail. We might have to sleep on the mountain tonight, but I'd rather get down. Can you take the packhorses for a bit and let me take lead?"

"Of course," she answered. "Would you teach me what you see and what to look for as we go?"

"Sara, I'm not sure how much there is to teach you. I've watched you this whole day, and you've done exceptionally."

"There is always something new to learn," she told him as they mounted the horses.

"Let's walk through the meadow a moment before we ride," he told her and took his bow and quiver from Stone Foot's back. Sara grabbed her bow as well and followed him toward the upper edge of the meadow. There, behind a line of trees, began a large field of fairly flat rock, mixed with boulders and tall spires of granite, flowing down the mountain from high above.

They reached the trees that separated meadow from granite, and Bren stopped short. "Look at the ground, Sara. Tell me what you see." Sara cast around the ground for several yards left and right. She looked up and into the rock field before returning to Bren and answering his raised eyebrows.

"I see droppings and sheep tracks everywhere," she told him quietly. "There are four rams forty yards up the grade, laying under the shade of that scrub tree. They know we're here."

He smiled proudly at her and told her, "You're much more than a farm girl, farm girl. You are a mountain wolf, no doubt!" Bren spoke quietly to her. "Would you like to try your bow, Sara?" Her eyes became lanterns as she produced an arrow from her quiver.

"Lead me to it, mountain man, but would you have an arrow ready as well? I wouldn't want the ram to suffer needlessly if I miss a killing shot."

Bren showed her how to nock an arrow ready on her bow and did so himself. They used the cover of trees to make their way to an outcropping of rock. From where they stood, they were within thirty yards of the tree that sheltered the rams.

Bren bent low and slowly broke the cover of the tree line, picking his footing carefully the last twenty feet. He looked back and was surprised to see Sara just over his left shoulder. She followed in his footsteps from the trees.

He smiled at the serious excitement in her face and motioned her alongside him. He whispered to the hair covering her ear, "Slowly now, raise your head above the rock and sight distance on the one you choose. Then hide yourself once more."

Sara did as he asked and bent down again. "There is a young ram standing between our rock and other three, still laying down. He isn't as large as the others but has almost a full curl and is the closest." She grinned at him with excitement as she began to pull her bow to full draw. Bren had to hurry to catch up with her, in case she missed the shot.

Sara stood slowly as she drew the bow back into position. The sun gleamed in her hair, and Bren wondered if the rams would see the shine. He watched her shooting posture but found nothing to correct. Sara's bow sang and answered the unspoken question. Sara sang out as well in triumph, and Bren jumped from behind the boulder.

The chosen ram stood twenty-five yards from them, with Sara's arrow deep into his side, exactly over the heart. He slumped onto the rocks as Bren watched the other three scatter up the mountain.

Sara made her way over the rocks to her kill. She bent over the ram and spoke in a quiet tone Bren couldn't make out. He cocked his head and simply looked on as this young mountain woman said her thanks to the ram. She looked back at him with a proud smile on her beautiful face. "Well done, Sara. Well done" was all he could find to say.

Bren found a stout limb laying cast off in the trees and tied the feet of the ram. He threaded the feet through the pole, and together they brought the animal off the rocks into the shade of the trees. Thunder and Winter lay in the shade nearby, watching with interest as Bren began to prepare the ram for the back of a horse.

"Shall we take the quarters and back straps and leave the rest?" he asked her.

"Yes," Sara said. "That will give the four of us more than enough meat for this trip, don't you think?"

Winter chuffed her answer, and Bren felt that was a sufficient response. The pelt was in fine shape for so late in the year. Sara scraped off as much fat as she could, and they wrapped two quarters in that.

Bren brought the horses to the trees and produced a cotton wrap cloth from his pack. The two remaining quarters were wrapped in the cotton. After tying the meat to the packhorse, they were ready to travel.

After they mounted, Sara looked over to Bren and said, "You're going to have a very hard time getting me to stay home when you go to the mountains to hunt!"

"Why would I want you to stay home, mountain girl?" he answered. "It's far too much fun watching you hunt!"

She laughed and blushed as they headed across the meadow.

The wolves caught up to them as they entered the wood on the west side of the meadow. Thunder had evidence of elk hair on his black nose, and Winter's muzzle was red with fresh blood. Sara noticed but said nothing. Bren spoke to the winter wolf. "No wonder you wanted none of the ram! I see you've both found your lunch on the mountain." Winter chuffed at him in answer, and they were both gone down the trail to the west.

"They're at home on the mountain. Are they overstepping bounds, going ahead as they are?"

"No, let them run and have fun, as long as I can call them back to us if something goes amiss."

"You won't have to, mountain man." She grinned at him.

It took them into the afternoon to find a suitable trail down the mountain. They came out of trees and could see the wolves laying in the path just ahead of the trail split. Winter looked pointedly down the new pathway, and her jaw dropped into a wide smile as they approached. Thunder lay in the sun with his eyes almost closed, enjoying the warmth. Bren and Sara laughed, and Bren said to them, "I should have known. You've been leading us along this whole trip, have you not?"

"They are my mountain wolves," Sara said as they headed the horses down a well-used game trail.

A little more than a mile down the path, they came upon a clearing in a flat meadow, on the high side of the trail. The thick green grass was ringed with large stones, standing as high as a man on horseback. Near the center of the small meadow was a cluster of rounded boulders. They appeared to have been placed there, not by chance. The boulders were spread apart just enough that a person could walk between them and large enough that once they did, they would be hidden from view outside the circle. Both Bren and Sara dismounted and explored the mountain meadow. Sara's expression one of awed wonder, Bren's more speculative.

Each stone in the outer ring was at least twice the height of a tall man, and most were wider than the front door of the cabin. "Come look," Bren said as he studied one of the tall, broad stones around the outer ring. Sara joined him and was amazed at what she saw.

A series of pictures was etched, or chiseled, across the breadth of the stone, from just above the grass and continuing toward the top of the stones. Sara recognized buffalo, elk, and horses. There were what appeared to be eagles represented, as well as designs of spirals and suns and shapes she could only guess the meaning of.

They walked from one monolith to the next and saw each one had some form of pictographic art on the inner face, while the outside surface of the stone was unmarked. Fascinated by what the stones revealed, they took their time wandering to each.

After completing their exploration of the outer circle, they walked into the inner circle of smaller, rounded boulders. They found evidence of a very old campfire. There was a ring of stones around very old, Bren thought, charred remains. The fire wouldn't have to be very big to heat the whole of the center ring. The boulders would reflect the heat well.

"I think we've found tonight's camp," Bren said. Sara agreed, and they went about unloading the horses and setting up their bedroll and dinner implements. They would have roasted sheep backstrap tonight. Bren produced ears of corn, potatoes, and onion from a panier on one of the packhorses.

As Sara was setting wood in the old fire ring, Winter and Thunder walked into the circle of boulders and plopped down to one side. Both wolves looked satisfied with the arrangement and watched the work proceed.

Bren left the circle to check on the horses in the meadow, and Winter followed him out. There was plenty of grass for all four horses through the night, and Bren was sure Stone Foot would keep the other three from straying.

He began to smell meat cooking and came back into the fire circle to see Sara cutting potatoes and onion into a skillet. He sat on one of the smaller boulders and watched her complete her tasks.

"Do you think this place is here by accident, or was it made by the hands of some long-ago people?" he asked her.

"I don't know, Bren," she answered. "It's a curious place!" She thought for a moment before continuing, "This is a stony mountain, and either one could be true. I would like to know the story behind the place. The wolves don't mind being here, and I trust their judgment in most things."

He watched Sara move around the small fire as she cooked their meal. He noticed the shadows cast against the rocks from the flames, and his breath caught. There appeared to be shapes in the shadows that weren't cast from Sara's movement. He saw what appeared to him to be dancers moving across the rock in slow, rhythmic steps. He called her to him quietly, and the dancers changed direction as she moved to where Bren was seated.

The dancers stopped as she sat next to him. Bren called the wolves to him from where they lay in the grass, across the small clearing. Thunder and Winter trotted to where the couple sat, and their shadows stalked toward Bren and Sara. Sara let out a gasp, and the stalkers stopped as the wolves lay their heads in her lap.

"Watch the rocks," Bren said as he stood. He walked from their seats to the far side of the clearing, and several dancers followed him across the rocks. They appeared to be holding bows, shields, and dances sticks and wearing headdresses.

Bren stopped, and the dancers paused as well, their shapes fading into the structure of the rocks. He looked back at Sara, who was staring in awe at the rocks surrounding them. Bren saw the wolves appeared to be unaffected by the dancing shapes.

"This is a magical spot, isn't it? I wonder what occurred here in the past." Sara looked at him and smiled. "Whatever has happened here seems to have happened long, long ago. The shadows don't threaten at all. Maybe there's a message in the dance. I think we should let them dance and see what comes. Let's eat!"

They ate dinner sitting on the buffalo robes and drank coffee, watching the stars come out above the circle of boulders. They talked about the stories on the stones until the moon was straight overhead and drifted into sleep, comfortable and close to one another. The coals of the fire lent a golden glow to the rock spires surrounding them.

Bren woke with the sun to see the wolves were gone from the circle. He checked on the horses and found them all content, cropping grass still green and lush, for this late in the year. He brought the still-warm fire back to flame and saw Sara watching him work from the warmth of the buffalo robes.

"Wolves are gone," he told her. Sara smiled and nodded.

"They're having fun on the mountain. They seldom get to run at will on the farm, and this is a welcome diversion. Don't worry about the wolves, Bren, they'll cause no mischief."

"Yes, ma'am," he said and tossed her an apple. "Coffee in a minute or two."

The wolves returned, while Bren poured coffee. Winter sniffed carefully around the base of every boulder as the packs were loaded and the horses made ready. By the time they were mounted and ready to ride, the sun was warm and halfway to noon.

It took the pair several hours to make their way down the switch back path. The day was bright and warm, with enough breeze to move the scent of mountain flowers to them. As they rode, they saw more and more sign of both large and small animals. Tracks of bear, elk, and deer were everywhere, as were martin and many other forest animals. They saw two porcupines laying on low branches, watching them pass from the shade of the trees.

"This area looks good for trapping and hunting both." Bren was thinking aloud as they reached the bottom of the mountain. They stopped when they reached the rolling wooded foothills. The trees were thick, mixed with pine of several species and aspen, but not so dense that a bull elk would have a problem getting through.

They followed their game trail west along the base of the mountain. They stopped at a broad, deep creek and sat on stones in the dappling shade of aspens while they ate a small lunch. Sara remarked to Bren how tuff this hunting life was as she lounged against a rock warmed by the sun. He smiled back at her. "Not always this easy, farm girl," he said around bites of apple. "Next spring after the grass comes back, we'll chase buffalo across the prairie. You'll earn a living then."

Sara's eyes widened in anticipation. "I've heard the stories, Bren. I was thrilled by the telling. I can't wait to be a part of it!"

As evening approached, they came upon a clearing in the thick of the woods, just a stone's throw from their path. The thick grass spread out in a rough oval. They saw water pushing up from a spring that bubbled quietly out of the ground. The spring creek flowed through the middle of the park like setting and disappeared gurgling into a second hole in the ground. It came out once again several paces along before falling over the face of a rock outcropping. It pooled at the bottom before traveling through the glade and continued somewhere out onto the prairie. It disappeared around a small hill a half mile or so distant.

"A perfect spot for an overnight shelter, don't you think?" Bren asked Sara as they surveyed the park from horseback.

"I think so, we could place the shelter there"—she pointed—"at the end toward the mountain, to keep us out of the wet. We could build a small fireplace with those stones from where the water comes back up. Shall we?"

They let the horses crop the dark-green grass while they unpacked what they needed, and the wolves explored. Bren cut several long lodge poles and tied them to standing trees to make a boxlike shelter with an opening facing the spring. He added poles to the top to support green bows for cover and slanted several out the back side. Sara gathered and placed the green bows from the fresh-cut trees, and soon they had a passable shelter. It would keep out most of the wind and hold the heat from the fire they would place right in front.

They both gathered stones to make a fire circle and in moments had a small fire burning. Their gear was stowed inside on a floor of the buffalo blankets. They cut generous-sized chunks of Sara's sheep. She seasoned the meat with salt and pepper she found in Bren's pack and skewered them over the small fire. Bren took Sara's hand, and they explored their park while dinner cooked.

The spring was clean and clear and tasted wonderful! The wolves had found a patch of blueberries where the sun hit a clearing, and Sara picked several hands full. The woods were alive with bird song, and squirrels barked at them from high in the aspen groves.

Soon it was time to check on their dinner, and they wandered back to the shelter. Shadow was melting into night through the trees, so Bren gathered more wood for the fire. Sara sliced the meat on a serving board from the packed provisions. There was a skin of wine she found tucked in the panier.

They sat in their shelter with the wolves spread out a few feet from the fire. They ate the meat with bread left from their picnic on the mountain. They drank wine straight from the skin. The night crept through the woodlands, with stars blinking down just above the trees. The fire glowed across their park and painted patterns of golden light upon the surface of the trees. Night birds and a bubbling spring sang them songs old as the slivered moon overhead.

"I want to remember every moment of this," Sara said simply. "When I was young, I wondered what life would bring me. Never once did I think I would be sitting in the forest, drinking wine with a wild mountain man, after hunting my first big horn high in the top of a mountain."

"I'm happy you're happy, woman of the wolves. I'm no wild man, though," Bren answered, pulling her gently to him. She leaned against him and sighed. The winter wolf raised her head from the grass and thumped her tail on the ground. Thunder breathed loud, content, as he lay facing into the coming night.

They lay warm in the buffalo robes, contemplating sleep, while Bren spoke to her about the next day. "We'll travel east toward home from here. We'll place pole sets in promising spots as we go. This winter when I come back through, I can bait them as I pass and check the traps on my way home."

"I'm sure that's the way of it, Bren, but you won't be alone." She spoke softly into his ear, biting the lobe just a little. "As I said on the mountain, you'll be hard-pressed getting me to stay home alone when there is so much adventure and beauty in these mountains. I'll not be denied the fun of it."

"Sara, I'm happy you want to come with me to hunt, but running a trapline is no pleasant hunting trip. The days are long and cold, and the nights are colder. I wouldn't want to worry about your safety while we are out on the trail."

"Oh, but, husband, I'll be with the bear killer! The healer of the circle and friend of eagles! I'll walk beside one who walks the red road. How much safer could I be than to walk through the world with this man?" She rose up and propped herself on one arm as she looked down at him. "Do you think for a moment, Bren Redhorse, that I would sit snug in our warm cabin to worry about your safety? I'm a mountain woman now. I am Sara of the wolves." Thunder chuffed from his spot on the grass, and Winter answered the same.

Bren slept deeply and dreamed of the winter trapping. He dreamed of all that had happened since the spring. In his dream, Wanbli was sitting on a branch above his head. His mate, the golden eagle Tayla, was by his side. He talked with the pair about the hides he had gathered and how that alone had given him all he needed to trade for what he needed at the fall gather. They talked of trapping and taking just what you needed and no more from the plains and from the mountains.

Morning found the newlyweds wrapped together in their buffalo blankets, warm under the protection of their shelter. Sometime during the night, the wolves had moved onto the buffalo robes to get away from a thin layer of frost covering their little park. They were curled tightly at the foot of the shelter. The horses were standing close to one another, their heads drooped in sleep.

Bren got up and coaxed the fire to flame. He placed the coffeepot on the rocks to brew and rolled against Sara's warmth once more. She moved into him, wrapping one slender leg across his hip and feeling the beating of his heart with her open palm.

He hesitated before he spoke. He wanted to put the words in just the right order. "I dreamed last night of Wanbli and of trapping. I believe I might have taken you away from the cabin for no good reason. Her hand moved down to his hip and stopped there. She was listening closely. I talked to Wanbli and Tayla in my dream of trapping and the winter. I won't be trapping this winter. I've made sufficient trade with the hides I took from hunting alone. I think I've been taking more than I should from the land, and that needs to change."

"So what you're telling me is we won't be sleeping on the trapping trail this winter?" She spoke quietly. "I won't be coming with you to check the traps?"

"I'm sorry, Sara. I think, at least for this winter season and probably from now on, I won't be trapping. We came on this trip for nothing."

"Oh no, Bren! This trip wasn't for nothing! You brought me to the mountain. I showed you I can track and use my bow. I brought down a ram, and we ate him! We discovered the life stories of an ancient people written in stone. We journeyed together with our wolves and saw the lands where we live! This is a wonderful trip! I believe this may have been bothering you for a time and came to the surface in your dream last night. I think you are finding healing the circle will take sacrifice, in some manner, from each of us. I am disappointed though, a little."

He turned to her under the blankets, ready to take her scolding. "Go ahead," he said as he looked into her eyes. She could hold back her smile no longer. She flopped back on the bedroll and said, theatrically, "I made such a wonderful speech last night, don't you think?"

Bren could only laugh with relief.

Winter stood from her spot at their feet. Facing them both, she stretched and shook her coat fluffy. She turned, giving them a look. She would give the pups when they were trying her patience. The white wolf turned and with raised tail trotted into the woods. Bren and Sara looked at each other. They smiled as only scolded children will and pulled the buffalo robe closer.

"Here's one more reason this trip to the mountain was not a waste," Bren said as he reached for his wife. Thunder went to the woods for a while as well.

When the wolves returned to the small park in the woods, they found it bustling with breakfast preparations. Bren was setting the coffeepot back on the coals, as it had boiled almost dry. Sara was placing meat from her ram in a cast-iron pan. Both were dressed, the camp almost packed and ready to move.

Bren and Sara discussed over breakfast what to do now since they wouldn't need to explore west any further to place Bren's trapline. They decided to stay within the forest line at the base of the mountain and work their way slowly back home. Sara pointed out how disappointed Aria would be if they returned too early.

They sat in the warmth of their shelter, watching the fire burn to coals as they ate. Sara seemed particularly happy and smiled when Bren asked about her mood.

"We're together in a beautiful wood. We have our wolves with us and nothing pressing to do with our day but enjoy it. We have a warm home and good friends waiting for us. We have everything we need."

They packed the camp and set off on a leisurely ride east toward home. Midday found them coming out of the trees and across the edge of the prairie. They saw high mountains far to the north, white with snow at their tops. There were hundreds of buffalo everywhere, and there was no mistaking the wonder in Sara's eyes.

"I've not seen buffalo in these numbers!" she said, her face lighting up as she looked across the low, rolling hills. She slowed her horse until Bren came along side. "We could ride through that herd all day and not see the end of it!"

"You're probably right," Bren answered her. "What else do you see on the prairie?"

Sara studied the herd a few moments, and her eyes lit up further as they began to reveal a story to her. "There are many antelope on the outer edge of the herd. I see a huge elk herd mixed in with the buffalo! There must be half a thousand elk!"

Bren grinned back at her excitement. "The antelope stay on the edge of the herd so they don't get trapped if the buffalo run. They are much faster and don't want to get trampled. The elk are comfortable inside where the numbers keep them safer. They know the wolves hunt mostly the outer edges of the herd, and the buffalo are wary of the antlers of the elk. Neither one pushes the other too much, so rarely is there a confrontation. The grass must be very good in this area, or they would have moved on by now. These things you can learn if you spend time on the prairie and look closely."

"Listen to the noise they make!" Sara said.

Bren explained, "The cows are calling to their young. The bulls are grunting at one another. Rut is just ending with the beginning of winter, and they are trying to build as much fat as they can to make it through the lean times ahead. We're skirting the reserved area now.

North of here, west and east for many miles, no one may build a village or even a single cabin. This place is set aside for the animals alone. We can hunt here, but only that. We can camp while we hunt but must move on when the hunt is done."

For the next three hours they rode past the buffalo herd. After a time, a large finger of foothills came down off the mountains on their right and jutted out onto the prairie. They were cut off from the herd and once again entered the forest. They rode in the cooling shade of the trees until dusk, both wrapped in their red wool coats.

The wolves walked alongside the horses or explored into the trees, never more than a shout away from Sara. Deep into the wood they found a quiet place to camp and unpacked the horses once more.

The place they chose was an aspen grove circled by a creek coming off the mountain. The creek almost doubled back on itself before dropping off the slight bench where they had dismounted. The water continued to wind through a thick pine forest.

They laid out their bedroll in the midst of a stack of downed pines that made a sheltering wall. Bren allowed the horses their freedom within the confines of the meadow created by the creek. Night was kept at bay by their small fire. The wolves came and went as they discovered what this section of woods had hidden in its depths.

"I can see why this life draws you to it," Sara said as they reclined against their makeshift wall. "Every day brings something new to look at. There's a new discovery around every turn in the path."

"Yes, and the foothills are different from the mountains. The mountains are different the higher you go, and the plains are different yet. Always something new. You could live on these great plains for three lifetimes and not see it all. I will always want to wander these places," Bren said this, looking from the corner of his eyes at Sara.

"It's good then you have someone who will always want to wander with you."

They woke to a leaden sky filled with low clouds. "Snow is coming." They agreed. "Good thing we'll be home today, I think," Bren said. They shared a cold breakfast of jerked elk and dried fruit and started on the trail early. Still air and fat snowflakes had them riding huddled in their coats until noon, when the sun broke free and warmed the world once more.

Bren began to recognize their path just after the sun burned its way through the clouds. They were in sight of the rock wall that separated the village from the plains by late afternoon and home two hours before dusk.

The Circle Healed

Aria, along with Winter and the rest of the wolves, met them in the middle of the meadow, in front of the cabin. The wolves jumped and danced, and Aria laughed and hugged. They unpacked and cared for the horses.

Bren and Sara made their way to the caves for a bath and were soon warmed and relaxed from the hot water. White Calf and Airik stopped at the cabin after seeing the horses out front. White Calf heated a pot of stew and made biscuits, while Airik took the horses to feed and get settled for the night. Soon Bren and Sara were dressed, and the friends sat to eat together.

Aria shared what little news there was of the village. She explained how most of the eagles had fledged, and many of them were still living on the mountain or in the trees around the village. The young ones were still closely connected to their human helpers. Everyone thought their close connection would continue through their lives.

The young villagers were still feeding the fledglings from time to time, although the young birds were fairly self-sufficient and hunting on their own. Ben was home from guiding Arden and Ellie to the stream. They found the stream and the area perfect for their needs and started off for home after resting overnight.

Bren and Sara told the friends of their trip and the reason for returning earlier than expected. Bren told of Sara's hunt for the big horn sheep and her skills in tracking on the mountain and through the woods.

He described the double ring of stones they used for a campsite and the images they found on the stones. White Calf was clearly interested in the pictographs, asking several questions about the shapes they had found. She described a few when Bren nor Sara could remember detail. She was extremely accurate in her description and asked if Bren and Sara would consider taking her back to this place after the winter was gone.

"We'd be happy to take you there, sister," Sara told her, and Bren concurred.

"What do you think this place might be?" he asked her.

"There are many places of power in the mountains" was her answer. "It's hard to say if this place could be one of them or just a place to spend a night on the mountain. What did the wolves think of the place?"

"They were content to sleep there for the night. They came and went as if at home," Sara said.

White Calf was thoughtful for a while, and the subject changed to the coming of winter snows.

The friends talked until the logs on the fire burned down. Their eyes began to droop with sleep and wine. The conversation turned to the falling snow and warm beds. White Calf and Airik followed Aria home to her parents' lodge, leaving the newlywed couple to themselves in their cabin.

They made their way to the bedroom, where Bren had lighted a fire to warm the room. They undressed and lay in the bed, watching the fire and talking quietly. They were both soon sleeping deeply. Bren dreamed the eagles were coming. The whole convocation. He saw them as they appeared to him from Bear Butte, winging their way toward him in formation.

Bren and Sara were awakened by an insistent knocking at the front door. The sun was up but just barely. Light of the new day splashed across the room, leaving shadows in the corners. Bren made his way to the door, putting on his pants as he went.

Airik stood with the wolves to his back. His face was ashen and worried. His eyes swollen and red. "White Calf sent me for you. Joseph is very sick and fading. He's asked to speak with you."

"Go, we'll be right behind you," Bren responded. He left the door open as he went to find his clothes. He explained to Sara what Airik had said while he laced up his winter moccasins. She was already half dressed.

"I thought something was to happen. I dreamed of the eagles in the night. They were flying to us in huge numbers," Sara told him.

Bren stopped with his shirt half on, staring at his wife. "I had the same dream. Just as they were when they approached me on the butte. I'm believing that was no dream but a message."

They went quickly through the wood. Their whole pack followed behind. The wolves traveled with a solemn stride, close behind their pack leaders. It seemed every tree was covered with eagles, both village eagles and birds Bren was not familiar with. Golden and bald eagles were everywhere.

Bren reached out to Wanbli with his mind and was touched immediately.

"I'm here, brother. We are with Joseph now. I gave you the picture in the night. Some things are better told face-to-face."

"Sara and I both got the message, Wanbli, but didn't know the reasoning. What happens here?"

"Joseph is leaving this world, Bren. His time is done. We've come for the honoring."

Bren stopped in the path, shocked.

"I've heard his words, Bren. We must go to White Calf. She needs us now," Sara said as she took his hand, gently urging him forward done the path. They continued across the wood. The villagers now lining the path were asking what was happening.

Bern and Sara approached Joseph's lodge and found Ben, Thora, Aria, and Airik sitting at the fire outside the door. The smoke flaps were open slightly on the lodge, venting smoke to the sky that smelled of sweetgrass and sage. Thora came to Bren and silently held him to her.

"Speak to the village, Bren. Tell them what's happening and ask them to give us room and prayer."

Bren nodded. He turned and walked to the crowd that was forming.

Sara was at his side. "Joseph is passing from our world." A hushed intake spread through the assembly. "I don't know more than that. I ask you to give us space and prayer. I'll tell you what I can when I can, but for now, respect his family and do him this honor."

"Yes, of course" and "Tell us if you need…" came from several voices in the crowd as they turned back to their homes.

White Calf came from Joseph's lodge looking very tired but upright and regal. Bren went to her and enveloped her in his arms. "We love you," he said, and he held her as she cried. "Your family holds you now. Lean on us and let us support you through this."

"I have no time for grief in this moment," she said, straightening herself. "He still lives, and I'm called to serve my grandfather. He's asked for you, Bren. The both of you. He looks fine, but he is very weak. Please don't keep him any longer than you must."

Bren and Sara entered the lodge and saw Joseph in his usual spot, at the rear of the center fireplace. He was wrapped in a buffalo robe and smiling at them. The smell of sweetgrass wafted through the space.

Sara sat next to the old man and took his hand. Bren knelt in front of him and asked, "Joseph, what can I do?"

"Some of that tea you bought me at gather would be nice, don't you think?" was his answer. As the words were spoken, White Calf pulled aside the door flap and entered with the same tea set she brought when they first met the old man at gather. "She knows my every thought, I think," Joseph said, as White Calf served the tea in silence and left.

They sat for a moment sipping at the tea before Joseph spoke. "I've lived two lifetimes of winters in this world, and it's at last my time to go. My tasks here are accomplished, and I'm old. I'm ready. I've seen the circle healed, Bren. It does my heart good to know I had a small part in this time of change." His foggy eyes appeared to sparkle as he spoke but became somber as he continued. "White Calf is being very strong, as she always has, but she's not taking my leaving well. I've spoken to Airik, who has made promises to be kind to her and to be a good husband."

Bren and Sara shared a glance.

"This year has begun a dawning of a new age for the world, but your road isn't traveled to its end. There's more for you to do, but you will have one another and many friends to help. I'm deeply proud of the both of you. The way you've conducted yourselves through this time has shined a light for many to follow. I would like to stay and see the paths you have to take, but the world turns." He sipped his tea and thought for several moments before continuing. "I would ask you both this favor. Don't put me in the ground, but somewhere high, so I can look on this place as I rest."

Bren was about to assure him it would be done when he heard the familiar voice of the eagle in his head. "It will be as you ask, Grandfather. You will rest high within the mountain. The eagles will be always near. So it was in the very old times, now it will be again."

"Ah," Joseph said, the sparkle coming back to his eyes. "Your eagle speaks to me once again. I think that will be a good place to be." Bren and Sara had both heard Wanbli as well.

The door flap moved, and Winter's nose pushed through. Sara was about to send her away, when Joseph's hand raised and motioned to the wolf. She entered the lodge followed by Thunder. Winter took her place at the side of the old man, gently dropping her head into his lap. His hand went softly to the crown of her head. Thunder lay down between the fire and Joseph's legs.

"Can I borrow your wolves for a while?" he asked.

"Of course, Grandfather," Sara whispered, her voice cracking as the words came.

"Sara, woman of the wolves, don't grieve over much for me. I've seen wondrous things in this life, and I'm ready to see what comes next. This is part of the circle as surely as the cycles of the moon and sun. Oh, before I forget, you have company in the meadow that fronts your cabin. They are four in number and very sacred. If you would see to it they aren't bothered through the winter snow, I would be grateful."

He reached for Bren and Sara, placing a small wrinkled hand on each of theirs. "Know that my love for you both and for all the people will continue as long as time turns the wheel. Please ask White Calf to come to me, and remember, don't be afraid of what's to come. You are together."

Before Bren or Sara could rise to their feet, White Calf slipped through the door and was at her grandfather's side. She knelt where Sara had been and took his hand in hers. Before they could leave, Joseph called to them again. "Wait, the both of you." White Calf looked at him with reddened half-lidded eyes. "I would speak to you as well, granddaughter. Much time has flown by me while I waited for the earth mother to heal and in her turn to heal the people. Know that time will lie to you if you don't listen very carefully to the words he speaks. It's hard to perceive the truth of time, it flows by us like a wind in the darkness. Love one another with much passion, and always let it be known who you love. Leave me now to rest, and let these wolves guide me from this place."

Sara and Bren stepped into the brightness of the morning. She buried her head into his chest, crying softly as he held her close. They sat by the fire through the morning in front of Joseph's lodge. Both waiting, wishing something could be done but knowing Joseph's time was short. Thora and Aria brought food though no one ate much of anything. As the sun reached its zenith directly over the lodge of the old man, there came a low mournful howl from within.

The song was taken up by the rest of the pack, who stood around the lodge facing the four directions. The eagles from every tree in the village raised in flight. They flew four times around Joseph's lodge then banked as one body toward the mountain and soon disappeared in its distant heights.

"Joseph is gone from this village but not from the hearts of the people," Bren said. "Before this day is gone, we will take him to rest in the high places."

Wanbli spoke to Bren, saying, "Come to the mountain, past the rooms where the new ones were born, and I will show you the resting place of the old ones."

Having heard the eagle's words, Bren and Sara both stood and made their way to the caverns. They climbed up the tunnels to the room where the children had waited and slept. It was empty now, cleaned of even footprints on the stone. They continued past the nesting ledges and found Wanbli perched on a ledge opened to the sky.

"Continue past this spot and into the mountain. There you will find rooms cut into a cavern. There are many of them sealed with rock and many that are open yet. The first one not sealed is the resting place of Joseph. He has served your people and mine well. We've guided his spirit to this high place to rest before moving on. He will be at peace here, as are many of your ancestors."

The couple made their way down to the village where White Calf and Airik waited outside Joseph's lodge. The village was gathered around as well. "We'll take Joseph to the top of the mountain." Bren spoke loud enough for the village to hear. "Once in the mountain, there won't be room for everyone, so the four of us will continue alone." Bren gestured to the circle of friends, White Calf, Airik, Sara, and himself.

White Calf had dressed Joseph in his finest clothes. Quillwork covered the front of his hide shirt and down the arms in red and white. Airik had wrapped the buffalo robe around two lodge poles to carry him with. Bren placed Joseph on the robe, and the two men lifted him. The village followed to the caverns, where they left the small party to continue into the mountain. Winter and Thunder would not be left behind and followed the friends into the mountain.

Several turns into the tunnel the poles of the litter would no longer fit the turns of the corridor. Bren took Joseph off the bed and carried the body of the tiny man in his arms as they continued to climb. Airik brought the buffalo robe.

Far past the nesting rooms they went and came to a small opening none of them had seen before. Bren was sure no one had been this far into the mountain for thousands of years. He watched White Calf bend down and through the small rounded opening and carefully followed her with his burden. He stood again and found himself on the edge of a vast cavern their lanterns could not light to its edges.

There was a path around the wall of the cavern polished smooth by the passing of many feet. They followed it, with lanterns held high by both Sara and White Calf. The air they breathed tasted clean and cold and dry.

Bren could feel the enormity of this space as they followed the path along the wall to their left. Their footsteps echoed off the floor and back to them from the walls. He thought that if he stood in the middle of this great cathedral-like cavern and shot his bow straight up, his arrow might clatter back to the floor without reaching the roof.

As they spoke quietly to one another, Bren got the feeling they could whisper from one side of the great room to the other and have no trouble being heard. The silence so complete, he could hear the soft rustle of his clothing when he moved. Looking around, he saw tool marks on the walls and knew the enormous hall had been worked to enlarge or at least to define the area.

They walked past many doors closed off with stacked rock until they found one door yet opened to the main room. Shining the lanterns inside, the friends saw a stone bench in the center of the small room. Here they placed the buffalo robe and wrapped Joseph's frail form in it.

White Calf placed Joseph's bow and quiver of arrows atop the robe, along with his shield and his medicine bag. "Rest well, Grandfather. I love you now and always," she said, and they backed out of the room.

Bren and Airik stacked rocks they found piled to one side, across the opening of the door, until it was closed off from the main cavern. They heard the quiet click of stone on stone echo back to them from the dark depths as they worked without speaking to seal the door on their grandfather's resting place. The four friends stood for a moment, holding one another. White Calf stepped to the door, placed her hand on the stone, and said a quiet prayer in the ancient language of Joseph Red Star's people. She finished, and taking Airik's hand, the four friends made their way from the cavern.

As they stepped into the light of day, they saw the eagles once more filled the sky. They circled the village four times in formation, then once again filled the trees. The villagers followed the group back to Joseph's lodge, dropping off a few at a time as they came to their homes. Aria, Ben, and Thora met them at the lodge that now belonged to White Calf.

Thora said, "We have a dinner gathered for us to honor Joseph. Aria and I will cook while we sit and remember. Would it be all right if we came to your home, Sara?"

"Yes, please. Let's do that," Sara said.

They carried the baskets of food and wine to Bren and Sara's home. As they entered the yard, Sara noticed the wolves looking intently into the meadow. She had forgotten Joseph told them they would have guests waiting. Standing at the center of the meadow were four white bison calves. The small party of friends stood wordless, looking out across the meadow.

Wanbli landed on his usual perch in the yard along with Tayla. "Yes, they are the ones you saw during the spring hunt. They've come to spend the winter in this meadow. I don't know what will happen come the spring, but for now, they're here," the eagle said.

"And here they will remain safely as long as they should want," Bren said.

White Calf walked into the meadow as Wanbli spoke. As she approached, the four white buffalo calves looked up at the young woman. She held her arms out to them, and they approached her. The yearling calves stepped into a circle enclosing the young woman as she touched each one. They appeared to be looking up into her face as she spoke quietly to them. White Calf broke the circle and walked back toward her friends, and the calves continued to graze.

The friends were speechless as she approached them and leaned once more into Airik's open arms, her eyes brimmed with tears. Airik wrapped his arms around White Calf. He held her as she cast a melancholy smile out over the white buffalo yearlings standing in Bren's meadow. Logan met the friends in the yard with his two herding dogs. He stood with Aria and quietly took her hand. Sara looked up into Bren's face and smiled. He nodded reassurance to her, smiling in return.

The group sat together in the cabin as the meal was prepared. Aria cuddled on the floor with Thunder and Winter. Ben sat quietly at the table, while Thora helped Sara to prepare the meal. Logan sat close with his hand on Winter's side. Logan looked at Sara and asked her, "Sara, did you know this wolf has pups in her? I would imagine about four, maybe six." Sara smiled and answered him, "Yes, she accepted one of the wild wolves when we were waiting for Bren in the northern camp. I would guess she will whelp in about a month and a half. Near the end of the month of quiet snow."

Aria followed the conversation with mounting joy and gave Sara such a look of question and glee that she had to respond. "Yes, Aria. At least one of the pups will be for you. We will train her together, and you will learn to run with the wolves." As she was saying this, Aria sprang from the floor and into Sara's arms.

"Thank you, sister, I've been waiting for this to happen since I first saw your wolves."

"I know, little sister," Sara said. "I've been waiting for this to happen as well. I see the way you are with my wolves. You'll be a good wolf woman one day soon. Now come to the table, all of us, and let's share this food."

They shared warmth and wine and stories of friends, absent from the table but not from their hearts or lives. They looked back on the past year with wonder and spoke of winter plans. All seven of Sara's wolves filled the room wherever they could find empty floor. Smoke and her pups appeared to be comfortable enough inside, for the moment. As they ate at the table Bren had built, the snowflakes began to drift to the cold earth, heavy and fat, outside the windows. The snow came down white and pure, deep into the night. The friends shared long hours of laughter and the warmth of a home fire.

It is said in stories of this time that the last wounded part of the circle was closed and truly healed on this night. It happened when friends of the human nation and the animal nations joined to become family, in a cabin at the edge of a meadow. It happened near a village filled with eagles, under a mountain where the spirits of the old world and the new rested together. This is not the ending of an old story but the beginning of a new age of the world and the people who lived within it.

Cast of Characters

Bren: Healer of the circle
Sara: Trainer of wolves
Ben: Bren's father
Thora: Bren's mother
Aria: Bren's sister
Arden: Sara's father
Ellie: Sara's mother
Airik: Bren's best friend
Don: Bren's uncle
Seela: Bren's aunt and Don's wife
Joseph: Elder of the plains people
White Calf: Joseph's granddaughter
Kennon: Village elder
Libby: Kennon's wife
Lanis: Village healer
Ashlen: Elder at gather
Lizzie: Girl at marketplace
Jon: Airik's elder brother
Tam: Jon's wife
Wil: Village elder

Translations

Wanbli (Wan-blee): Golden Eagle

Eagles

Wanbli (Wan-blee): Bren's eagle
Tayla: Wanbli's mate

Young Villagers

Jamie
Daniel
Mika
Toren

Sara's Wolves

Thunder (Male)
Winter (Female)
Smoke (Female)
Summer (Male)
Dusk (Male)
Spring (Female)
Midnight (Female)

Northern Villagers

Long Runner: Sara's kidnapper
Black Moccasin: Elder of the northern village

About the Author

Richard L. Gibson was born in Oklahoma and spent his childhood in Northern California.

He finished a tour in the United States Army infantry and then a year in the National Guard as a military police officer. He put himself through the Reserve Police Academy and then was sponsored through the regular police academy before spending twenty-six years in law enforcement in California.

He retired to Montana, a place that had been pulling on his soul since his first visit. He lives in Montana with his wife, Teri, where he currently works as a city court judge. He also practices often and aspires to become, one day, a fly fisherman.

Richard's love and respect of Native American art, stories, and people were born in him as a child.

His hope is that this story reflects these deep feelings.